Please don't tell what train I'm on
They won't know what route I'm going

Cotton, Elizabeth. "Freight Train." Circa 1906-1912.

Also by Alfred M. Struthers:

THE THIRD FLOOR MYSTERY SERIES

The Case of Secrets

The Phantom Vale

The Curse of Halim

The Demon Tide

The Stone Ghost

The Grim Fugue

The Watchman's Keep

The Tears of the Empress

CHAPTER BOOKS

Did You Hear That?

(illustrated by Cathy Provoda)

PICTURE BOOKS

Pepperoni Macaroni

(illustrated by Cathy Provoda)

Ms. Fuzzburt's Nap

with Madelyn Rose Stone

(illustrated by George Amaru)

Cats Can't Read

(illustrated by Sarah Adam)

THE BARNYARD RULES

(illustrated by Sarah Adam)

Available at:

Thirdfloorbooksllc.com

The Shadows Grieve

A Third Floor Mystery

By Alfred M. Struthers

Third Floor Books

thirdfloorbooksllc.com

Cover design by Third Floor Books

ISBN: 979-8-9913941-0-9

10 9 8 7 6 5 4 3 2 1

Published by Third Floor Books, LLC

thirdfloorbooksllc.com

For Les Weiner

Poet, spiritualist,
civil rights activist,
loving father and grandfather

"Unchanging Love"

Unchanged by its flow are the depths of God's sea
Of love that's eternal, unvaried.
Yet choppy the waves, and turbulent be
Life's forces by which we are carried. (Weiner, 1-4)

Prologue

June, 2002
Hammond Books, Cambridge, MA

It was just before 8 a.m. when Helen appeared at the front window. The bookshop wasn't due to open for another hour but Henry Hammond was already inside, busily stocking new titles on one of the front end caps. When he heard her rap on the glass, he turned and looked, recognizing her at once. But something was wrong. Gone was the signature Helen Bainbridge smile. In its place was a look of utter desperation.

She gestured urgently with her hand. *I need to talk to you!*

Without delay, he set the books aside and rushed over to unlock the door.

"I'm sorry for disturbing you at this hour but I need your help," she said. "I wouldn't ask if it weren't frightfully important."

"No apology needed. Please, come in," he said, motioning her inside. She stepped into the shop and he quickly locked the door.

When he turned around to face her, she had started to pace. "What's wrong?" he asked. "Did something happen?"

She stopped pacing and faced him directly. "I'm not sure if you read about it in the paper, but a good friend of mine was critically injured in an accident this past week. His name is James Donnelly and he's a detective with the Boston Police Department. For almost a year now he's been leading a task force investigating corruption at local construction companies."

"James Donnelly? Yes, I *did* read about that. You say he's a friend of yours?"

"Yes. I've been conferring with him about police procedures for a new book I'm writing."

"The newspaper article implied that what happened to him wasn't an accident. Isn't there a perceived mob connection?"

"There is, and while he refuses to discuss who was behind the accident, they're not finished. They've been pursuing his daughter, Ann, and I'm afraid of what they'll do to her if they find her. She's convinced that her only chance to survive is to run. James has even devised a method for her to communicate with him wherever she goes."

She began to pace again.

"Henry, I fear for that girl. I really do. If the mob really was responsible for the accident, how long do you think it'll be before they find her?"

"Where is she now?" Henry asked.

"She's staying with my agent in East Cambridge."

"Okay, good," he said. "You're right about the mob. With their reach, she'll be lucky to last a week on her own. What she needs is a completely new identity. In essence, a whole new life."

"Can you make that happen?" Helen asked, knowing that he'd come to the aid of those who had been wrongfully persecuted.

"I can," Henry replied, "but I can also teach *you* how to do it."

"I'd like that very much," she said. "No one should have to live in fear."

"Agreed. Now, you need to understand the risk. If word gets out to the wrong people that you helped this woman disappear…"

"I'm prepared to take that chance," she said, "but I'll do everything in my power to make sure *nobody* knows."

"Very well. In addition to a new identity, I'll connect you with a person who can safely transport Ann out of the area. There's also the matter of where she'll go. I can help with that too. But before we get started, tell me more about this communication plan that James set up."

"James is a rock hound. His idea is to have her send him a rock from wherever she's staying, one that is tied directly to that geographic location. As part of the plan, she'll send them to a secret drop site that he set up in a professional building in Waltham."

"That's very clever, but I have two immediate concerns," Henry said. "First off, who's going to retrieve the rocks? Wasn't James was left paralyzed by the accident?"

"I've agreed to pick up Ann's packages and deliver them to him," Helen said.

"Okay, good. The second issue is, how is Ann going to know that he's getting them? Writing to her is out of the question."

"James didn't say anything about that. As you can imagine, he's very distraught about his daughter being hunted by these gangsters.

His sole focus has been on getting her to safety."

Ye Geffray Chaucer   1

Don't Look Back

Wednesday, 6:30 a.m.

They came for her at dawn. As Rachel Goudas stood at her bedroom window, cradling a cup of tea in her hands and watching the first ribbon of sunlight spill over Neddy Mountain, she saw them slinking through the woods. Bolan, the leader of the team, was in front. Slightly behind him, and fanned out to either side, were Cafferty and Rodano. Menacing in their physical build, each one seemingly chiseled from a block of Mecklenburg County granite, it was the guns they carried that betrayed their sinister intent.

They weren't there hunting native black bear or coyote.

They were hunting her.

But how could that be? The plan Helen Bainbridge had put together to help her disappear had worked flawlessly. And ever since then she'd been so careful.

She could still remember the day, seven years ago, after weeks of running, when she'd sought out the noted author and clandestine savior of women in peril. After hearing Rachel's desperate plea for protection from the ruthless men who were pursuing her, Helen agreed to help her. Soon thereafter, Harper Denny, the successful real estate agent from Walpole, MA, had vanished like a wisp of early morning mist. In her place was Rachel Goudas: a nobody, from nowhere; a loner with no appetite for social interaction.

As part of her new life, Helen had secured a remote home for Rachel in the Bear Lake Reserve, a heavily wooded and elegant gated community in the Blue Ridge Mountains of North Carolina. In the years that followed, Rachel quickly embraced her newfound life of peace and solitude, never once imagining that the evil forces that had plagued Harper Denny would ever resurface. But now, for reasons she couldn't fathom, the threat was back.

Working quickly, she raced through the house stuffing clothes and personal items into a backpack before sneaking out through the basement slider.

Into the deep woods.

And back to a life of running.

From Bear Lake she headed north, staying out of sight as best she could and always paying with the cash she had squirreled away during the years when the real estate market was exploding and homes were selling faster than she could list them.

The good times.

They almost had her in Celina. If not for the kindness of a long-haul trucker who offered to take her as far as Falls Creek, PA, she would've been done for.

From there she continued east, but once again they caught up with her, this time in Weston Mills, NY. Under the cover of darkness she managed to slip away, and by early afternoon the next day she reached Coolidge, VT. Weary from the road, and starving from a lack of food, she found a small bistro café tucked away on a small side street and slid into a booth in the back corner.

By the time she was done eating, the skies were darkening with an impending storm. Feeling renewed from the food, she exited the café through the back door and found herself in a narrow, brick-lined alley. And that's when she saw Cafferty standing out near the street.

The moment he spotted her he turned and whistled loudly, waving to Bolan and Rodano who had taken a position on either side of the front door. *OVER HERE!*

With his eyes momentarily averted, Rachel ducked behind a dumpster to her left and knelt down, out of sight. The air was thick with the stench of rotten garbage, and as she crouched there a deafening clap of thunder jolted her senses. Then came the rain, a torrent of heavy droplets that pelted her body like hard plastic pellets. A crack of lightning lit the sky, and in that brief moment she saw them, standing three across, forming an impenetrable barrier at the mouth of the alley.

After all this time, with their failed attempts to apprehend her, it struck her as odd that they were still tasked with the job, considering who they worked for. Almost on cue, they each took out a pistol and began a slow and methodical march forward.

"You might as well give up," Bolan shouted, his words barely audible over the pounding rain. "There's no way out."

They were 30 feet from her position when a heavy metal door to their right swung open and a short gray-haired shopkeeper emerged, backside first, hunched over as he struggled to drag two bulging trash bags through the doorway.

Bolan, Cafferty and Rodano spun around at once.

When the shopkeeper turned and saw three guns pointed in his direction, he froze.

For several seconds no one moved.

And that's when Rachel squeezed out from behind the dumpster and ducked back inside the café. Less than a minute later she pushed through the front door, unseen, and sprinted up the sidewalk.

Back in the alley, Bolan waved his gun at the shopkeeper. "Get lost!"

At that, the old man abandoned the trash bags and hurried back inside, quickly closing the metal door behind him.

Rachel knew that within minutes they'd realize what she had done and would turn their attention to the café—a logical decision, and one that would buy her an additional three, maybe four minutes. But then what? Where could she go where she'd be safe? They knew she was here in town and they'd turn it upside down until they found her. What she needed was to *leave* town while she still had the jump on them.

She reached Main Street and turned right, ignoring the driving rain that stung her eyes as she raced along the abandoned sidewalk. Two hundred feet away she saw a large UPS truck parked at the curb. The driver had his back to her as he quickly wheeled a dolly loaded with boxes into a nearby store. By the time he returned to the truck, she had already climbed inside and was wedged underneath a low shelf, completely obscured behind a wall of large boxes.

The driver stowed the dolly in the back and pulled down the rolling door, the clatter momentarily blotting out the sound of the raindrops peppering the roof of the truck. He climbed in behind the wheel and pulled away from the curb just as Bolan, Cafferty, and Rodano charged out of the café, frantic.

Several minutes later the UPS truck crossed the town line into Union Falls and the driver navigated to Central Street, a wide thoroughfare lined on both sides with offices and small retail shops. He parked in his usual spot, roughly halfway down the street, which allowed him quick and easy access to each of his delivery points.

By now the rain had stopped and silver bands of afternoon sunlight were knifing through the clouds as he loaded his dolly and quickly wheeled it away. Once he was out of sight, Rachel crawled out of the truck and started up the sidewalk, walking briskly as she plotted her next move. At the next intersection she stopped. Halfway down the adjoining street to her right she saw a Greyhound bus idling at the curb. She hurried down the sidewalk and reached the bus station just as the bus was pulling away.

The station was a modest glass-front building. Inside, she saw rows of plastic seats, partially filled with travelers, some with backpacks on the floor near their feet, awaiting their bus. Positioned on the back wall was a counter where a clerk was busy helping a customer with a connecting route. On the wall overhead was the

company's iconic logo: a long, slender greyhound in full sprint—
the same logo that adorned each of their motor coaches.

From this small room she had access to virtually any town
in America. But the question was: where to go? What location
would offer her safety from the men who, somehow, unthinkably,
kept finding her? More than just a ride, she realized she needed
someone to help her—someone she could trust. But who? All of
her close friends were a faded memory. And despite having a good-
sized family, she couldn't reach out to them; the potential danger
to them was simply too much to risk. Helen Bainbridge had made
that abundantly clear.

"Once you're gone, you're gone," Helen had told her. "You
don't look back. You don't contact any family or friends. And you
don't contact *me*. If you follow my exact instructions, there won't be
any need to do so."

"Ma'am?" someone said, breaking her train of thought.

She spun around and saw a slender man in his late 20s with
a guitar case in hand and a backpack slung over his shoulder. The
weathered brown fedora on his head did little to hide his mop of
long stringy hair.

"Oh, sorry," she said, quickly stepping aside to let him pass.

As he made his way to the counter, she went to the far corner
of the room and took a seat well away from everyone else. Then,
amazingly, it came to her. There was one person who could help
her: Helen Bainbridge's agent, Louise Hayden. She had been a
trusted ally, offering counsel at a time when Rachel needed it most.
She was also the one who had processed the legal documents for
the Bear Lake Reserve property.

From her backpack, Rachel pulled out a small clutch. Buried at the bottom was her address book. She flipped to the back and found Louise's private number, scribbled there years earlier and referenced only by the letter "L." She pulled a handful of change from her pocket and hurried over to the public phone on the near wall. She fed it all the quarters she had and then dialed Louise's number. After what felt like an eternity, if finally began to ring. But no one was answering. She was just about to hang up when a voice came on the line.

"Hello?"

"Louise?" Rachel said, desperately.

"Yes, this is Louise. To whom am I speaking?"

Rachel looked around to make sure no one was close enough to hear. "It's Rachel," she said.

"I'm sorry, miss. I don't know anyone by that name. Now if you don't mind I have—"

"Wait!" Rachel blurted out. "You helped me. It was years ago. The paperwork. Remember? Harper Denny? You helped me with the paperwork."

"And what paperwork might that be?" Louise asked, calmly.

"Bear Lake Reserve."

For several seconds Louise said nothing. Then, in a clearly annoyed tone, she said, "Why are you calling me? That wasn't the arrangement, which as I recall was made very clear to you at the time."

"I know," Rachel said apologetically, "but…something went wrong. They found me. And now they're chasing me again. I've managed to lose them several times but…I can't keep doing this…

17

they're going to catch me…I know they will…and then…" she said, letting the implication hang in the air.

Again, Louise said nothing.

"I need Helen's help," Rachel said. "She's my only hope if I have any chance of surviving."

"You don't watch the news?" Louise asked.

"What are you talking about?"

"There is no Helen."

"WHAT?" Rachel exclaimed.

Several travelers looked in her direction, then went back to playing with their phones.

"Helen died…years ago."

Rachel's heart sank. "She *d-died?*"

"It was on the news," Louise said. *Where have you been?*

"I don't watch the news," Rachel explained. "I don't even own a TV. When I went into hiding, I shut the world out completely. I stayed away from crowds. I talked to no one. I made no friends."

"As you were instructed," Louise said.

"Yes, I know, but I'm desperate," Rachel told her. "These men…they just keep *showing up.* I don't know how much longer I can elude them."

"I'm going to give you a name," Louise said. "You're not to share it with anyone, is that understood?"

"Yes, of course," Rachel said, relieved.

"You contact this person, *carefully.* Do you know what that means?"

"Uh…secretly? Privately?"

"Very privately," Louise said. "I'm not sure what she'll be able to do, if anything, but at this point I'd say she's your only option."

"That's fine," Rachel said, growing impatient. "Who is it?"

Overhead, through a speaker mounted in the ceiling, came a tinny voice announcing the imminent arrival of a bus arriving from Albany with a connection to Boston.

"Her name is Gina McDermott."

"I'm sorry, there's too much noise here," Rachel said. "Say again?" She turned and saw the nose of the bus come into view through the large plate glass windows at the front of the room.

"Gina. McDermott," Louise repeated, slowly.

As Rachel wrote down the address, a number of people got up and trailed out the front door in a single line, the smell of diesel exhaust leaking into the building. She slammed the handset down in its cradle and raced over to the counter to buy a ticket, praying she wasn't too late. Twenty minutes later she was tucked in a seat near the back of the bus, on her way to Boston to find someone named Gina McDermott.

Whoever that was.

2

Lafayette Street

Saturday, 11:30 p.m.

Gina was curled up on the living room couch, nose deep in a new puzzle book, when she heard her parents pull into the driveway, returning home after a late night out with friends. Moments later, the back door opened and they shuffled into the kitchen, debating the efficiency of the restaurant waitstaff, or the lack thereof.

Gina's mother appeared in the hallway. "Oh, you're still up," she said, surprised.

"Yes, Mom. It's Saturday, remember?" Gina groaned.

Something clicked in her mother's mind and she began patting both coat pockets.

"Did you lose something?" Gina asked.

"I…seem…to…have…misplaced…my…phone…"

Gina's father walked up behind her and stopped. When he saw Gina sitting on the couch, he stepped into the room and began a thorough search, as if an unwelcome person was hiding there at 11:30 on a Saturday night.

Someone like Nathan Cole.

They were convinced that he was nothing but trouble and would eventually lead her to a grisly end. For that reason, they had forbidden her from associating with him.

If they only knew, she had mused, time and again. The list of unsolved mysteries they had untangled was impressive and known to only a handful of friends and select family members.

"What's wrong?" Gina said, annoyed, as her father checked behind the curtains.

"Nothing," he mumbled, surveying the room one last time.

Gina's mother had given up on her coat and was checking each of her pants pockets.

When Gina saw that she shook her head in disbelief. *Unbelievable.* "Did you leave it in the car?" she asked.

"Well, let's see. Did I?" her mother said, staring off into that mystical void on the far side of the universe where answers to difficult questions resided.

Oh, brother, Gina thought. She rolled her eyes, then got up from the couch. "You wait here while I go check." *I wouldn't want you to get lost in the back yard.*

The night air was brisk as she pushed through the back-porch door and hurried across the lawn to the driveway. She checked the front seat of the car and found her mother's phone in the map pocket on the door, hidden behind a half-filled bottle of water and a package of tissues. How it got there she could only imagine.

She had just closed the door when she heard something stir in the bushes next to the house. When she turned, she saw a dark figure emerge, stumbling forward before eventually standing upright.

"Don't be afraid," Rachel said quickly. "I need your help. I'm looking for Gina McDermott. She lives here, right?"

"Yes," Gina replied, her fear suddenly replaced by a burning curiosity. "Who are you and what do you want?"

Rachel eyed the street nervously. "For your own safety, it would be better if I spoke with Gina directly."

"You are," Gina said sternly.

Rachel's eyes went wide. "Excuse me?"

"I'm Gina McDermott. What's this all about?"

The sound of an approaching car made Rachel duck back into the bushes.

"What are you *doing?*" Gina asked, watching the car pass the house. It was the woman who lived at the far end of the street in the cinnamon-red cape. They'd spoken so long ago that she'd forgotten the woman's last name. Pinchuk? Pinard? Peterson? *Whatever.*

Once the car had passed, Rachel emerged from the bushes. "It's not safe out in the open where anyone can see me," she said, panicked. "We need to hide."

Gina heard the genuine fear in her voice. The woman had the look of someone on the run. Her hair was a tangled mess and her clothes looked like she'd been sleeping in them for a week. The backpack she was holding looked like it had been used in a rugby scrum.

Gina sized up her options, eyeing the house, then the garage. *No, and no.* There was only one viable alternative. "Wait here," she said, then hurried back into the house. Her parents had gone upstairs so she left the phone on the kitchen counter, in plain sight where her mother couldn't possibly miss it.

Then again…

When she got back outside, Rachel was wedged between two hydrangea bushes. "Follow me," she told her, then hurried across the strip of lawn that divided her house from Nathan's, making a beeline for his garage. Once inside, the eerie darkness was unsettling. Gina could only make out the woman's silhouette, which was backlit by the moonlight filtering in through the side door. Suddenly she wondered if she'd made a tactical error.

What if she's a deranged killer?

I just led her into a place where no one can see us…

Or hear me if I scream for help.

"My name is Rachel Goudas," the woman said. "I got your name and address from Louise Hayden."

"*Louise* gave you my name?" Gina asked, baffled that her grandmother's former literary agent would do such a thing.

"Yes," Rachel said. "I came all the way from Ohio to find you."

Gina didn't ask why she would make such a trek; she was too busy working out the machinations that had delivered this woman to her in the middle of the night. *Louise worked with my grandmother… who secretly came to the aid of women in danger…which means…* "My grandmother helped you," she said.

"Your grandmother?"

"Helen Bainbridge."

"Yes," Rachel said. "Seven years ago she helped me escape from some very bad men who were chasing me. She created a whole new

23

life for me. New name. New place to live. She saved my life. But a week ago they managed to find me again."

"They being the same men from before?"

"Yes."

"Who are they?"

A car drove by the house and slowed, the throaty sound of the muffler echoing off the houses on either side of the street. When Rachel heard it, she panicked. She ran to the side door, eased it open in time to see red brake lights paint the street in front of Nathan's house. "Oh no!" she said, quickly closing the door. "It's them."

Gina went to her, took her arm, and gently guided her away from the door. "Relax. That's just my neighbor, *Franklin*," she said, uttering his name with disdain. "He comes home from work every night at the same time and wakes up the whole neighborhood. We think he's deaf."

Rachel took in a deep breath and let it out, feeling her fear evaporate.

"You still haven't answered my question," Gina said. "Who are these men chasing you?"

"Hired guns, enforcers, triggermen, call them whatever you like. When they showed up at my home in North Carolina, guns in hand, I fled…I grabbed what I could and then—"

"Wait," Gina said, cutting her off. "They just showed up at your house?"

"Yes?"

"Why? What do they want with you?"

"They think I have something that belongs to their boss."

"You *stole* something from their boss?"

24

"Nathan!"

He stopped walking and looked in her direction, scanning the trees that lined the back yard.

"Over here!" she yelled, louder.

"Gina?" he said, walking slowly toward the garage. When he got to the side door he saw her standing inside, holding the door open just enough to allow her to look out.

"What are you doing?" he asked.

"I need your help," she told him. There was fear in her voice.

"My help? Right *now?*"

She grabbed his arm and yanked him through the doorway.

"Hey! What are you doing?" he said, stumbling forward.

She let go of his arm and closed the door.

He instinctively reached for the light switch when she pulled his arm back.

"No lights."

A soft shuffling sound in the corner made him turn and look. In the murky shadows he saw the rough outline of a person. "Uh, Gina?" he said. "Who is that?"

"She's nobody you know."

"Then, what's she doing in my garage in the middle of the night?"

"You're going to help me save her life."

"I'm going to do *what?*"

"Just listen, and don't interrupt," Gina said. *Like you always do.* "Her name is Rachel. Some very bad men are chasing her and she needs our help."

"You mean, *my* help," Nathan countered.

"Interruptions?" Gina said.

"Go on," he said quietly.

"We need to find a place to hide her. Someplace safe where these goons won't find her."

"Is that all?"

"Yes…for now."

"All right. But first I have some questions. For starters, why did she come to you?"

"That's not important."

"Not *important*? A complete stranger approaches you in the middle of the night, in desperate need of help, and the reason why she picked you isn't important?"

"I'm not going to talk about it so *let it go!*" she said, loudly. "And don't ask me again."

He eyed her warily. Her refusal to talk about it sounded oddly familiar. "Does this have something to do with what happened six months ago?" *When you were acting strange and refused to explain why, and Kendra and I found you sneaking around outside the Bank Square Mall in Waltham?* he wanted to say.

She held her ground.

"Well?" he said, pressing.

Finally, she offered him a crumb. "Yes and no."

"What's that supposed to mean?"

"It means that, yes, this has something to do with that, and no, I'm not going to explain it. Now, can we please focus on the problem at hand?"

"Very well," he replied. "You want me to help you save her life, okay, fine. What exactly did you have in mind? And may I remind you, it's almost one o'clock in the morning."

She took his arm and pulled him over to the near corner of the garage. "Are you forgetting that you have a whole team of people at your disposal now?" she said, keeping her voice low.

The team in question was a secret group of specialists his grandfather, Henry Hammond, had assembled years earlier, to assist him in helping those in need, much like Helen Bainbridge had done during the remaining years of her life. The team, which his grandfather had nicknamed "Facilitators," included an expert in legal matters, another in electronics, one in transportation, one in safehouse acquisition and someone to keep them clean and stocked with food.

"Wait! How did it go tonight?" she said, referring to the events that had transpired three hours earlier, when Nathan and a handful of others exposed two members of the Facilitator's team as the ones responsible for the death of his grandfather, Henry Hammond.

"Our plan worked like a charm," Nathan replied, traces of the anger he'd felt for those who betrayed his grandfather heating his words. "My hunch was right. We got a full confession and the killers responsible are sitting in a jail cell as we speak."

Gina desperately wanted to hear more but now wasn't the time. "When we're done with this mess you're going to tell me what happened," she said. "Every single detail. But right now, can we get her into one of your safehouses?"

One of your safehouses.

The words hit him like a storm surge. He was about to turn 13 years old and he had a collection of safehouses at his disposal, none of which he could talk about with any of his friends.

Only Gina.

"Hold that thought," he said. He pulled his flip phone from his pocket and hit the speed dial number for Kendra.

"Hey," she said, picking up after the first ring. "Did you forget something in my car?"

"No. I need your help."

"O-kay," she said slowly. "Can this wait until later? You know, after the sun comes up?"

"No. It has to be done right now."

Kendra heard something unsettling in his tone. "Are you all right?"

"I'm fine," he said, "but there's a woman here who needs our help."

"A woman? What woman?" Kendra asked as she accelerated around a car that was slowing to make a turn. It was late and she was tired so she skipped her usual berating of the driver.

"I'll explain when you get here," Nathan said. "We need to find a place to hide her."

"You know who to call," Kendra said, implying that any safehouse request needed to come from him. Moreover, it was something he would have to learn to do using his newfound resources.

"I do," he said, "but the person we're helping will need a ride."

"You make the call. I'll be there in 10 minutes," Kendra said. She cut the wheel and made a tight U-turn in the road, the sound of screeching tires coming through the phone.

Nathan disconnected and quickly found the number for the facilitator in charge of the safehouses, a woman with the code name Sidney. As he punched in her number, he turned and faced the wall.

Sidney answered at once. "Nathan?" she said. "What's up? After the day you've had I figured you'd be fast asleep by now."

"Something's come up," he told her. "I need your help hiding someone. And, yes, I know, it's almost one o'clock in the morning."

Sidney didn't have to ask if he was serious. She could hear it in his voice. "The time of day has nothing to do with it," she said. "It never has and it never will. You call with a request and we make it happen, just like we did for your grandfather. Did you call Kendra for a ride?"

"I did. She's on her way."

"Good. When you see her, have her call me."

"Will do."

He closed the phone and turned around to see Rachel standing at the side door, face pressed to the glass, peering out at the street. Gina had walked over to join her and was standing behind her, craning her neck to see outside.

"What's wrong?" he asked.

"Someone just drove by the house, very slowly," Gina replied.

"It's probably just Mrs. Gilbert looking for her cat."

"There!" Rachel exclaimed. "They just drove by again." She turned from the door, panicked. "We need to get out of here, *now!*"

"Hold on," Nathan said, walking over to the door. "Let's not freak out just yet. You two stay here while I go take a look."

He stepped outside and ran around the back of the house. When he came to the front corner, he ducked behind the rhododendron bushes that lined the front porch. Moments later, a black Chevy Tahoe crept past. Through one of the side windows came a powerful flashlight beam that scoured every home, car port, and garage. Whoever it was, one thing was certain: they had no interest in flowering shrubs or suburban architecture.

31

As it continued down the street, he climbed out of the bushes and ran back to the garage where Gina and Rachel were waiting just inside the door. "Come on, let's go," he said. "Follow me and stay close."

Without a word they followed him outside. He hurried along the side of the garage and then climbed over a section of ragged wire fence into the patch of woods that lined the back of the property. From there, he sprinted across the neighbor's yard and stopped behind a small garden shed. By the time Rachel and Gina caught up to him, he had his flip phone out and was pressing the speed dial number for Kendra.

"Almost there," she said, answering right away.

"Forget my house," he said. "We're not there. We're one street over, on Lafayette."

"You're *where?*"

"Someone is casing the neighborhood. We think they're looking for...hold on." He lowered the phone and said to Rachel, "What's your name?"

"Rachel."

"We think they're looking for—"

"Rachel. Yes, I heard," Kendra cut in before he could finish.

"We're about halfway down Lafayette Street. Look for a large two-story colonial with a swing set and garden shed in the side yard. Flash your lights one time as you get close. Oh, and Sidney wants you to call her."

"All right, you three stay out of sight and watch for me. I'm calling Sidney now."

The line went silent and Nathan closed his phone. "Wait here," he told Gina. Then, to Rachel, "When I motion to you, you run like crazy to the car. Got it?"

"What are we doing?" she asked.

"We're getting you out of here," Gina said. "Our friend Kendra is going to take you to a safehouse where these thugs can't find you."

Rachel gave Nathan a look. "*You* have a safehouse?"

"Actually, I have a few of them," he said. "They belonged to my grandfather."

"Your grandfather," Rachel repeated, growing even more confused. Since when did a grandfather give his grandson a safehouse, let alone 'a few of them'? A train set or some tools, maybe. But *safehouses*? She shook her head and mumbled, "What kind of fantasy world is this?"

"Nathan's grandfather was Henry Hammond," Gina explained, giving legitimacy to Nathan's words. "He and my grandmother were good friends."

"Wait a minute," Rachel said, staring at Nathan with a look of awe. "Henry Hammond was your grandfather?"

"Yes," Nathan said. "Why? Did you know him?"

"Well, yeah...sort of..." she said, then paused, realizing she'd said too much.

"Sort of?" Nathan repeated, unwilling to let it go.

"Never mind," Rachel said, looking away. "It's nothing."

Nathan eyed her suspiciously. Something strange was going on here — something about Gina's grandmother and his grandfather. But what was it? Did Gina know? Even if she did, would she tell him? He stored that nugget away for another time, then darted over to the edge of the yard that skirted the street. He ducked down behind a white hydrangea bush, which gave him a clear view of the street in both directions. As he waited, the only sound to be heard was the sporadic traffic on Rt. 2A two blocks away.

Kendra kept her foot heavy on the gas pedal as she raced down the Alewife Brook Parkway, weaving around taxis and happy couples on their way home from a late-night dinner date. As she swerved around them, cutting from lane to lane, she kept one hand on the wheel and used the other to dial Sidney's phone number.

"Sidney, this is Kendra," she said, speeding through a traffic light as it changed from yellow to red. "You spoke with Nathan?"

"Yes. Are you familiar with "The Beach?" Sidney asked.

"Yeah, I heard my father mention it a few times. South Boston, right?"

"Correct. Given Nathan's location, it's the closest option and it's currently vacant. I'll give you the address and two entry codes. One for the back door and one for the door that leads up to the second floor. Be sure to go in the back, not the front. Once inside, you want the door to the left."

"Back entrance. Door to the left. Got it," Kendra said. "Address?"

"1480 Colombia Road. Look for the striped awning on the second-floor balcony. You can't miss it. It's rolled up and looks like a giant candy cane. Best to park one street over, on East 8th, or beneath the apartment complex on the next block."

"Understood."

Sidney recited both entry code numbers and had Kendra read them back to her. "Okay, good," she said, when Kendra was done. "That leaves just one more thing."

"What's that?"

"How to leave the building without being seen."

Rachel got tired of waiting and began to pace in a tight oval. She was convinced that any minute now Bolan and his associates would appear, guns drawn, and finish the job they'd been hired to do.

"Relax," Gina told her. "Kendra will take good care of you. Later today, I'll call her with a plan. *Once I figure one out.*

"You promise?" Rachel asked.

"Yes. Don't worry, I'll make it happen." *Somehow.*

"Don't forget what I told you in the garage," Rachel said. "You need to find him. It's the only way this thing has a happy ending. These people are ruthless. You need to avoid them at all costs. That goes for your friend Nathan too. If they somehow discover you're involved…"

She couldn't bring herself to finish the thought but Gina got the message loud and clear.

Nathan saw a car make the turn at the opposite end of the street. As it grew closer, the groan of the engine told him it was Kendra even before she flashed her lights. He stood at once and flagged her down, then called to Gina and Rachel in a voice loud enough for them to hear but low enough to keep from waking the whole neighborhood.

"Let's go," Gina said, taking Rachel by the arm. Together they sprinted across the yard and got to the street just as the Volvo came to a stop. With the dexterity of a hotel valet, Nathan opened the rear door and motioned Rachel inside, then spoke to Kendra through the open driver's-side window. "You know where you're going?" he asked.

"I do," she said.

"You'll call when you get there?" Gina asked.

"Yup. Should be about 20 minutes from now."

Out of the corner of his eye Nathan saw the flash of headlights as another vehicle turned onto the street. It was driving slowly, a powerful beam like a theater spotlight blasting from the passenger-side window.

"Go! Now!" he told Kendra.

When she glanced up at the rearview mirror and saw the driver suddenly accelerate, she stomped on the gas pedal, sending the Volvo racing away, tires squealing.

Nathan grabbed Gina's arm and ran back to the garden shed. They had just ducked behind it when the Tahoe sped past, the moonlight reflecting off its polished snowflake rims. Nathan watched it speed past then dug the phone from his pocket and called Kendra. "The Tahoe," he said, trying to keep his voice calm. "Those are the same guys who were casing the houses on my street. Are they still following you?"

"Uh, you could say that," Kendra said. There was an edge to her voice.

He heard her tell Rachel to grab hold of something and hang on tight. That was followed by the painful screech of tires and the roar of the Volvo's engine.

"Kendra?"

"Gotta go," she said.

CLICK!

"What's going on?" Gina asked, when she saw the look of concern on his face.

"Those were the same guys," he said.

The air went out of her lungs and she fell back against the shed.

"Are you sure you don't want to tell me what this is all about?" Nathan asked.

"No!"

"Okay, fine. What happens next? You know your friend can't stay in the safehouse forever."

"Assuming she gets there alive," Gina muttered under her breath. And she's not my friend.

Nathan heard his phone ring and quickly pulled it out of his pocket. When he saw Kendra's name on the call screen he tapped the talk button. "Yeah?"

"We're good," she told him.

In the background he heard the usual sound of the Volvo's engine. It wasn't racing. There were no screeching tires. Just a steady rumble as it cruised along at what he could only assume was a speed well above the posted limit. "You lost them?" he asked.

"Uh-huh," she said. "It wasn't that hard."

In his mind he pictured her smirking.

"Must've been out-of-towners," she said, not impressed. "They hung with me for a bit but I lost them at Tufts University."

"Nice work. And, oh, by the way…thank you."

"No thanks needed," she said. "I'm the new driver, remember? This is how it works."

"Right," Nathan said, once again staggered by the notion of the Facilitators group, and the variety of specialized services that were now at his beck and call, including a driver.

"You never told me what this is all about," Kendra said. She was racing south on Rt. 93, watching the road ahead while systematically checking the rearview mirror.

"Honestly, I have no idea. This is a Gina thing," he said, looking at her as he spoke.

"Well, tell her I'll stay with Rachel at the safehouse tonight. But somebody needs to call me in the morning with a plan of action."

"Will do," Nathan said. "Until then, be careful."

"Aren't I always?" Kendra joked.

"No comment," he said, then clicked off the call. "They're okay. Kendra lost them, which brings us back to my question. What happens next?"

"We need to keep her safe while I look for someone."

"Someone?"

"The only person who can make all this go away, that's all you need to know."

"Can I at least get his name?"

"He has no name," she said, pushing past him and heading for the trees.

"No name? Wait!" he said, running to catch up. "Without a name, how do you expect to find him? Do you know where he lives?"

"No. He's a phantom."

"A phantom? Oh, that's nice," he muttered as he followed her into the patch of trees.

When they reached the wire fence, she pushed it down and hopped over it with ease.

"If he's a phantom," Nathan asked, doing the same, "how are you supposed to find him?"

"I have my ways," she said.

As they walked past the garage his curiosity continued to churn. "What's that supposed to mean? Without a name or an address, you have nothing."

Wrong, she thought to herself. What Rachel had said was vague, but there was someone who might be able to help her decipher it—a man named James Donnelly. But before she sought him out, there was an important stop she had to make.

Alone.

Like a ghost.

Unseen by anyone.

3

The Beach

Sunday, 6:00 a.m.

Gina awoke at six o'clock to a quiet house. Factoring in travel time for the job at hand, roughly a half hour each way, she knew that leaving now would put her back home in less than two hours—well before her parents pried themselves out of bed for the day.

At 6:15 she snuck out the back door and walked briskly up the street. All around her, everything was eerily still. There was no breeze. Tree branches hung motionless as if made of injection-molded plastic. There were no human forms to be seen, not a single person walking their dog or out for an early morning power walk.

When she reached Mass Ave she rode the Mass Transit bus to the Upland Road stop, then made the short walk to Porter Square

Station where she took the Fitchburg Line out to Waltham.

With the commuter rail car jostling her from side to side, questions began to flood her mind. Why did Rachel Goudas suddenly appear at her house now, after all these years? What went wrong with the new life her grandmother had carefully constructed for her? More importantly, what was she, Gina McDermott, going to do to return Rachel to a life of total obscurity without anyone else knowing? Is this what her grandmother had in mind for her when she entrusted her with the book notes for the Helen Bainbridge Mysteries—a six-book collection that followed the exploits of her main character, a fictional police detective named Nikki Nolan—which doubled as a secret messaging system for the women she had helped to hide.

Fortunately, Nathan had agreed to help. But how much further would he go without knowing every last detail? Would she have to reveal her grandmother's secret after making a vow to herself never to do so?

She pushed those nagging questions aside, which felt like trying to slide heavy furniture across cracked asphalt, and then recounted the conversation she'd had with Rachel in Nathan's garage. Specifically, Rachel's interaction with Helen Bainbridge years earlier as she was about to leave behind everything and everyone she held precious.

"She told me we were going to meet someone," Rachel had said. *"She never mentioned his name. According to her he was a transporter, nothing more. He wasn't interested in who I was or my dilemma that had required his services. His one and only job was to deliver me to a specific location, safely, and without incident. Your grandmother assured me that*

he was very good at it because in all the years she'd worked with him, he'd never lost anyone."

Gina reached into her backpack and took out her leather-bound notepad, a gift from her grandmother, and one of her most treasured possessions. The jarring motion of the car disrupted her ordinarily flawless penmanship as she scribbled a single word.

Transporter?

When she was done, she stared at what she'd written and recalled what Rachel had said next.

"It was after midnight when we left. I was totally exhausted and fell asleep. When your grandmother woke me sometime later, I had no idea where we were or how long we'd been driving. All I remember is, we were parked on a narrow road in some city. At least I think it was a city. I was sleeping when we arrived, and when I woke up, it was so dark that I couldn't be sure. I just remember the sensation I had. It was like I was dreaming, but I was fully awake."

Gina made another entry in her notepad.

City?

"There was an alley across from the car. Your grandmother was watching it when out of nowhere this figure appeared wearing a heavy cloak with the hood pulled up over his head."

"Appeared?"

"Yeah, it was eerie. He wasn't there and then he was. He stepped right out of the darkness, into the moonlight. When your grandmother saw him, she said, 'It's time,' then reached over the seat and grabbed this backpack. It was jam packed with bottles of water, sandwiches, power bars, you

name it."

"For the trip."

"Yeah. Little did I know at the time, it was the only thing I'd eat or drink for the next two days."

"And then what happened? You went with this...courier person?"

"Yeah, but before I got out of the car, your grandmother handed me an envelope and instructed me to give it to the man in the cloak. Then she looked me in the eye and muttered something that made no sense."

"What was it?"

"I don't know. It was seven years ago. You really expect me to remember back that far?"

"Yes, as a matter of fact I do," Gina remembered saying, her voice rising in volume. "This woman is about to save your life and you forget the things she tells you?"

"Hey, it was late!" Rachel had countered, equally miffed. "I was afraid for my life. And here I was about to go who-knows-where with some creepy guy that looked like he might dismember me with a chainsaw the first chance he got. What was I supposed to do? Take out a pen and write down the cryptic things she was saying?"

Gina made a third entry in her notepad.

Cryptic words?

She felt the train slow, the brakes emitting a high-pitched squeal as the Moody Street platform came into sight. Ten minutes later she was walking down Green Street, just as she'd done six months earlier at the desperate urging of James Donnelly.

Modern office buildings with finely manicured lawns and strategically placed ornamental trees and flowering shrubs lined both sides of the street. As it curved to the left, she saw the large two-story office building with alternating bands of pale concrete and dark mirrored glass that made it look like a giant piece of layered chocolate cake. Lining the perimeter were Dogwood trees and Littleleaf Boxwood shrubs. She went as far as the center walkway, then turned in a slow circle, surveying everything in sight. Just like her street at home, she was completely alone.

She started up the walk, past the polished black-marble slab that identified the property as the Arthur M. House Professional Building at 17 Green Street. When she reached the large front doors, made with thick tinted glass set in a heavy steel frame, she pulled one handle, then the other.

They were both locked.

At 7 a.m., Nathan's father David rapped softly on Nathan's bedroom door and then stepped into the room.

Nathan was lying on his side in bed. Not asleep. Not awake. He was somewhere in that middle place, his mind swimming in a dark fog as he contemplated the dramatic turn his life had taken, punctuated by the events of the previous day. With Gina's help, along with a few select others, he had concocted a clever ruse to expose those who had betrayed his grandfather years earlier, a selfless and deadly act that had resulted in his untimely passing. For years it had been an unsolved mystery that had haunted the Hammond family. But no longer.

For Nathan, catching the two masterminds behind the plot was an emotional victory, but it served as a cruel reminder that the carefree life he once enjoyed was gone forever. Those simpler times had been swept aside the day he stumbled across his grandfather's book-case in the attic, a discovery that had pulled him into a shadowy world of misfortune, deceit, and evildoers from which there was no turning back.

"Did I wake you?" David whispered, as he eased the door shut.

Nathan blinked hard, scattering the dark thoughts that had plagued his sleep into oblivion. But they'd be back, and in greater number. It was only a matter of time. "Dad?" he said, confused.

David brought the chair over from the desk and sat down. "We need to talk," he said.

"About what?"

"You."

"What about me?" Nathan asked. He kicked away the bed covers and sat up.

"We've reached the point where a decision has to be made."

"A decision? What are you talking about?"

"Before I answer that question, I think we need to come to an agreement on something."

"And that would be...?"

"Each of your adventures," David said, bracketing the word with air quotes, "has steered you into very dangerous and uncharted wa-ters."

"Uh...*yeah*...you could say that," Nathan said, leaning back against the headboard. *Didn't exactly have much of a choice, did I?* he wanted to say, recalling the enchanted things the bookcase had done, otherworldly occurrences, that had initiated each of his so-called ad-ventures. In that moment, he wondered how much his parents really knew about the bookcase and the spirit of his grandfather that had

45

taken up residence there.

"Your mother and I have discussed this and we both agree," David said slowly, unsure of how Nathan would react. "If you want, you can stop. Just walk away."

And there was the answer.

They *didn't* know.

He couldn't just walk away. He had already tried and it didn't work. His grandfather's spirit had badgered him relentlessly through a series of ghostly and spine-tingling incidents that made Nathan's options painfully clear: he had none. They were his grandfather's way of saying, "I have chosen you and you will continue."

"What about the family legacy?" he asked, referring to the generations of family members who had used the bookcase as an instrument for justice.

His father looked down at the floor, saddened, as one tragic family event after another stabbed at his memory. "The legacy you speak of has resulted in a mixture of triumphs and unbearable sorrows," he said softly.

Nathan knew full well that he was referring to the various family members who had perished over the years, and for several seconds neither of them spoke as the painful loss of those loved ones hung in the room like a fetid odor.

Finally, his father broke the silence.

"Your mother and I know that, before he died, your grandfather chose you to be the next guardian of the bookcase, to continue the work that he and his predecessors had done."

There was so much Nathan wanted to say at that moment but he remained silent. As dangerous and life-threatening as each of his endeavors had been, he had never experienced anything like the bookcase—to be part of something so worthwhile, so powerful. So *important*.

"We also realize that you've inherited certain…tools…" David began, referring to Beck, Nathan's de facto body guard and personal trainer; Jameson, the Hammond family's longtime friend and trusted advisor; Kendra, his tougher-than-nails daughter; and the remaining members of the Facilitators group—the secret team Henry Hammond had assembled, each with their own specialized set of skills. "They've helped to ease our anxiety, but only just a little."

Again, Nathan said nothing. In his own defense, his actions held true to everything the bookcase stood for following its arrival in America five generations earlier.

Wrongful acts require corrective action.

Good must triumph over evil.

Regardless of the risks involved.

His father stood and returned the chair to the desk. "I'll fully understand if you don't want to continue," he said, "but if you decide otherwise, then your training with Beck needs to be taken to the next level. Immediately."

"I'm ready," Nathan said without hesitation. *Bring it on.*

His father walked over and gave him a hug. "This family has suffered far too much loss."

"I'm going to change that, Dad," Nathan said.

His father broke their embrace and placed his hands atop Nathan's shoulders, eyeing him intently. "You already have, son, which is why it's okay if you just forget about the bookcase and get on with the rest of your life."

Nathan gave him an incredulous look. "Forget about the book-case? Get on with my life? Dad, the bookcase *is* my life. I don't want less. I want more! I'm older now. I'm stronger. I have help…"

"Okay, okay," David said, gesturing with both hands. "I'll call Beck." He walked as far as the door and stopped to look back. "You're sure about this?"

Nathan nodded emphatically. "Call him."

Gina stepped back from the doors, unsure what to do next. During her previous visit they were open and she was able to duck inside, unnoticed. But that was a Friday. This was Sunday, which for most people was a day of rest. She was scolding herself for not antic-ipating such a contingency when the sound of an approaching vehi-cle made her turn and look. Seconds later she saw a cleaning-service van turn the corner. Hoping the driver hadn't noticed her standing at the door, she scrambled along the side of the building and ducked down behind a grouping of Boxwood shrubs.

The van came to a stop in front of the building and two men climbed out. Both were clad in blue jeans and matching polo shirts with a small company logo embroidered on the breast pocket. As the driver unloaded cleaning equipment, his partner sauntered up the walkway, a ring of keys jingling in one hand. He unlocked the front doors and propped them open using the kick-down door stop mounted to each one. As he walked back to the van, Gina crept out from behind the shrubs and darted into the building.

The front foyer was just as she remembered it: cavernous, with a floor of polished marble tile and walls paneled in an exotic dark wood. She ignored the elevator and stairs directly ahead and took a sharp left, sprinting down the empty hallway until she reached the second office on the left. There was no sign on the door. It was simply marked Suite #3.

She dug the key out of her backpack and quickly opened the door. Junk mail, retail catalogs, grocery flyers and direct mail pieces had infiltrated the room through the mail slot and were spread across the floor like an invading army. *Note to self,* she told herself, *next time bring trash bags.*

She turned her attention to the large cardboard box that was taped to the back of the door. In the six months that had passed since she was last there, the box was roughly half full. She was fishing through the contents when her hand grazed a thickly padded mailer. Feeling a bolt of nervous excitement, she pulled it from the box, checked the handwriting, which she recognized at once, then put it in her backpack.

Should anyone open the envelope, the gemstone sealed inside was nothing more than a unique rock. But, in fact, it was part of a covert system Donnelly had set up with his daughter, Ann DeBartolo, to be used as a secret method of communication after Helen Bainbridge had helped her escape a North Shore mob family and a crooked FBI agent. The gemstones she sent were from specific locations across the country, which let her father know where she was. They were also a confirmation of her continued safety.

When her further search of the box yielded no more mailers, she zipped her backpack shut and slowly eased the door open, checking the hallway in both directions. The cleaning crew was nowhere in sight.

Well that wasn't so hard, she though as she left the building. She rode the train back to Porter Square, her arms wrapped around her backpack that was nestled in her lap, contemplating what she needed to do next. Not just how to do it. But how to pull it off without getting an innocent woman killed.

When she got home, she entered through the back porch, creeping slowly toward the kitchen door as she listened for the sound of her parents talking or making breakfast. Hearing neither, she stepped into the kitchen, fixed herself a bagel, then hurried upstairs. As she passed her parents' bedroom she heard snoring. Two erratic patterns. Like a pair of old lawn mowers in desperate need of a tune up, trying their best to out-sputter one another. Judging by the sound, she figured they wouldn't wake up for another two hours.

She sat down at her desk and began eating, all the while plotting how she would deliver the padded mailer to Donnelly. Just like before, the problem was how to get to the facility where he lived, Sutton Woods, in Weston, without having to explain it to anyone. At the moment, her options were severely limited.

Kendra was indisposed.

Walking or riding her bike to Weston was out of the question.

Mass transit would take too long.

There was Ellie, her aunt, who knew of her collaborations with Nathan and who had helped her on numerous occasions, but...*wait a minute!* She was in her current predicament because of one person: Louise Hayden. She was the one who had thrust Rachel into her life, along with a trio of thugs who apparently were dead set on finding her. Emphasis on the word dead. By Gina's way of thinking, Louise owed her.

She set the bagel down on her plate and tiptoed out of the room, her stocking feet barely registering a sound on the hardwood floor as she padded down the hallway. When she got downstairs she grabbed the wireless extension from the end table in the living room, then hurried back up to her room. Months earlier, she had taped Louise Hayden's business card to the underside of her desktop where prying eyes wouldn't find it. On the back of the card was Louise's personal phone number. Ignoring the early hour, and the fact that it was Sunday, she quickly dialed the number.

As she waited for the call to connect, her thoughts drifted back to the moment she saw Rachel emerge from the bushes next to the house, desperation in her voice and fear in her eyes. *What in the world would possess Louise Hayden to give her my name?* she wondered. *Why would she blindly pass that firestorm on to me without so much as—?"*

"Hello?"

"Louise?" Gina said, the image of Rachel fading away in a flash.

"Yes, to whom am I speaking?"

"This is Gina McDermott."

Silence.

"Hello?" Gina said.

"I'm here," Louise replied, cautiously. "Are you all right?"

"All right? No, I'm not *all right!*" Gina said. There was fire in her words. "Last night a woman named Rachel Goudas showed up at my house. I believe the two of you have met. The reason I know this is because she claims *you* gave her my name. Said she was being pursued by three thugs who've been after her for some time now. Years, in fact. As it turns out, she wasn't making it up because they arrived just moments later. If it wasn't for the help of a friend, who shall remain nameless, there's no telling what might've happened, to

Rachel, or to me, or to my friend…but it wouldn't have been good!"

"Nathan," Louise said.

"Huh?"

"Your friend. You're talking about Nathan."

"Yes, but how—?"

"Not on the phone."

"Excuse me?"

"I'll explain, but not on the phone."

"Okay, fine," Gina shot back. "I need a ride to Weston…*today*… and you're the perfect person to drive me there. It'll be just the two of us. You can explain on the way."

"Weston," Louise confirmed.

"Yes. And don't ask me why."

"Very well. When would you like to go?"

"How soon can you get here?"

Just after eight o'clock, Kendra pushed through the door of the second-floor apartment carrying a cardboard beverage tray loaded with two large styrofoam cups of coffee, a dozen creamers, and a small mountain of sugar packets.

Rachel was sitting on the couch in the next room, rummaging through her backpack. At the sound of the door opening, she quickly zipped it shut. "Oh, it's you," she said, hand to chest. "I thought you abandoned me."

"Nope," Kendra said coolly, as she walked into the living room. She set the cardboard tray on the oblong coffee table in front of the couch. "You were still sleeping when I left and I didn't want to wake you." She twisted each of the cups from the tray and handed one to

Rachel. "There's a small market a couple blocks over. I love those places. Family run by good hard-working people who take pride in everything they do." She removed the lid of her cup and inhaled the aroma. "This isn't as good as what I serve in my shop, but it's not bad."

"Your shop?" Rachel asked, peeling the lid off her cup.

"Yeah, I have a coffee shop. A serious one, mind you," Kendra replied. "Not like these chain joints that keep popping up like weeds everywhere. We only grind the best beans, my staff is awesome, and we source our pastries from a local bakery. Lucky for me, the place practically runs itself." *Which is why I'm here right now and not there,* she didn't say.

She walked over to the slider that opened onto a spacious balcony, then used the tip of her finger to part the sheer curtain. The sun was shimmering off the rippled surface of Old Harbor, creating a thin haze that partially obscured Carson Beach, and further out, Thomson Island.

Rachel was busy doctoring her coffee with sugar packets and nearly all the creamers. When she was done, she took a cautious sip, then another, before replacing the lid. "So what happens now?" she asked.

"We wait here until Gina calls with a plan," Kendra said.

Rachel grunted something, barely audible.

Kendra let go of the curtain and turned around to face her. "What was that?"

"I've got hired thugs chasing me and my life is in the hands of a 12-year-old girl!" Rachel exclaimed.

"Actually, she turns 13 next month," Kendra noted.

"Thirteen? Oh, well that changes everything."

"I wouldn't be so quick to judge her," Kendra warned. "She and Nathan have taken on some pretty serious gangsters and have lived to see the following day. And when I say serious, I mean the type of criminals who prompt global manhunts. They make the goons chasing you look like shoplifters."

"Gangsters, huh?" Rachel said. "Like who?"

"I'm not at liberty to say, but trust me when I tell you that—"

Her words fell off and she jerked her head toward the kitchen.

Rachel was mid-sip and pulled the cup away from her mouth, nearly spilling coffee in her lap. "What is it?" she asked. "What's wrong?"

Kendra hurried back to the kitchen, set her coffee cup on the counter, then crossed the room and disappeared down the narrow hallway that led to the bathroom and a series of bedrooms. Years earlier, one of them had been converted into a mini communication center. There were no lamps or overhead lighting. A series of narrow LED light bars were set into the wall just above the baseboard molding, giving off a soft glow that clung to the floor like swamp fog.

Positioned in the middle of the room was a "banana table console" with an ergonomic design that, true to its name, resembled the curved shape of a six-foot-long banana, or an equally large cashew. On the lower level was a single keypad, wirelessly connected to four 32" monitors that sat directly above it on a matching shelf. They were linked to cameras mounted up near the roof, right below the eaves, providing a bird's-eye view of each side of the building.

A proximity alarm, integrated into the computer system, was

emitting a sharp beeping sound and making all four screens flash an intruder warning. Kendra hurried over to the desk, pressed a series of keys on the keypad, and the beeping stopped. With another keystroke she turned on the live feed to all four monitors. "Well, well, who might you be?" she said, her eyes jumping from screen to screen.

The first one showed a man somewhere in the low six-foot range, with sandy brown hair, standing just inside the front gate, surveying the front of the house. On the next was a slightly taller man with jet black hair, walking cautiously down the driveway, eyeing each of the windows. Another man could be seen on the third monitor, inspecting the back door. He had a medium build and wiry brown hair in desperate need of a trim.

The fourth monitor had a view of the narrow strip of grass and tall wooden fence that lined the eastern edge of the property. All clear there.

Rachel appeared in the doorway. "What's going on?"

"We have company," Kendra said, watching the man at the back door. He had pulled a small leather case out of his back pocket and was kneeling down, preparing to pick the lock.

Rachel hurried into the room, her eyes locked on the monitors. "NO!" she exclaimed.

"Are these the guys who've been chasing you?" Kendra asked.

"Yes," she said, panicked. She pointed at the first monitor. "That one's Cafferty. That one in the driveway is the boss, Bolan. That guy there, at the back door, is Rodano."

"You know their *names?*"

"Yes. It's a long story, and one I'd rather not share at the moment, *if-you-don't-mind!*"

"Okay, fine. Bolan, Cafferty, and Rodano. Got it," Kendra said, committing their names and faces to memory.

"How do they keep finding me?" Rachel shouted, her frustration boiling over.

"Never mind that," Kendra said. "We gotta go."

"Go? Go where?"

Kendra shut down the system and one by one the monitors went dark.

"I'll show you."

4

Marote Gari

With the kitchen clock showing 8:20 a.m., Gina snuck out the back door for the second time that morning. Unlike her earlier trek, she knew there was no way she'd be back before her parents awoke, so she left them a short note on the kitchen counter—a strategy she'd used previously and with good result.

It's a nice day so I
decided to take a walk.
Be back in awhile.
-G

She knew if she didn't give them something, they'd automatically assume that Nathan had convinced her to join him on another life-threatening escapade.

As she cut across the lawn toward the street, she could hear him in his garage, punishing the heavy bag that hung in the corner, his fists making a distinctive *whap-whap, whap-whap, whap-whap* sound as they repeatedly pounded the leather.

With her backpack hanging off her shoulder, and the neighborhood showing signs of human activity, she walked briskly up the sidewalk. Two houses down, she passed Mr. Griffey, an obsessive gardener, out in his front yard, clippers in hand, fussing over his pristine rose hedge. Another neighbor, Mrs. Toomey, was walking her dog, a copper-colored Pomeranian named "Penny," who insisted on stopping to leave a little something on every lawn they passed.

When she reached the end of the street, Gina crossed Mass Ave and waited on the sidewalk in front of the Family Dental Center. Precisely seven minutes later, Louise glided to a stop at the curb in her starch-white Mercedes Benz sedan.

"Hello again," she said politely as Gina climbed in the front seat.

Gina ignored her attempt at civility, stowed her backpack on the floor between her feet, and then looked over at Louise, her expression boiling hot. "Why?" she demanded.

Louise motioned with her hand…*hold that thought*…then pulled away from the curb and reversed direction, executing a surgically precise U-turn in the street. "You want to know why I gave Rachel Goudas your name and address," she said as she drove back to the Alewife Brook Parkway. Her words were silky smooth, showing no hint of regret.

"Uh…*yeah*," Gina replied.

"When we first met, there were things I didn't share with you,"

Louise explained.

Gina flashed back to that day, and their lunch meeting when Louise gave her the key to the safety deposit box where Helen Bainbridge had secured the book notes for her mystery series.

"You knew that my grandmother was secretly helping women in trouble, didn't you?" she asked. She already knew the answer but she wanted to hear Louise say it.

"Yes."

"But why didn't you tell me?"

They came to the Alewife Brook Parkway intersection and Louise turned right. "Your grandmother wanted you to be the guardian of her book notes," she said. "Should you ever attempt to contact me, I was instructed to give you that envelope."

Again, Gina already knew this. "And…" she said impatiently.

"When you think about it," Louise said, casually, "the fact that you called me completely out of the blue only confirmed what she already suspected."

"Which was…?"

"That you were the perfect person to safeguard her files."

"You mean, keep them from the dangerous people who might use them to find the person she had helped to hide."

"Exactly."

"Because there's a secret message hidden in each book."

"Yes."

"That's touching, but you still haven't answered my question," Gina said.

"I was following your grandmother's instructions. She told me to give you the envelope. Period. I wasn't to say anything about the women she was helping or the books."

"Why would she do that?" Gina asked. "Why not just tell me what she was doing?"

"I think your grandmother knew you far better than you think," Louise said as she merged onto Rt. 2 West.

"Meaning…?"

"She knew that you had an excellent, analytical mind, and that you'd figure it out for yourself, all in good time, and on your own terms."

Gina said nothing. As it turned out, her grandmother had called it correctly.

"You also want to know how I figured out it was Nathan who helped you last night?"

"It was more like one o'clock this morning," Gina grumbled. She had turned her attention to the highway ahead, watching for the Rt. 95 exit that would take them south to Weston.

"Oh, that's right. One o'clock. I forgot."

"You *forgot?* Wait a minute. When we spoke on the phone, I never mentioned the exact time."

"That's right."

"So, how could you possibly know that it was one o'clock, or that it was Nathan who helped us?"

"Gina…" Louise began. She paused momentarily to take in a deep breath and then let it out. "It's time I let you in on a little secret."

"What secret is that?"

"I'm quite familiar with Nathan Cole and the various exploits the two of you have managed to, how shall I put it…survive?"

"*What?*" Gina exclaimed. "No one is supposed to know about that stuff, except for Nathan's parents."

"Aren't you forgetting a few people?" Louise asked, eyebrows raised.

"No," Gina insisted, put off by the question.

"Really? What about Jameson?"

Gina furrowed both brows. "You know Jameson?"

"I do," Louise said, easy as you please. "And Kendra, too."

"Wait! You know Kendra?"

"Well, I certainly hope so," Louise said, unable to keep from smiling.

"Why is that?"

"Because she's my niece."

Kendra took hold of Rachel, turned her around, and pointed her toward the doorway. "Go get your backpack!"

"What are you going to do?" Rachel asked, stumbling forward.

"Just go!" Kendra shouted.

As Rachel hurried back to the front room, Kendra followed her as far as the kitchen and then made a beeline for the broom closet that had been built into the back corner of the room. Following Sidney's instructions, she opened the door and knelt down, feeling along the inside edge of the door frame on the left side. An inch from the floor her fingertips grazed a small square button. She pressed it and the entire shelving unit, bottles, brushes, brooms and all, slid to the right, revealing a mini-lift elevator on the left.

Rachel came back into the kitchen carrying her backpack. "What are we doing?"

"We're leaving," Kendra said, climbing to her feet. She opened the lift door and pointed inside. "You first."

"But…how…?"

Kendra grabbed her arm and jostled her through the closet doorway and into the lift. "When you get to the bottom, get out, shut the door, and send it back up. There'll be a panel somewhere close by. Is that clear?"

"Wait…what if…?"

"Is that clear?" Kendra repeated, nearly shouting.

"Yes, yes, it's clear."

"Good. Now go!"

Kendra pushed the door shut and pressed the arrow-down button on the panel built into the wall to the left of the lift. With a sound no louder than a gentle puff of wind, the car gradually descended. As she waited for it to return, she went to the door and placed her ear against the wood. She heard nothing. If the three intruders had made it inside, they hadn't gotten past the second door. Or maybe they'd opted for the one on the right and were checking the first-floor apartment. *Good luck with that,* she told herself.

The first floor was staged to look like someone lived there when, in fact, it was vacant. If the three goons bothered to look in the refrigerator, they'd discover that it was just for show. It wasn't running and the shelves were completely empty; not so much as a stick of butter to be found.

A soft *ding!* told her that the elevator car had returned. She gulped down the last of her coffee and dropped the empty cup in the trashcan under the sink, then stepped through the closet door and onto the lift. Before she shut the lift door, she reached out and pulled the closet door shut, then used her foot to nudge the button that returned the shelving unit to its original position. As it slid closer, she shut the lift door and punched the control panel behind her, sending the car gliding downward to the basement.

Moments later, the car dipped below the first floor and came to a gentle stop in the basement. When the door opened, she stepped out into the darkness, the only light coming from the web-covered casement windows set just above the foundation.

Rachel was nowhere in sight.

Gina stared at Louise, slack-jawed.

"What's wrong?" Louise asked. She signaled, then changed lanes and took the exit for Rt. 95 south.

"Kendra," Gina said, making sure they were talking about the same person. "She's your niece?" Maybe if she said it out loud enough times it would make her head stop spinning, but she was several hundred thousand repetitions from that happening.

"You look surprised," Louise said.

"Surprised? That's hardly the word *I'd* use," Gina muttered.

"Oh, I almost forgot," Louise said. "Give me the address of where we're going and I'll put it in the car's navigation system. It'll be much easier than—"

"No," Gina said abruptly, before Louise could finish. Like her first visit with James Donnelly, they weren't going to Sutton Woods where he lived; they were going to the Freeman Library next door. Using the same ploy as before, when Ellie drove her, she'd instruct Louise to park in front of the library and wait while she went inside. Once there, she'd slip out the back and cut through the small forest of trees that separated the two properties. Louise would be none the wiser, and Donnelly's anonymity would remain intact.

"Are you familiar with the Freeman Library?" she asked.

"I am," Louise said, cheerfully, like she'd spent many an hour there as a young child, curled up in one of overstuffed chairs with a picture book.

"Good," Gina said, "because that's where we're going."

Nathan was still working the heavy bag, throwing a series of lightning-quick jabs in varying combinations, when the side door opened and Beck stepped into the garage. The former Marine was a human skyscraper, standing over 6' 5" tall with the kind of bulk that would deter any would-be attacker who didn't want to spend a week inside an intensive care unit. He was an associate of Jameson's friend Sully, an evidence tech for the Portland, Maine, Police Department, and at Nathan's urging had agreed to be his private fight instructor.

Nathan stopped punching when he heard the door open. His face was glowing red and his brow was glistening with sweat. "Hey," he said, when he saw Beck's massive frame. "I'm guessing my dad called you?"

"Yup."

"And he told you about stepping up my training?"

"He did," Beck replied, in his usual clipped tone. In each hand he was carrying a cast dumbbell with the number 10 imprinted on the hexagonal ends. He crossed the room and handed them to Nathan. "Before we get to that, try these," he said.

Days earlier, Nathan had rejected Beck's offering of two 6 lb. weights, claiming they were too light. He took each of the 10 lb.

versions and pumped them up and down in an alternating motion. Right hand, left hand. Right hand, left hand. "Now *this* is more like it," he said. After several reps with each arm, he set them on the floor next to the wall. The dumbbells could wait. He and Beck had more important things to get to. "So where do we start?" he asked.

"I'm going to show you some basic martial arts moves," Beck said. "But before we begin, are you sure you're ready?"

Nathan smirked. "Am I ready? Are you kidding?" He closed his fists into a tight ball and brought them up to his chest, then raised his right knee and lashed out with his foot, sending it up in the air toward Beck's head.

With cat-like reflexes Beck grabbed Nathan's ankle with one hand and then swept his leg, sending Nathan falling backward onto the concrete floor.

Nathan lay there for several long seconds, staring up at the ceiling, stunned by the ease in which he'd been put down.

Beck raised an eyebrow. "You were saying?"

Nathan gave him a disgusted look, then rolled over on his side and pushed himself up off the floor.

"Martial arts training isn't just a bunch of kicking and punching," Beck said. "Many of the different styles use grappling techniques to control or defeat an opponent."

"Grappling?" Nathan asked.

"Come on, I'll show you."

They went outside to the backyard where the lawn would be more forgiving than the garage floor.

"Okay," Beck said, "let's start with a basic technique called 'ma-rote gari'."

"Uh…in English please?"

"A double-leg takedown," Beck said. He positioned Nathan across from him, then stepped back, staying within punching distance. "I want you to come at me with your arms extended, like you're going to attack me."

"O-kay," Nathan said slowly, unsure of what was coming next. He reached out with both arms, palms open and fingers spread, and took a step forward.

"Good. Now stop right there," Beck said.

Nathan froze.

"The first thing you do is change your level," said Beck. He bent his knees, lowering his frame closer to the ground. "Notice how I'm keeping my head to the outside of your body?"

"Yeah?" *What about it?*

"Head position is key if you want this to work."

"Head to the outside, got it," Nathan said.

"Next, I'm going to clear your arms," Beck said. He moved forward in slow motion and ducked beneath Nathan's arms, then pressed the side of his head against Nathan's rib cage. With his hands cupped around the back of Nathan's knees, he said, "At this point, you're not going to take your opponent's legs out from under him, especially if he's bigger than you. The objective is to get him off balance. To do that, you use your head to force him sideways. Once his weight shifts, you lift his legs with both hands and drive him backward onto the ground. As you're doing it, remember to keep your back straight."

"And once he's on the ground, then what?" Nathan asked.

"You disengage and run like hell."

"Disengage?"

"It's called 'The Detachment Principle'. It deals with knowing when to let go. As you get bigger and stronger, you can stick around and brawl if you want, but until then, once your opponent is down, you separate yourself and get out of there."

Without another word, he used his head to force Nathan sideways onto his left foot. At the same time, he lifted him up by the legs and dropped him on the ground.

Nathan landed with a thud, grimaced, and then sat up. *Well that wasn't fun.*

"Your turn," Beck said. He pulled Nathan to his feet and they took their original positions. Face to face. Punching distance apart.

As Beck advanced, arms extended, Nathan bent forward to change his level. When Beck saw that, he grabbed him by the shoulders and flung him down on the grass.

"Why did you do that?" Nathan shouted. He rolled over onto his back and exhaled, staring up at the cloudless sky overhead.

"You never lean forward," Beck said. "If you do, you make yourself vulnerable to your opponent."

"And you couldn't tell me that before we started?" Nathan griped. He climbed to his feet, fuming, and took his original position. *Grappling…tell me again, why are we doing this?*

"This time, to change your level, bend your knees," Beck said.

Nathan flashed him a phony smile, squinty eyes and all. *Yeah, thanks, I got it.* He waited until Beck reached for him, then bent his knees and took two steps forward. When he had cleared Beck's arms, he unleashed his anger and launched himself into Beck's midsection. He dug his left foot into the ground and grabbed Beck's legs, then used his head to push the giant's massive frame to the right. Beck teetered sideways onto his left foot and Nathan lifted him just enough to topple him over onto the ground. As Beck fell, Nathan let go and stumbled backward, struggling to maintain his balance.

"Nice," Beck said, as he quickly got to his feet, unfazed by the fall. "See how getting your opponent off balance worked in your favor?"

A surge of adrenaline rippled through Nathan's body. Maybe this grappling thing wasn't so bad after all.

"Now, it won't always be that easy, especially if your opponent is an experienced fighter," Beck said. "To prepare for that eventuality, you'll need to learn a different set of skills."

"Not grappling?" Nathan asked.

"Not grappling," Beck replied.

Phillip Roman was sitting in a golf cart in the middle of the 17th fairway at the Ledgemont Country Club in Seekonk. He'd crushed his tee shot, leaving him another 150 yards to the green. As he was considering his club selection, his cellphone emitted four short electronic beeps—the ringtone he'd assigned to a single contact. He snatched it from the cubby storage compartment in the dash and answered it before it could ring again. "This is Roman."

"Did you get her?"

"Not yet. We're still tracking her. The last report put her in South Boston."

"So go get her."

"We will. It won't be long now."

"Yeah, you keep telling me that."

Roman took a breath to calm himself. "We had a small setback."

"So deal with it. Or should I get someone else to do it?"

"That won't be necessary," Roman said. "It appears she's getting help from someone."

"Okay, so find out who this someone is and eliminate them. How hard can that be?"

"We'll get it done," Roman assured him.

"See that you do. This has gone on far too long."

Roman ended the call and dialed Wicks, who answered after the first ring.

"Yeah, this is Wicks."

"Do you have an update for me?" Roman asked.

"She hasn't moved. She's still in South Boston."

"All right, let me know the second that changes."

Kendra moved away from the lift and paused, scanning the murky gloom from left to right. *Where did she go?* "Rachel!" she hissed, keeping her voice down.

From somewhere close by came a muffled reply. "Over here."

Kendra turned in that direction. "What are you doing?" she asked, annoyed. Did this woman not understand the gravity of their current situation?

"I'm hiding," Rachel said, barely above a whisper. "Just in case."

"Just in case what?"

"They look in the windows."

Kendra did a quick visual check of each casement window on the driveway side of the house, expecting to see at least one of the three men kneeling down, nose to the glass, attempting to see through the thick webbing that coated each of the panes. She saw no one.

69

"There's no one looking in the windows," she said. "Now, come on. We have to keep moving."

"Are you sure?"

"Positive," Kendra said. She heard a scuffing of feet on the rough concrete floor and then Rachel appeared, clutching her backpack to her chest.

"Follow me and stay close," Kendra told her.

"Where are we going?"

"This way," Kendra said. She extended her arms and walked cautiously toward the back end of the basement. With every step she took, her eyes grew more accustomed to the dark and what had started as a complete blackout gradually became a murky haze. They were 10 feet from the end wall when she saw them.

Three distinct outlines.

Standing side by side in the dark.

Waiting for them.

5

12-to-6

"The thing is," Beck said, "grappling is very effective, until it isn't."

Nathan looked at him, confused. "Then what do you do?"

"You strike."

Nathan had been putting in serious hours on the heavy bag, perfecting his straightaway jabs, hooks, and crosses, in a number of different combinations. Not only was it making him stronger and tougher, it helped him to work off any anger or frustration he was feeling. But when he heard the word "strike," his pulse quickened and he clenched his fist. *Yes!*

He'd had enough of this dancing around.

It was time to get serious.

Beck saw his reaction and raised a cautionary palm. "Don't get too excited," he said. "You still have a long way to go before you're ready for advance striking techniques. What I'm going to show you is a basic maneuver designed to buy you some time, that's all."

"Fine by me," Nathan said. *Let's go!*

"Okay, let's run through the double leg takedown again. I'll be the attacker and you'll be…you."

Once they had resumed their starting positions, Beck said, "Ready?"

"Ready," Nathan replied. He was in his defensive posture: hands up, slight crouch, ready for whatever Beck was going to throw at him.

Beck nodded, then advanced, faster this time. As he closed in, Nathan bent his knees and repeated his earlier series of moves: exploding forward; pushing off with his left foot; driving his right shoulder into Beck's rib cage, then using his head to force him off balance. What came next was the best part: lift and drop.

Simple.

Only this time, as Beck fell backward, he grabbed Nathan's shirt with both hands and together they fell to the ground. When they landed on the grass, Beck didn't let go.

"What are you doing?" Nathan said. He struggled to break free but it was no use; Beck's grip was too strong.

"Don't worry about what I'm doing," said Beck. "Your focus should be on taking control of the situation."

Again, Nathan struggled to break free of Beck's grip and failed.

"Squirming isn't going to work," Beck said.

Nathan exhaled, frustrated, then relaxed his muscles and rested his hands on the ground.

"Okay, so what do I do?" he asked.

"You strike and strike fast."

"And how do I do that?"

"With your elbow."

Nathan frowned. "My elbow?" *How could that possibly work?*

"That's right. The bones in your elbow are harder and stronger than the bones in your hand. If your opponent takes you down with him, you respond with a circular elbow strike. The move is called 'mawashi empi uchi'."

"Elbow strike?" Nathan said. "Isn't that a bowling thing?"

"Make jokes if you want," Beck said, "but it's highly effective at close range and very hard to block."

"O-kay." *If you say so.*

"Are you right handed or left handed?"

"Right handed."

"Okay, make a fist with your right hand and bring it up to your chest."

Nathan did as he was told.

"Perfect. Now, with your right elbow extended outward, twist your body and sweep your elbow slowly from right to left until it touches my jaw…. *slowly!*"

Again, Nathan responded as instructed, rotating his torso as he swung his elbow in a circular motion from right to left. When it reached Beck's jaw, he stopped.

"Good," said Beck.

"That's it?" Nathan asked.

"In a real-life situation you'll do it much quicker and with more power. Depending on where you make contact, it can knock out your opponent. At the very least, it will disorient him long enough for you to disengage and make your escape."

Elbow strike. Cool. Nathan thought. He rolled off Beck and stood up.

"I want you to practice it," Beck said, as he got up off the lawn. "I'll bring you a tackling dummy that you can use. Remember the sequence: fist to chest; elbow out; swing from right to left...hard. Make sure to practice it with your left elbow too."

Nathan straightened and tried it. Right elbow, left elbow, right elbow, left elbow. With each rotation he increased his speed.

"There's one more thing I need to show you," Beck said.

"What's that?" Nathan asked.

"What you do if that doesn't work."

Positioned against the back wall of the basement, sitting less than a foot apart, were three double-walled Roth fuel tanks. They were made from seamless polyethylene and encased in a galvanized weld-free outer shell. Each one sat in a tubular-steel "cradle base".

The tank on the far left held heating fuel for the first-floor apartment. The middle tank, for the top floor. The tank on the far right was a decoy, an exact replica of the other two, put there to simulate an excess-fuel reservoir for those brutal winter storms that could paralyze the entire city of Boston in a matter of hours. The only clue that it was a fake was the lack of a fill or vent pipe. Kendra took hold of it and pulled it straight out. With no fuel in it, the entire unit slid easily across the concrete floor.

Rachel stood behind her and watched, speechless, as Kendra stepped up to the wall and ran her fingers across the surface that had been sheathed in 3/4" vertical boards made to look like cheap 1/8" Home Depot paneling. As she moved her hand from left to right, her fingertips brushed a thin seam between the boards. *"Find the seam,"* Sidney had told her. *"When you do, give it a firm push. One shove should do the trick."*

Kendra leaned into it with her shoulder and a section of the wall sprung open, revealing the entrance to a tunnel that ran under the back yard and ended beneath the detached garage at the back corner of the property. She peered into the darkness, another wall of pitch black, and recounted the other thing Sidney had told her. *"You'll find a flashlight affixed to the back of the fuel tank."*

She ran her hands over the back of the tank until she found it, held there by a small magnet. With a flick of her finger she turned it on, then pointed it into the opening of the tunnel.

"*That's* our way out?" Rachel asked, in a skeptical tone.

"Yup," Kendra said. She took one step into the tunnel and then stopped to look back at Rachel who hadn't moved. "Well? Are you coming or not?"

When Louise and Gina reached the Freeman Library, the parking lot was barely one third full. Louise parked in the middle row, then turned off the car and eyed the front entrance. "I haven't been here in years," she said. "It'll be interesting to see if it's changed or if it still looks like I remember it."

She reached for the door handle when Gina said, "Uh, I'd rather you didn't come in."

Louise pulled her hand back. "I see," she said, taking no offense. "I'll be a while. Forty five minutes? Maybe an hour?"

"Take all the time you need," Louise told her. She looked straight ahead, a thought forming in her mind. "I have an old friend who lives nearby. Maybe I'll go pay her a visit. She'd like that. I'll be sure to return by the time you're done."

Gina shrugged…*whatever*…then grabbed her backpack off the floor of the car and climbed out. She was walking up the front steps of the library when she heard Louise start the car and drive out of the lot.

Unlike her previous visit, when the library had attracted a voracious horde of fans for an author event, the front lobby was graveyard quiet. She turned left and followed the stairway down to the lower level. From there she ducked out the back door and raced across the staff parking lot. She cut through the woods to the back of the Sutton Woods property, a huge, gently rolling lawn dotted with oak benches and flower beds that were brimming with color. Since her last visit they had added more stone paths that wound through plots of roses, delphiniums, foxglove and hollyhocks, giving the entire lawn the look of an English garden.

Stretching along the back of the facility were three spacious patios: the Brookings, the Ellison, and the Davenport. It was on the Davenport patio that she first spoke with James Donnelly, and it was such a gorgeous day, she fully expected to see him sitting there, head back, eyes closed, the bright sunshine warming his face.

She continued around the end of the building to the front entrance. When she pushed through the doors she was met by the unmistakable smell of cooked bacon. On the far side of the lobby, through a large entryway, she saw a crowd of residents in the dining room, enjoying the Sunday morning breakfast buffet. Their voices filled the room amid a backdrop of classical music that played from small speakers built into the ceiling.

She went to the front desk, which was currently vacant, and waited for the receptionist to return. In her mind she tried to dredge up the woman's name from her memory. *It's Martha. Or is it Marie? Muriel? No, that's not it. It definitely begins with M.* She bit the edge of her lip, thinking. *Margaret? Marjorie? No, wait! Mary. Yes, that's it!*

A minute passed. Then another. She grew tired of waiting and switched to Plan B: act like you're a regular visitor. She used the pen on the desk to sign the visitor's log, scribbling a fictitious name in an outlandish and barely readable scrawl.

In the destination box, she did the same.

She left the room number blank and dropped the pen on the desk, then followed the long hallway past the elevator to Donnelly's room. Standing at the door, she did a quick check of the hallway in both directions and then knocked. When there was no reply she knocked again. Suddenly, the door swung open and there he was, in his wheelchair, turned sideways with the wheel keeping the door from opening any further.

"It's you!" he said, a smile crossing his face.

"In the flesh," Gina replied.

He rolled his wheelchair away from the door and motioned with his hand. "Come in, come in."

She checked the hallway for a second time. Seeing no one, she ducked inside and quickly closed the door behind her.

A detective with the Boston Police Department, Donnelly had overseen a high-profile corruption task force until he'd been paralyzed in what had been termed "an accident of suspicious nature." To this day he had refused to make any public comments on the incident, but some on his task force believed the party responsible for the accident was the crime family they'd been investigating at the time—the same crime family that Donnelly knew was searching for his daughter, Ann DeBartolo. With the help of Helen Bainbridge, their search had yet to produce any results.

"Do you have something for me or is this just a social call?" Donnelly asked, his face a picture of unbridled anticipation.

"As a matter of fact, I *do* have something for you," Gina said. She walked over to the couch and sat down. Then, with her backpack sitting squarely in her lap, she unzipped the center compartment and took out the padded mailer. "Just one this time," she said, waving it in the air like a winning lottery ticket.

Donnelly wheeled over to the couch, unable to control his excitement at the prospect of what was enclosed in the thick envelope. Based on the covert system he'd put into motion years ago, he knew the contents were a confirmation that Ann was still alive and well. Six months ago she was in Louisiana. The package she'd sent had an Alabama postmark, which told him she was heading north. The question was, how far had she gotten?

The answer was seconds away.

Nathan and Beck recreated their earlier stance, where Nathan had just executed the perfect double-leg takedown and Beck had pulled him down to the ground. Beck grabbed Nathan's shirt with both hands as he'd done before and said, "First, the elbow strike."

Nathan extended his right elbow and brought it down slowly in a sweeping motion, stopping at Beck's chin.

"Okay, hold right there." Beck said. "You've just executed a powerful elbow strike, but for whatever reason your opponent is still conscious and he still has a hold of you. This is when you use a *downward* elbow strike, or, what's commonly referred to as a '12-to-six elbow'." He took hold of Nathan's elbow and pushed it up and over until it was positioned directly over his chest. "Twelve o'clock." Then he pulled it straight down until it was touching the area right above his solarplexius. "Six o'clock."

Nathan was speechless as he eyed the tip of his elbow, then the target area in the center of Beck's chest. Unlike the punches he'd been practicing in his garage, this had lethal, potentially fatal consequences. The thought of delivering such a strike was unsettling. But, if Beck was right, and he found himself matched against a highly skilled and murderous adversary...

"The vertical delivery allows you to use your entire bodyweight to deliver a lethal blow concentrated on one area," Beck explained. "The higher you raise your elbow, the more powerful the impact. And just like the circular strike, a downward hit to the head can knock out your opponent, especially if it lands on his temple or his jaw, or even his neck. Hit his solarplexius and he could go into shock

79

and have difficulty breathing."

"And then I run," Nathan said.

"Yes. You run like the wind."

Kendra handed Rachel the flashlight, then stepped out of the tunnel and slid the fuel tank back into position. When she pulled the wall panel shut, everything in the basement returned to its original position, giving the outward impression that no one had been there.

"What is that *smell?*" Rachel asked, running the beam of the flashlight over the walls and ceiling.

Kendra sniffed several times. "If I had to guess, I'd say apple crisp."

"Very funny."

Kendra took the flashlight and started down the narrow corridor, the beam of the flashlight illuminating the webs that stretched across their path like long strips of cheesecloth. To their left and right, rocks of every size jutted out from the packed dirt walls, along with spindly roots on a never-ending quest to find water.

The going was slow. Draped in webbing that they continually had to stop and peel from their faces, it took them nearly five minutes to walk 20 feet.

Rachel's trepidation, which had flickered to life the second she stepped into the tunnel, quickly reached its peak. She grabbed Kendra's arm and said, "Stop."

"What's wrong?" Kendra asked. She turned around, pulling a fresh layer of webbing from her hair and forehead.

"How much farther?" Rachel demanded.

"If my calculation is correct, about another 30 feet. Give or take."

"Thirty feet?" Rachel groaned.

"Relax," Kendra said. "Bolan, Cafferty, and Rodelo—"

"Rodano!"

"Whatever," Kendra said. "They have no idea where we are. My guess is, they already gave up and left."

"Guess again," Rachel muttered.

"Excuse me?"

"They don't give up. They never have and they never will."

"We'll see about that," Kendra replied. She aimed the flashlight at the tunnel ahead and resumed walking, leaning forward and waving her free hand in front of the flashlight to clear the webs out of the way. They walked another 20 feet when the tunnel turned sharply to the left. Ten feet later it ended. Leaning up against the sidewall at a 60° angle was an old iron ladder that looked like it had once been an inner city apartment-house fire escape. "Wait here," Kendra said.

She handed Rachel the flashlight and then grabbed the sides of the ladder and began to climb. When she reached the top, she saw a panel roughly three feet square, made from thick wooden floorboards. She placed her hand on the edge of it and pushed up. It barely moved. She tried again, this time with more force, and it eased it up another inch. On her third try it broke free, sending needles of light spilling down into the tunnel.

She stepped up onto the next rung and peered through the opening. Straight ahead was a wall with exposed studs. Nailed to one of them was a short board that held a coiled garden hose. On another, an old seven-blade reel mower hung on a curved iron hook. To her right was an old workbench that had been pushed up against the back wall. To her left, a pair of tall carriage-house garage doors with X bracing, straight out of the 1950s. Each door had a large window set at the top, two horizontal rows of panes, four over four. Their height from the ground made them too high to see through without a ladder.

"What do you see?" Rachel whispered. "Is it safe?"

"Yeah I think we're good," Kendra said, "but you wait there while I make sure." She placed her hand in the center of the wooden panel and lifted it straight up. The noise it made when she slid it onto the garage floor sounded like two sanding blocks rubbing together.

She climbed out of the tunnel and eyed the small four-pane windows on both sides of the building. They were set high up where the wall met the roof. A longer transom-style version had been built into the back wall, high above the workbench. She walked to the front of the garage and pulled a six-foot stepladder off the wall. After positioning it next to one of the doors, she climbed up and peeked outside, taking care to keep back from the glass to avoid being seen.

All three men were standing at the mouth of the driveway. Bolan had his phone to his ear, listening to the voice on the other end of the line, while Cafferty and Rodano stood nearby, smoking cigarettes and watching the beach walkers across the street. Moments later, Bolan ended the call. He didn't look happy. After a brief conversation with the other two, they split up and began checking the windows on the first floor of the house.

Kendra figured it would take them roughly 10 minutes to complete that task, which was more than enough time for her and Rachel to slip away. Moving quickly, she climbed down, hung the ladder back on the wall, then hurried back to the tunnel opening. "They're still here," she said. "But if we move fast we can leave without them seeing us."

Rachel hooked her backpack over her shoulder and started up the ladder, muttering a string of "I-told-you-so" comments under her breath. When she reached the top, she handed Kendra the flashlight and climbed up onto the garage floor. "The garage?" she groaned, doing a quick scan of the space. "*This* is your brilliant plan of escape?"

There was no time to argue. As much as Kendra wanted to toss her down into the tunnel and be done with her, she set the flashlight on a fireblock and then slid the wooden panel back into place. "Let's go," she said, moving quickly toward the workbench.

Rachel's eyes jumped from the bench to the transom window directly above it. "You are *not* serious."

"As serious as a corpse," Kendra said. "Which is what *you'll* be if we don't get moving. Now, come on!" She reached under the workbench and pulled out an old five-gallon metal pail of roofing tar that looked like it had been there since World War 1. After hoisting it up onto the bench, she slid it back against the wall and centered it directly below the window.

Why did I get on that bus? Rachel asked herself.

Kendra climbed up on the workbench and then stood on the metal pail. With a flick of her thumb she released the latch at the base of the transom window and it swung outward with ease.

Rachel walked over to the bench, shaking her head. "This is crazy."

"Crazier than letting those three dirt bags get their hands on you?" Kendra replied.

Rachel said nothing as she pealed the backpack off her shoulder and then climbed up on the bench.

"You first," Kendra said. She stepped off the pail and reached for Rachel's backpack. "Here, let me hold that for you."

Rachel jerked it away. "I'm *fine.*"

"Have it your way," Kendra said.

Rachel climbed up on the pail, pushed the window open, and shoved her backpack out through the opening. Using both hands, she grabbed the window frame and jumped up, resting one elbow on the sill, followed by the other. As she leaned forward, her head pushed the window outward and she got a good look at the ground below. "You've got to be kidding me," she said. It had to be at least a seven-foot drop. If she was lucky, she'd only sprain an ankle.

"Tick-tock, tick-tock," Kendra said.

Rachel cursed and swung her right leg up onto the sill, then used it to bring her body up and over the frame. She teetered there for several seconds, trying to maintain her balance, before tumbling helplessly through the opening and landing on the lawn with a heavy thud.

For Kendra it wasn't that difficult. She repeated the maneuver with the speed and agility of an Olympic gymnast. Up, over, and down, landing squarely on the lawn with both feet. "Playing in a softball league has its advantages," she said. "You should try it."

She pulled Rachel to her feet and together they broke into an all-out run through the yard that abutted the back of the property. When they came to East 8th Street, Kendra took the lead, jogging down the sidewalk with Rachel doing her best to keep pace. Two minutes later they were sitting in Kendra's Volvo, one block away, in the ground-level parking lot of a giant apartment complex. With a twist of the key, the Volvo's engine roared to life.

'Time to get out of Dodge," she said.

Donnelly took the padded mailer from Gina and tore off one end. There was no letter tucked inside. No short note. There was no written correspondence of any kind, only an inch-thick chunk of dull-white quartz. It was barely three inches long and less than two inches wide, streaked with varying shades of blue.

"Interesting," he said, turning it over in his hand.

"Do you want me to get the book?" Gina asked.

Donnelly nodded. "You remember where I keep it, right?"

"Yup. Bottom shelf. Seventh book from the left."

"Very good."

She set her backpack aside and jumped up from the couch. The book in question was *Parker's Guide to Gemstones: A Field Guide.* Donnelly kept the rock hunter's sourcebook hidden in the bookcase next to the window, cleverly concealed within a dustjacket for *Cannery Row,* by John Steinbeck.

Because Donnelly suspected he was being watched by the FBI, who wanted very much to question his daughter, the rocks she sent, and any printed matter relating to gemstones were a carefully guarded secret.

Gina found the book and brought it back to Donnelly. With one hand he flipped through the pages in search of one image in particular. He was nearly halfway through the book when he stopped. "Ah, just as I suspected," he said, turning the book so Gina could see the picture on the page.

"Kyanite," she said, reading the caption.

Donnelly handed her the book so she could read the description.

"Kyanite is a typically blue... I hope I say this right... *alumi-no-silicate* mineral."

"Very good," Donnelly told her.

"It is found in aluminum-rich metamorphic *pegmatites* and sedimentary rock."

Donnelly nodded his head, waiting patiently for the information that he knew was soon to follow.

"It is the high-pressure polymorph of *andalusite* and *sillimanite*," Gina said, pronouncing the words slowly. She skipped down through the next paragraph, which described the various colors of the stone that ranged from light to dark or indigo blue, with less common variations that included white, gray, green, orange and black. Then she found the information they were both anxious to hear. Reading it slowly, she said, "Kyanite and other sillimanite minerals are commonly found in metamorphic rocks in the Piedmont geologic province of Virginia."

She looked up from the book, awestruck. "She's in Virginia."

"Is she?" Donnelly asked, already knowing the answer to the question.

"Oh, right," Gina said, realizing the error in her thinking. On cue, she closed the book and handed it to Donnelly, who, in turn, gave her the padded mailer.

As Donnelly had counseled her, Ann never mailed anything from the state where she was hiding. Instead, she mailed her packages from a different state, a clever ruse that would throw off any of the mobsters who were looking for her should they manage to intercept on one of her envelopes.

Gina pulled it close and read the postmark. "Saratoga Springs, New York."

"And what does that tell us?" Donnelly asked, like a teacher quizzing his students.

"She was in Virginia," Gina said, "then she went north, stopping in Saratoga Springs to mail the envelope."

There was no need to explain the rest.

They both knew.

Ann DeBartolo was somewhere close by, hiding out in any one of the six New England states: Maine, New Hampshire, Vermont, Massachusetts, Rhode Island, Connecticut—take your pick.

Donnelly handed Gina the kyanite and she dropped it back in the padded mailer. In the days to come, she'd give it to Nathan, to hide in his grandfather's old fish tank.

Out of sight and out of mind.

After she buried it in her backpack, she said, "There's something I need to ask you."

"Shoot," Donnelly replied. He had wheeled over to the bookcase and was sliding Parker's guidebook back on the shelf.

"Before Ann left, did she talk about my grandmother?"

"Uh...not really. In fact, the only time she mentioned your grandmother was when she snuck into my hospital room. That was a week after my accident. She was convinced that the people responsible for what happened to me were gunning for her next. She told me that your grandmother could help her escape them once and for all." He paused and stared absently at the bookcase as he recalled their conversation. "I'll never forget that moment," he said. "There was a glint of hope in her eyes, and as it turned out, your grandmother's help was instrumental in saving my daughter's life."

"Did she happen to mention if my grandmother said anything cryptic?"

"Cryptic? No."

"How about Ann. Did *she* say anything that seemed unusual?"

"Not that I remember. But then again, she didn't stay long. We spoke briefly about how she'd stay in touch, then she gave me a hug and…"

"And what?" Gina asked.

"I take that back," he said, slowly, as the memory slowly came into focus. "She *did* say something unusual."

Gina's heart raced and she quickly opened her backpack and pulled out her notepad. "What was it?" she asked, turning to the first blank page.

"After she hugged me, she was walking to the door when she muttered something. Her back was turned to me and I only caught part of it."

Gina had the tip of her pen resting on the paper, poised to start writing.

"I distinctly heard her say the word Jericho."

"Jericho?" Gina said, writing it down. "You're sure that's what she said?"

"Yes. I only remember it because it's not a word you hear every day, and, obviously, there's the biblical connection."

"Jericho," Gina repeated, wondering what relevance it had.

"It sounded like she said, 'I have three days to get to Jericho'."

6

The Third Act

When Gina emerged from the Freeman Library, she saw Louise parked in the first row.

"How did it go?" she asked, after Gina climbed in the car and pulled the door shut.

"Fine," Gina said plainly, making it clear she had no interest in discussing what she'd been doing for the past 50 minutes. She buckled her seatbelt and looked out the side window, staring absently at the next car as the word "Jericho" raced through her mind. Running a close second was the bombshell news that Louise had shared about Kendra being her niece. *What else hasn't she told me?* she wondered.

Louise sensed Gina's hesitation and didn't push it. "Home, then?" she said.

"Yes, that would be fine," Gina said curtly, like she was talking to the butler.

As Louise pulled out of the lot, Gina reviewed what she knew thus far, starting with what Rachel had told her: how she'd been driven to some unknown city in the middle of the night; Helen's cryptic words; the cloaked figure stepping out of the darkness. Added to the list was Ann DeBartolo's mention of something or some place called Jericho.

Gina knew each of her grandmother's books contained a hidden message for the woman she was helping at the time. She also knew that Rachel Goudas was the second woman she'd rescued, which meant that somewhere in the second book was a clue of some sort. After all, wasn't that the purpose of the books? To use them to further communicate with the women she had saved? But what clue did she create for Rachel? More importantly for Gina, would it lead her to the person that Rachel had begged her to find—the alleged phantom who she claimed could end this ordeal once and for all?

Kendra drove out of the lot and followed East 8th Street toward Dorchester Ave. Since they'd climbed into the car, neither woman had uttered a word. They'd used the garage to shield their escape through the neighboring yard, but what if Bolan, or Cafferty, or Rodano had spotted them as they were running away? What's more, Bolan's crew had seen the Volvo, followed it for a good distance in the wee hours of the morning, long enough to memorize the make and model, along with the plate number.

"Thank you," Rachel said, breaking the prolonged silence. "I shouldn't have doubted you."

"Don't worry about it," Kendra replied, her eyes jumping back and forth between the road ahead and the rearview mirror. So far there was no suspicious vehicle chasing them in a frantic attempt to catch up.

Rachel twisted around in the seat and scanned the road behind them, then faced forward again. "So, what now?" she asked.

The same question had been swimming in Kendra's thoughts from the moment they sprinted through the apartment complex parking lot. "Let's find out," she said.

She grabbed her phone from the cupholder and dialed Nathan's number.

Nathan and Beck were done for the day. But there would be others. Many others. In the weeks to follow, Beck would provide further instruction. But for the time being Nathan had plenty to work on before he could handle the rigors of what would come next.

They were standing next to Beck's truck in the driveway, talking, when Nathan's mother came out the back door of the house.

"Nathan!" she shouted.

He looked over at her. "Yeah?"

She held up the wireless extension from the kitchen. "Kendra's been trying to get a hold of you. It sounds important."

Instinctively, he patted his pockets with both hands and realized that he'd left his flip phone in his bedroom. In that moment, a series of thoughts rocketed through his mind in rapid succession.

Kendra...

At the safehouse...

Trying to contact me...

Sounds important...

"You want me to wait?" Beck asked, seeing the look of concern on Nathan's face.

"Yeah, maybe you should," Nathan said. *Just in case.* He sprinted across the lawn and took the phone from his mother. "Kendra," he said quickly. "Is everything okay?"

"Funny you should ask," she said. "Early this morning those three creeps showed up at the safehouse."

"They *what?*" he blurted out.

Elizabeth rested a hand on his shoulder. "What is it?"

He pulled away from her, gesturing with his hand. *Just wait.*

"I have no idea how they found it," Kendra said, "but lucky for us they tripped the perimeter alarm."

"Are you two all right?"

"Yeah. We managed to get out through the tunnel and now we're—"

"Wait!" he cut in. "There's a tunnel?"

"I'll explain it later," she said. "Right now, we need to come up with another place to hide Rachel."

"Any ideas?" he asked.

"It's your call."

"Where are you now?"

"We're still in South Boston."

"Give me five minutes and somebody will call you back. In the meantime, find a safe place to hunker down." He didn't wait for a reply and clicked off the call, his mind spinning.

"What's going on?" Elizabeth asked.

"I need my phone," he told her, then tossed her the wireless and raced into the house.

She looked over at Beck. "Do you know what's going on?"

"Not a clue."

Nathan ran up to his room two stairs at a time. He grabbed his flip phone from his bedside table and hit the speed-dial number for Sidney. As he waited for it to connect, he began to pace. *Come on, come on!*

Sidney picked up after the first ring. "Good morning," she said, upbeat.

"We need another safehouse."

The words came out of his mouth like they were glued together.

"Okay, okay, slow down," she said. "What happened?"

"Some people found the safehouse. Some very *bad* people."

"When was this?"

"Early this morning."

"Not good," she said.

"Yeah, tell me about it," he said, as a troubling thought sprouted in the back of his mind.

"Is Kendra okay?"

"Yes. She and our …guest…escaped through some tunnel."

"That it is."

"Huh?"

"Some tunnel," she repeated. *It should be for the time and money it took to make it.*

"You lost me," Nathan said.

"It's a story for another time. I'll call Kendra with another location."

"Could you? Would you? I mean, thank you!"

"No thanks required, remember? I'll have her contact you once she and her *guest* are settled in."

He closed the phone and went back downstairs, wondering how three total strangers had managed to find the South Boston safehouse. How was that even possible? And for that matter, how did they know the exact day and time that Rachel would be at Gina's house? Something didn't add up. This was like a bad stage production, and by sending Kendra and Rachel to yet another location, he'd just written the third act.

There was another matter to tend to as well: Gina. He had to relay this newest devleopment to her, but how? He had yet to see her that morning. Was she even home? She wasn't the type to sleep late, so where was she?

He continued down the back hallway. When he pushed through the screen door and stepped outside, his mother and Beck were standing there waiting for him.

"Is there something you'd like to tell me?" his mother asked.

Kendra came to Dorchester Street and turned right. She followed it for a short distance and then turned left on West Broadway. She was approaching D Street when she spotted a Burger King on the corner. "Perfect," she said, slowing to make the turn.

She drove to the back of the parking lot, such as it was, and backed up beside the dumpster. From there she could monitor the entrance from D Street to her left, and the secondary entrance from West Broadway, directly ahead. Her instincts told her not to take anything for granted so she kept a steady eye on the traffic flow on both streets, cellphone in her hand, as she awaited a callback.

"So…we're just going to sit here?" Rachel asked.

"Yup," Kendra said. A silver Ford Taurus pulled up to the drive-through menu board, but the glare of the sun off the windshield made it impossible to see the driver or if there were two additional passengers in the car.

Rachel began to fidget. "I need to use the bathroom," she said.

"Go," Kendra told her, keeping her eyes trained on the Taurus.

Rachel pushed the door open and climbed out. As Kendra watched her scurry across the lot, she got the callback she'd been waiting for. "Sidney, talk to me," she said. "What 'cha got?"

"That depends on where you are," Sidney replied.

"We're still in South Boston, about halfway down West Broadway."

Sidney knew all the safehouse properties having secured them for Henry Hammond. "You're not that far from Canton," she said. "Ever been there? The house is right next to the Pequit Brook Conservation Area."

"I remember it well," Kendra said, remembering her first visit to the property. "Is Burgess still there?"

"Yes, he is. Remember, when you pull around back, don't get out of the car until he comes out to greet you."

"Right," Kendra said, recalling how Jameson had uttered those exact same words.

"I told Nathan you'd call him once you get there."

"Okay, will do," Kendra said.

"By the way, how was the tunnel?" Sidney asked.

"It was…interesting," Kendra said, unsure of how else to describe it.

"Did you come across any snakes?"

"Snakes? No." *Spider webs? Yes.*

95

"Good," Sidney offered. "That means the cinnamon oil worked."

"Oh, so that was what we smelled."

Elizabeth held her ground, glaring at Nathan with a stern look that indicated he wasn't going anywhere until he told her what was happening.

"Early this morning, Gina had a visitor," he said. "Some woman named Rachel."

"Rachel? Rachel who?"

"I couldn't tell you."

"What *can* you tell me?" Elizabeth said, exasperated.

"Not much."

She raised an eyebrow. *Uh, you want to try that again?*

"It's true," he said. "All Gina would tell me is that the woman was being chased by three men and she needed a place to hide."

"Three men."

"Uh-huh. They showed up while we were in the garage."

"And what were you doing in the garage?"

Nathan looked at her like she was daft. "Hiding?" he said. *Hello?*

"Then what happened?" Beck asked, speaking for the first time.

"I made a couple of phone calls and arranged for her to go to one of the safehouses."

"You called Kendra and Sidney," Elizabeth said.

"Yes."

"Okay, that was good." The sooner he learned how to use the assets he had available to him, the safer he would be.

"Well, yes and no," Nathan replied.

"What do you mean?"

"Somehow, the three men chasing Rachel found the safehouse."

"When?"

"Sometime this morning."

"Well that certainly explains the frantic call from Kendra," Elizabeth said.

"Yeah, well, they escaped without being seen and now we need to find another safehouse."

"And what does this have to do with Gina?"

"I have no idea."

She did the eyebrow thing again.

"Mom, I'm telling you, I *don't know!*" he groaned. "She refuses to talk about it."

"You say these three men showed up last night, and then again this morning?" Beck said.

"Yeah. Weird, right?"

"I was thinking more like, a little too convenient."

Nathan thought for a moment, then said, "Are you thinking what I'm thinking?"

"Uh-huh."

They spoke for several minutes, and when they were done Beck took his phone out of his pocket and called Kendra.

"Beck!" she said, answering right away. "How's *your* day going so far? I bet mine's been crazier."

"It's about to get even more interesting," he said. "Where are you?"

"I'm just about to get on Rt. 93 south."

"Turn around."

"What was that?"

97

"Turn around. There's somewhere I want you to meet me."

"Nothing would please me more," Kendra said, "but first, I've got some cargo to deliver."

"Yes, so I've been told. I'm calling because I want you to bring that cargo to a different location."

"And why is that?"

"I can give you three good reasons," Beck said, "and I'm guessing none of them have showered in a few days."

"You spoke with Nathan?"

"He's standing right in front of me."

"Understood," Kendra said. "Where am I meeting you?" She was driving past Moakley Park, approaching the dreaded Kosciuszko Circle.

"Braden Street," Beck said, referring to his small ranch-style house in Arlington.

"Turning around now," she said. She came to Kosciuszko Circle and sliced into a seemingly endless line of cars, shouting curses at each of them before taking her first right. She went a short distance and took another right, putting her on Rt. 93 North. "Change of plans," she told Rachel, as she rocketed into the left lane.

"So I gathered," Rachel mumbled, unable to take her eyes off the road ahead, or loosen her iron grip on the armrest.

"Kendra!"

She put the phone to her ear again. "Still here."

"Are you going to be okay?" Beck said, all too familiar with her erratic driving habits.

"Me? I'm fine," she replied. "BUT THESE OTHER MO-RONS NEED TO GET A LIFE!" she shouted, as she cut back into the right lane and sped past a slow-moving bakery van.

"Okay, well, try not to damage the cargo," Beck said. He ended the call and shoved the phone back in his pocket. "This could happen faster than we think, so we need to be ready."

"Let's do it," Nathan said.

Phillip Roman was finishing his second Bloody Mary in the clubhouse lounge when he got a call from Wicks. "Yes?" he said, watching the other club members hunched over the bar like a pack of hungry livestock at a feeding trough. The bartender had put out a platter of chicken fingers, fried pickles and Jalapeño poppers, all of which were being voraciously consumed.

"She's on the move," said Wicks.

"What?" Roman blurted out.

"She's still in South Boston, but she's moved north of her original location."

Roman turned away from the bar and lowered his head. "You're telling me she managed to slip them *again?*" It took every ounce of restraint he had to keep from shouting.

"It would appear so," Wicks said.

Roman took a calming breath. "Give them her new location," he said, tamping down his anger, "and call me back when it's done." With that, he ended the call and lifted his empty glass in the air, motioning to the bartender for a refill.

On the ride home Gina said nothing. Her head was still turned toward the side window, the landscape flying past in a blur as she continued to wrestle with her odd collection of clues. They were disjointed at best, like pieces to several different puzzles mixed together in the same box.

Louise could see that she had no interest in discussing their trip to the Freeman Library, so she refrained from pressing her for details. But 15 minutes later, as they were approaching the street where Gina lived, her curiosity bubble burst. "How was he?" she asked, sounding more like a concerned friend than a nosy neighbor.

"How was who?" Gina asked, without turning from the window.

Louise flicked the directional lever and then slowed to make the turn. "Her father," she said.

Gina spun around and looked at her, blindsided by the question. "What did you say?" But before Louise could answer, Gina saw Beck's monster truck coming up the street toward them. Nathan was sitting in the front passenger seat. "Pull over," she told Louise.

"I'm sorry, what?"

"PULL OVER!"

Louise touched the brakes and came to a stop at the curb. "Is something wrong?"

Gina ignored the question and jumped out of the car, sliding her arm through the strap of her backpack as she raced into the oncoming lane. When Beck saw her, he slammed his foot on the brake, making the truck tires screech on the pavement. She went directly to the passenger-side door. By the time she got there, Nathan had already lowered the window.

"Have you spoken with Kendra today?" she asked. "Please tell me they made it to the safehouse."

"They made it to the safehouse. But…"

"But what?"

"This morning they had to leave unexpectedly when those three guys showed up again."

"NO!"

"Yes."

"So, where are they now? Kendra and Rachel, I mean."

Nathan looked over at Beck. "We should bring her with us."

Beck made an uneasy face. "I don't know," he said, shaking his head. If Nathan's hunch was correct, things were bound to get bloody.

"Bring me with you where?" Gina asked. When Nathan hesitated, she grit her teeth and grabbed his forearm, digging her fingernails into his skin. "Bring me with you *where?*"

"OWW!" he said, prying her hand off his arm. "We're going to meet Kendra and Rachel."

"Oh, I am SO coming with you!" She stormed around the front of the truck and stopped in the middle of the street. "We're not done!" she shouted, stabbing a finger at Louise, who was still parked at the curb with her window down.

"Call me when you want to talk," Louise said smoothly.

"Oh, I will," Gina fired back. "You can count on it!"

Ten minutes later they pulled into Beck's driveway on Braden Street. He clicked the wireless remote clipped to the visor and waited for the garage door to rise.

"So, let me get this straight," Gina said, recounting what they'd told her on the ride over. "You think these three killers are tracking Rachel through her cellphone?"

"Yes," said Beck. "There are other methods of tracking, but using the signal from a cellphone is the most common." The door reached its apex and he pulled into the garage.

101

"How would they even do that?" Gina asked.

"That's what we need to find out," Beck said. He tapped the remote again and the door slid down to its original position. "We need to talk to Rachel, but before we do that we need to get ready."

"For what?"

"Some rough company."

Gina nodded her head slowly, a spooked look on her face, as she realized the rough company he was referring to.

Beck jumped down from the truck and went over to the gray metal door that led into the house. He entered a code on the small numeric keypad next to the frame, then opened the door and stepped back to let Gina and Nathan enter first.

Gina walked in and stopped next to the center island in the kitchen, surveying the open-concept layout that included a large adjoining living room. The entire space was spotless. Every lamp, every table, every cushion was perfectly arranged. She got the immediate sensation of standing in a furniture showroom.

Beck checked his watch. "Assuming Kendra hasn't caused a multi-car pileup on Rt. 93, they should be here any time now," he said. "The question is, are they being tracked to this location by Mo, Larry and Curly."

"Who?" Nathan and Gina said at the same time.

"The Three Stooges," Beck said. "You've never heard of them?"

Nathan looked at Gina, confused. *Do you know what he's talking about?*

She shrugged. *Couldn't tell you.*

"Never mind," Beck said. "Both of you, come with me."

He crossed the kitchen and followed the narrow hallway that

led to his office. Pushed up against the wall on the right was a large desk with two 24" computer monitors. Sitting on the desktop in front of them was a wireless keypad and mouse. He sat down at the desk and went to work on the keypad, entering a command that brought the monitors to life. With another keystroke the desktop images were replaced by panoramic views of the yard, provided by cameras mounted on each corner of the house. On one monitor was the front and back. On the other, each side yard.

"This is new," Nathan said.

"I figured it was time I beefed up the security," Beck said. As he watched the screens, he saw Kendra's Volvo pull into the driveway. From the looks of it, it didn't appear to have any new dents. "Here they are," he said. He pushed away from the desk and stood up. "Let's go meet this friend of yours."

She's not my friend, Gina thought. *I inherited her.*

Bolan was nearing the end of West Broadway when he pulled in to an open space directly across the street from the former SS. Peter and Paul Church. It had been converted years earlier to a beehive of condos and loomed high over the street with a stately grace that made all who passed it look up at its classic gothic construction.

So far their search of West Broadway and the surrounding streets had yielded nothing.

"How hard can it be to find a beat-up Volvo?" he said, keeping an eye on the passing traffic.

"Maybe they switched cars," Rodano said, from the back seat.

"I doubt it," Cafferty chimed in. "There wasn't enough time. Besides, if they did, we'd see the Volvo sitting somewhere, abandoned."

Bolan cut a tight U-turn in the street and retraced their route. "Where *are* you?" he asked, fearing they might not survive another blunder.

Beck went out through the garage to escort Kendra and Rachel into the house. As Nathan and Gina waited in the living room, Nathan asked, "Who was that woman in the white Mercedes?"

"Kendra's aunt."

Nathan furrowed both brows. "Her *aunt?* Wait, that means she's…"

"Yes," Gina said. "She's Jameson's sister."

"What were you doing with Jameson's sister? And how did you even meet her?"

Thinking quickly, Gina said, "She's an old friend of the family."

"Really. And you never thought to tell me that?"

I just found out today, Gina wanted to say. Instead, fearing it would only lead to more questions, ones she didn't want to answer, she just shrugged and said, "Sorry, I thought I told you."

The gray metal door opened and Beck stepped inside. Trailing him were Kendra and Rachel who looked like they'd been leopard crawling through an inner-city construction site. Their hair was tousled and full of grit, and their clothes looked like they'd been pulled from the bottom of a laundry hamper.

Gina went to Rachel at once, relieved to see her alive. "How are you holding up?" she asked.

"I'm alive, thanks to her," Rachel said, nodding at Kendra.

"Thank you," Gina told her.

Kendra responded with a customary fist bump. "Any time, sister."

Next, Gina turned and addressed the group. "Everyone," she said, "there's something I need to say to all of you."

All eyes turned to her.

"First, to Nathan and Kendra, thank you for your help, last night and again this morning. Without your quick thinking…"

"And expert driving," Kendra added, proudly.

"Yes, without that, there's no telling what might've happened."

Heads nodded.

"I know you have questions, but I beg of you…please… *please*… don't ask. All I can tell you is that there are things at work here that…well…I'll just leave it at that. There are things at work here."

"Okay, fair enough," Beck said. He turned to Rachel. "I'm sorry, we didn't get formally introduced. I'm Beck."

"Rachel Goudas," she said, taking her full measure of him. He looked like he could rip oak trees out of the ground with his bare hands, roots and all.

"I'm not sure how much time we have, so I'll be direct," he said. "Who is it?"

"Excuse me?"

"The person you've been calling. Who is it?"

She gave him a guarded look, like he was several degrees left of crazy. "I have no idea what you're talking about."

7

Extra Mushrooms

"You want to try that again?" Beck said.

Rachel looked at Gina, feigning confusion. *What is it with this guy?*

"Is it true?" Gina asked.

"No! I gave my phone up years ago. It was right before—"

"STOP!" Gina blurted out, cutting Rachel off before she could say another word. "Uh, we need a minute," she said, then took Rachel by the arm and dragged her down the hallway. When they came to Beck's office, she steered her inside and closed the door.

"What's going on?" Rachel asked.

"Do *not* talk about my grandmother," Gina said.

"Why not?"

"None of these guys know what she did for you, or for any of the other women."

"There were others?"

"Yes. And I'd rather that information stay between the two of us."

"No problem," Rachel said. "But what am I supposed to tell King Kong if he—"

"Beck," Gina said.

"Huh?"

"His name is Beck."

"Okay, fine. If *Beck* keeps pressing me with questions, like, why I'm on the run, and why I have three hired killers looking for me, what am I supposed to tell him?"

"If Beck questions you, you say nothing. As far as your cellphone, you gave it up years ago for reasons that you'd rather not discuss. That's it."

"And you think that'll work?"

"I'll *make* it work," Gina said. "But just so I understand, you didn't just give up your phone voluntarily. I'm guessing my grandmother took it from you just before you went into hiding?"

"Yes."

"So, what phone have you been using?" Gina asked, remembering what Beck had said about tracking methods.

Rachel looked away.

This was something Gina had seen Nathan do on multiple occasions, whenever he wasn't being completely forthcoming. She called it his 'no-look, no-tell' act. "What are you hiding?" she said.

Rachel looked up at the ceiling, feigning boredom. "It's nothing. Just forget it."

"No. I won't forget it. Now, answer the question!"

Rachel picked at the dirt beneath her fingernails, stalling.

"We can stand here as long as you want," Gina said. "I have all the time in the world. You? Not so much. Those three men chasing you are probably going to show up any minute now."

"I have another one," Rachel muttered, under her breath.

Gina cupped her hand behind her ear and leaned forward. "What was that?"

"I have another one!" Rachel growled, annoyed that she had to repeat it.

"*What?*"

"The real estate company gave it to me when I started working there. I thought I gave it back but I found it buried in some of my old stuff."

"And you've been *using it?*" Gina asked, her voice growing louder. Rachel nodded.

"ARE YOU *CRAZY?*" Gina shouted. She began to pace. "Nathan was right. You've been broadcasting your location to three killers!"

"Will you stop?" Rachel said. "All I did was *text!*"

There was a knock on the door, then it opened and Beck stuck his head in the room. "Is everything all right in here?" he asked.

"No," Gina said, incredulous. "You and Nathan were right. You just had the wrong phone."

"I don't follow," Beck said. He stepped into the room and shut the door.

"She doesn't have a personal cellphone," Gina said. "She's got a work phone, and she's been texting with it!"

"And what's wrong with that?" Rachel protested.

"What's wrong is that every time you use that phone, the signal can be traced," Beck said. "It doesn't matter if you call or text."

"Oh really," Rachel said, not buying it. "You expect me to believe that?"

"Every phone is assigned what's called an IMEI number. It's stored in your phone's hardware and it can't be changed. If someone gets a hold of it, they can use it to track your location. I know because I've done it before."

Rachel's jaw fell open and she began to teeter. If Beck hadn't grabbed hold of her she would've collapsed on the floor. He walked her over to the desk and eased her down in the chair. "Go to the kitchen and get some water," he told Gina. "The glasses are in the cupboard to the left of the sink."

Gina nodded...*on it*...then hurried out of the room.

Rachel sat back in the chair, wobbly, threatening to topple over at any moment.

Beck knelt down and held her arms to keep her upright. "I'm going to ask you something and I need you to tell me the truth," he said. "This is extremely important."

"It's all my fault," she mumbled, oblivious to his words. "I-I had no idea..."

"Rachel! Listen to me," he said, tightening his grip. He spoke the next words slowly and clearly. "When was the last time you used the phone?"

"All this time..." she muttered. She was sobbing now.

"Rachel! Focus!

"I-I'm sorry...what?" she said. The room was spinning out of control and she felt like she might throw up.

Beck repeated the question, speaking even slower. "When-was-the-last-time-you-used-the-phone?"

The door swung open and Gina came in carrying a glass of water. Following behind her were Nathan and Kendra, their expressions tight with concern.

"Here," Gina said, handing the glass to Beck.

He wrapped Rachel's fingers around it and steadied her hand as she raised it to her mouth and took a sip. "The phone," he said. "When was the last time you used it?"

Rachel took several gulps of water, then pulled the glass from her mouth. "It was…after…" she said, trying to catch her breath.

"After what?"

"After we left the safehouse."

Beck looked over his shoulder at Kendra. *Are you following this?*

"I didn't see any phone," she said, shaking her head.

"It was when we stopped," Rachel said. She had regained some composure and was holding the glass on her own now, cupping it with both hands like it held a magic elixir that could make everything right again.

"You mean, at Burger King?" Kendra asked.

"Yeah, there."

"She went inside to use the bathroom," Kendra told Beck.

He turned back to Rachel. "That was the last time? In the bathroom at Burger King?"

Rachel nodded her head, mid-sip. "Mm-hmm."

Beck breathed a sigh of relief and then stood up.

"You know, this may actually be a good thing," Nathan said, upbeat.

"Nathan…I swear…if this is another one of your stupid jokes," Gina said, fiercely.

"Wait," he said. "Hear me out."

She slumped her shoulders and let out an exasperated breath. "What?"

"You want to help her, right?"

"What kind of stupid question is that? You know I do."

He kept on. "You're going to need some time to…you know…" he said, referring to the mysterious 'phantom' she claimed she needed to find to set things right.

"Yeah?" she said, suddenly intrigued.

"Well, you just got all the time you need, and then some."

"What makes you think that?"

"We can assume they've been tracking her phone, right?" he asked Beck. "I mean, it's the only thing that explains how they just keep showing up."

"Yes," said Beck.

"Then it's simple. We use that to our advantage."

Beck saw where Nathan was headed and slowly nodded his head. "Misdirection. I love it," he said, grinning.

"The question is where to send them," Nathan said.

"Oh, I have the perfect place in mind," Beck replied. He held out his hand and said to Rachel, "I'm going to need that phone."

In the blink of an eye the tension in the room evaporated. Knowing that Rachel hadn't used the phone since she arrived at Braden Street, the threat of Bolan's crew showing up was no longer a concern. Suddenly, the nickname Beck had given them, "The Three

111

Stooges" was about to take on a whole new meaning.

He began by explaining the target location, a popular restaurant owned by a good friend and military veteran.

"Are you sure that's wise?" Kendra asked. "From what I hear, that place is usually packed."

"That's the whole point," Beck said. "It has to be a place where Rachel would logically be on a Sunday. If they show up and it's an abandoned warehouse, they'll immediately become suspicious."

"Plus, we have the perfect bait," Nathan said.

"And what's that?" asked Kendra.

"Your car."

"Yes!" Gina said. "They saw Rachel get into it early this morning on Lafayette Street. When they see it again they'll know they found her."

"I like it," said Beck.

After that, while the others waited in the living room, Beck stood at the kitchen sink and stared out the window at the back yard as he called Elizabeth and told her the plan. He assured her that Nathan wouldn't be near any of the actual "dirty work" as he called it, although his participation would be key.

Next, he phoned Jameson and explained the situation in general terms: how he and Nathan were helping Gina protect a woman in need; the three thugs chasing her and tracking her phone signal; and Nathan's ingenious idea to use the phone to lure them into a trap.

"And you say Gina is *helping* this woman?" Jameson asked.

"Yes."

Jameson didn't ask why. "What do you need from me?" he said.

"We're going to need your guy with the van."

"You're referring to the Repository driver?"

"Yeah, him."

"Very well," Jameson said. "Call me when you're ready and I'll see that he arrives promptly."

"Thank you," Beck said, glad that the disposal portion of the plan was once again going to be handled by one of Jameson's associates. The Repository was still a mystery, one Jameson had never divulged until just recently. Beck made a mental note to press Jameson for more details once the current crisis was resolved.

"The kids," Jameson said. "How are they?"

"Like hardened steel," Beck replied.

"Good. You'll keep them safe?"

"You know it."

"How are you set for manpower?"

"We're good," Beck said. "The place we're going is, how shall I say, *advantageous?* For us, that is, not for our three visitors."

"In that case I'll be very interested to hear how it turns out."

Beck ended the call and walked into the living room. "Okay, listen up," he said to the group. He stood with his back to the giant flat screen TV and reviewed what would happen next. "Nathan, you'll ride with me. Gina, your work here is done. Kendra will drive you home and rendezvous with us at the restaurant." He looked at Rachel and said, "Do these guys have names?"

"The leader is Bolan. The other two are Cafferty and Rodano. But…"

"But what?"

"You guys need to rethink this," she said. "These guys are savages."

"We'll deal with it," Beck said, undeterred. "Once we're in position, I'll use Rachel's phone to make a random call that will lead Bolan and his two associates straight into our trap."

"Define random," Kendra said.

"I was thinking of calling Vercelli's."

"You're going to order a *pizza?*"

"Sure. Why not?" Beck replied. "I get hungry after a workout. Don't you?"

"Good point," Kendra said, tipping her index finger at him. "Be sure and get extra mushrooms."

"Extra mushrooms. Got it."

"Guys," Rachel said. "I'm serious. This isn't a joke."

"I agree," said Beck. "What's your point?"

"You make it sound like you'll just slip in, take them down, and then slip out."

"That's the general idea."

"Just the two of you?" Rachel said, pointing at each of them. "That's suicide. You're outgunned and outmatched."

"I think you're forgetting something," Beck said. "We have Nathan, too."

She shook her head, frustrated. "I'm serious," she said. "Don't do it."

"Why not?" Kendra asked, shrugging.

"Because you have no idea who you're dealing with okay?" Rachel exclaimed. "These guys are—"

"What?" Kendra barked. "Big? Tough? Mean as a snake?"

"Try cruel, heartless, and barbaric."

"Good! I can't wait to meet them," Kendra said. She smiled at

Nathan and rubbed her palms together in anticipation. "This is gonna be fun."

Rachel stared at her, incredulous. *Lady, you are absolutely, positively, 100% crazy.*

"Uh, Beck?" Gina said, uttering her first words in a long while.

"Yeah?"

"What about Rachel? While all of this is happening, what is *she* doing? I, for one, don't think she should be left unprotected. We still don't know who we're dealing with."

"You can say that again," Rachel mumbled.

"I agree," said Beck. "Any suggestions?"

"She can't come back to my house," Gina said, "but there *is* someone who can safeguard her until this is over." She turned to Kendra. "Ready to go?"

"Yup, but what about her?" Kendra asked, pointing at Rachel.

"She's coming with us."

"Huh?"

"I'll explain on the way."

Phillip Roman stowed his clubs in the trunk of his metallic-green Jaguar F-type S and then climbed in behind the wheel. Wicks had called every 30 minutes, as instructed, but the message had been the same each time: Rachel Goudas was nowhere to be found.

He backed out of the parking space and drove to the back edge of the lot. Parked in the cool shade of the maple trees that lined the 14th fairway, he pressed a speed dial number on his phone and sat back in the seat, breathing in the soothing smell of freshly mowed grass. Was there anything better?

As usual, Magnus answered after the first ring. "Didn't happen?" he said, his voice deep and frighteningly calm.

"No," Roman said. "The hunters have lost the scent."

Two weeks earlier, Roman had put him on standby, pending Bolan's success, or lack thereof, at capturing Rachel Goudas. What continued to baffle him was how three seasoned trackers, armed to the teeth, couldn't find a woman who had been broadcasting her location at every turn.

"What do you need me to do?" Magnus asked.

"Sit tight and wait for my text."

Beck let the three women out through the garage door. They had just piled into the Volvo, Gina in the front seat, Rachel in the back, when Kendra said, "So, what's the plan?"

"I'll let you know in just a minute," Gina said. She took Kendra's cellphone from the cupholder. "May I?"

"Uh…sure," Kendra said, confused. In all the time they'd known each other, Gina had never asked to use her phone. "Who are you calling?"

"Your aunt."

Kendra gave her a guarded look.

"Yeah, I just learned who she is," Gina said. "Imagine my surprise."

Kendra said nothing.

"The question is: why didn't you tell me?" Gina said.

"Uh…I guess…I…didn't see the *need?*" Kendra muttered, hoping the dodge would work. In truth, Louise had ordered her *not* to share their family connection. What prompted her to make such a demand was a mystery, but Kendra didn't question it. From a very early age she'd been taught that her aunt's rules were unbreakable.

"The need? Yeah, right," Gina said, scowling as she punched in Louise's number. She raised the phone to her ear and then motioned with her hand. "Come on, let's go. Chop, chop."

Kendra slid the key into the ignition and paused. "Where are we going?"

The call connected and Louise answered. "Hello, this is Louise." As always, the calm tone in her voice suggested she was reclining in a clawfoot tub, neck deep in a lavender-lime bubble bath.

"Yeah, this is Gina. Hold on a sec." She pulled the phone aside. "Library."

"You want to go to the *library?* Now?"

"Yes," Gina said, calmly, then pressed the phone to her ear. "Okay, I'm back."

Kendra turned the key and the Volvo's engine roared to life.

"Is everything all right?" Louise asked.

"It will be," Gina said. "Look, I'm sorry about before. It's just… this whole day…dealing with…you know…"

"Rachel," Louise said.

"Yes. Then, what you asked me…completely out of the blue like that?"

"I can understand how that must've confused you," Louise said.

Confused me? Gina thought. *Ya think?*

"How about this?" Louise said. "Once we get Rachel squared away, we'll sit down for a much-needed and long-overdue chat. There are a number of important things we need to discuss."

"We?" Gina said.

"Yes, we. I'm here to help in any way I can."

"You may come to regret that decision," Gina replied.

Louise said nothing.

Kendra came to the end of the street, paused momentarily, then shot out into traffic ahead of a coffee-colored Honda Civic packed with teenagers. The driver accelerated, his hand never leaving the horn, and proceeded to ride Kendra's bumper.

"KEEP IT UP MORON!" she shouted, staring at the rearview mirror. "I'LL MAKE YOU EAT THAT BUMPER!"

"I know that voice," Louise said, not so cheery this time.

"Sorry about that," Gina said. She glared at Kendra, eyes wide, and held up the phone. *Uh hello? I'm trying to talk on the phone here!*

Kendra shrugged, confused...*what did you expect me to do?*...as the Honda cut around them and accelerated, the passengers pressing their middle fingers against the windows as they raced past.

Gina saw it but said nothing, knowing it would only send Kendra into a low Earth orbit.

When Kendra looked back at the road, the Honda was speeding out of sight.

"All better now?" Louise asked.

"Yes, for the moment," Gina said, shooting Kendra a disapproving look. "Can you meet us at the library? Like, now?"

"The library? In Arlington?"

"Yes."

"Sure," Louise said. "What's up?"

"The three men chasing Rachel? They're about to go away, permanently."

"Let me guess...Beck?"

"That's right," Gina said, slowly. *Is there anyone this woman doesn't know?*

"Say no more," Louise told her. "I'll meet you there shortly."

After Kendra left, Beck went to his office and grabbed a black plastic carrying case from a shelf in the closet. When he returned to the kitchen, Nathan was sitting on a stool at the center island waiting for him.

"What's that?" he asked.

"This," Beck said, patting the side of the case, "is our secret weapon."

8

Smitty's

The library parking lot was virtually empty when Kendra pulled in. She backed the Volvo into a space in the back corner, well away from the street and any would-be onlookers. After she turned off the car, she eyed the library building with its weathered bricks that were being over-taken an incursion of Boston Ivy. "Why here?" she asked.

"You mean, why did I choose the library as a place to meet?" Gina replied.

"Yeah. Why not just have her come to Braden Street?"

"There's a book I need to get."

"A book," Kendra said, sounding surprised. By her way of thinking, reading printed pages had gone out of style decades ago. Today, libraries were museums, the books they housed nothing more than a reminder of what she called, "ye goode olde days of lore."

"Yes, a book," Gina said, strongly. *You might try reading one some-time.*

What she didn't say was that the book in question had been written by her grandmother, and that buried inside it might be the only information that could lead her to the person she needed to find.

Rachel's cellphone confession had answered at least one of Gina's questions: how this whole debacle started after Rachel had enjoyed years of peaceful anonymity. Unearthing her previous work phone, only to unwittingly charge it and start texting with it, bore the stamp of utter stupidity, and brought with it a signed and sealed death decree.

A glint of light broke her train of thought and she turned to see Louise's Mercedes pull into the lot. The bright white finish was as clean as new-fallen snow, the car seemingly immune to the tiniest spec of dirt or grime.

"We'll be right back," she told Rachel, then she and Kendra got out of the car.

Louise wasn't planning on staying long and didn't pull into one of the vacant parking spots. Instead, she looped around and came to a stop in front of the Volvo where Kendra and Gina were waiting. With the engine still running, she lowered the window and took Kendra's hand, pulling her closer for a cheek-to-cheek kiss. "My impatient niece," she said softly, resigned to that quirky part of her personality.

"Impatient? Me?" Kendra replied.

"Uh, we need to make this quick," Gina told them.

"Yeah, I have a date with three groovy dudes," Kendra said.

121

"Groovy?" Louise asked, suspiciously.

"Well, maybe 'groveling' would be a better description. Something tells me that's what they'll be doing when we're done with them."

"I hate to break up this little grammar exercise," Gina said, "but we need you to keep an eye on Rachel for a little while." She looked to Kendra for guidance. "What do you think, an hour?"

"Better make it two. Beck likes to play with his food."

"Take all the time you need," Louise said. "I can assure you that Rachel will be well protected." She pressed a button on the armrest releasing the door locks and that's when Gina turned around and motioned to Rachel with a frantic wave of her hand. *Let's go!*

Without so much as a word to the others, Rachel climbed out of the Volvo and slid into the back seat of the Mercedes.

"One of you will call me when it's done?" Louise asked, looking from Kendra to Gina.

"Yes," Gina said. She nudged Kendra's arm. "Come on, we gotta go."

Small talk and pleasantries would have to wait until later. She'd been gone for more than four hours, on a Sunday no less, and she had to get back home for what she assumed would be a grueling interrogation by her parents. She could just imagine her father's wild tirade.

"In what universe would a 13-year-old girl just up and disappear for four hours?" he'd yell.

What universe indeed.

Beck set the plastic case on top of the island but didn't open it.

"Ever hear of a cavalry scout?" he asked.

Nathan thought for a second then shook his head. "Nope."

"In the military, cavalry scouts act as the eyes and ears on the field of battle. They relay information about enemy positions, vehicles, weapons, and troop activity. That information is critical in helping those in charge make informed decisions about when to strike or when to pull back."

Nathan nodded his head slowly, envisioning a smoke-filled battlefield and the sound of bullets whizzing through the air.

"You're going to be our cavalry scout," Beck said. "Your primary job will be to observe and report."

"Observe and report," Nathan repeated. "I can do that."

Beck opened the case. Inside were several Motorola UHF 2-way radios, each equipped with a wired earpiece and an inline push-to-talk (PTT) switch. He took one out and handed it to Nathan. "That right there is how you'll relay what you see. If they go in the side door, you tell us. If they spread out and circle the building, you tell us. If reinforcements show up to help them…"

"I tell you," Nathan said.

"Correct. Now, I don't think that's going to happen, but you get my point. Everything you see, you report."

He showed Nathan how they worked by outfitting him with one while he took another and went out to the garage. After several successful transmissions, he came back inside, checked the time, and repacked the radios in the case.

"You ready to do this?" he asked.

Nathan's smile was blinding. "You better believe it."

After Louise drove away, Gina said, "I'll be right back," and cut across the lot, trotting toward the front of the building.

"Make it quick!" Kendra shouted, then went back to the Volvo to wait. There was a fight coming and she had to prepare—get herself in that dark place where anger would be her fuel— where justice would be levied one powerful rip of her bat at a time.

The wait turned out to be more like 15 minutes.

Gina hurried to the fiction section of the library and found her grandmother's books. That took all of two minutes. There were multiple volumes of each title, including the one she wanted, *The Crown Killer.* After a quick check of the publication date, which coincided with the year her grandmother was contacted by Rachel Goudas, she went to the front desk.

Another two minutes gone.

The librarian was the same one from last time. Patty. Her lips formed a perpetual smile that looked oddly like wax lips. Her black hair was cut so short that Gina wondered why the woman didn't just shave her head and get it over with.

When she set the book on the counter, Patty picked it up and pressed it to her chest like it was her favorite doll. "I *love* this book!" she said.

That's when Gina lost her race with time.

Patty's smile fell away and she looked at Gina, pointing as she spoke. "I recognize you. Weren't you in here about six months ago?"

"Uh…six months ago?…yeah," Gina said. *Now can you please stamp the book so I can get out of here?*

"I knew it, I knew it, I knew it," Patty clucked, bouncing up and down like she'd won the grand prize on an afternoon game show.

Gina imagined balloons and confetti raining down from the ceiling, and an announcer's voice saying, "Congratulations Patty! You're a winner!"

"Admit it!" Patty said. She was pointing again. "You're a Helen Bainbridge fan. Come on, you can say it."

"Yes," Gina said, in a tired voice. *You got me.* "I am a Helen Bainbridge fan."

Patty leaned across the counter. "So am I," she said with a devilish grin.

No, really? Gina thought. *I never would've guessed.*

Patty put the book down and stamped it, then slid it across the counter. Gina went to pick it up when Patty clamped her hand down on top of it. "Promise me!" she said.

"Promise you?" Gina asked, unable to pry the book free.

"When you're done reading this, you'll come back and tell me all your favorite parts."

"Sure…no problem," Gina said. *Can I have the book now?*

"Ooh, I can't wait!" Patty said, clapping her hands together.

Gina snatched the book off the counter and backed away. When she saw a young mother approaching with a short stack of books and her four-year-old daughter in tow, she turned and made a beeline for the front door.

Beck climbed up into his truck and took a moment to run through his mental checklist, making sure he had everything he'd need for the job. On the back seat was the case of two-way radios. He popped open the glove box and saw his binoculars and a K-bar knife. Next, he checked the large center console, home to his SIG

125

Sauer M17 service pistol. He reached under the seat and felt his eight-sided club and collapsible baton. Satisfied that he hadn't forgotten anything, he started the truck and backed out of the garage, stopping halfway down the driveway to watch the door close.

"Will they see me?" Nathan asked.

"Not a chance," Beck said. "You'll be directly across the street, three stories up, in a parking garage that's covered with vines. Your elevation, plus the overgrowth, will give you the perfect cover. Trust me, when they see Kendra's Volvo, their full attention is going to be on the restaurant."

"Which reminds me," Nathan said. "Why did you choose a restaurant? What's it called again?"

"Smitty's Backyard Barbeque," said Beck. "I chose it for two reasons. Number one, it's owned by an old service buddy of mine."

"And he's okay with what we're doing? I mean, you *did* tell him, right?"

"I let him know that we'd be stopping by to sample his legendary dry rub. While we're there, I told him we'd gladly remove any unruly patrons."

"Remove. I like that," Nathan said, smiling. "It's sounds serious but not too violent."

"Oh, if they put up a fight, things will definitely get violent," Beck said. "But it'll be a very short fight."

I don't doubt it, Nathan thought. "What's the second reason?"

"These guys are serious players, which means they're sure to have guns. But there's no way they'd march into a restaurant, guns drawn, unless they were planning to rob it, which they aren't. That should give us a momentary advantage."

"You mean, you'll have them on the ground before they have time to take out their guns."

"Very good," Beck said, impressed. "I'm going to make a warrior out of you yet."

Kendra was sitting with her head down, eyes closed, and her arms crossed, conjuring dark thoughts, when the passenger door squeaked open and Gina slid into the front seat. She took one look at Kendra and said, "Are you okay?"

Kendra sat up as if awoken from a dream. "Huh?"

"Were you *sleeping*?" Gina asked.

"Not quite," Kendra said. "Did you find what you're looking for?"

"Yes. Sorry it took so long". *I was being held prisoner by a psycho librarian.*

Kendra glanced down at the cover of the book. "*The Crown Killer*, I remember that book."

"You *read* it?"

Kendra started the car. "No," she said. "I saw it on the desk in my aunt's office."

Gina paused briefly, then said, "Did your aunt ever talk about my grandmother?"

"Every now and then," Kendra said as she pulled out of the parking space. She drove to the exit, threw a quick glance to her left and right, then punched the gas and shot out into the street.

"What kinds of things did she say?" Gina asked.

"This and that. You know my aunt was her agent, right?"

"Uh-huh."

"And not only that, they were good friends."

"Right."

"They used to do a lot of stuff together."

"Stuff?"

"Yeah, you know, lunches, author events, book conventions…"

"Sure," Gina said. *Louise never told her the rest of it,* she thought. *Good.*

When they came to Gina's street, Kendra stopped at the corner to drop her off. Gina knew if her parents saw Kendra, they'd immediately get suspicious and start peppering her with a barrage of questions. *Who was that person? Why were you riding around in her car? It looks like a deathtrap. You could have been seriously injured. She's not one of Nathan Cole's friends, is she?*

As they sat at the curb, Gina said, "Thank you for everything you did for Rachel. She wouldn't be alive right now if you hadn't taken her to the safehouse."

"Don't forget Nathan," Kendra said.

"Yeah, him too."

"Once these three lowlifes are out of the picture, what's the plan for her?" Kendra asked.

"I'm working on that," Gina said.

The sudden blare of a car horn made them both flinch. Kendra looked to her left and saw a red Lexus coupe just inches from her door. The driver, an irate man dressed in a tired gray business suit, was waving his hand wildly in the air and yelling.

"YOU GOT SOMETHING TO SAY TO ME BUDDY?" Kendra shouted through the open window.

The Lexus driver lowered his window. "YOU HAD TO PARK RIGHT THERE? WHAT ARE YOU…A MORON?"

"HOW ABOUT I PARK SOMETHING UPSIDE YOUR HEAD?" Kendra yelled.

The Lexus driver waved her off. "AW...GO BACK TO BRIGHTON!"

"Jerk," Kendra said, as she watched him drive off. "I love Brighton." She turned back to Gina and said, "Listen, don't worry about Rachel. I'll talk to Beck. We'll figure something out."

"And you'll let me know?"

"Of course. I'll have Nathan relay the information."

"Thank you. There's one more thing."

"Yeah? What's that?"

"Please be careful today."

"You know I will," Kendra said, like it wasn't a concern.

"I'm serious," Gina said. "These three guys are really bad. From what Rachel told me, they take great pleasure in hurting women."

And there it was.

The fuel Kendra needed.

She took a deep breath and looked straight ahead, her fists white-knuckled on the steering wheel.

"I'm sorry," Gina said. "Did I say something wrong?"

Kendra's reply came out slow and methodical, each word simmering with anger. "No, that's exactly what I needed to hear."

Smitty's Backyard Barbeque was located on a narrow side street off of Webster Ave in Somerville. The former carpet store had been gutted and retrofitted with shiny new tile flooring, a pair of family friendly bathrooms, and a state-of-the-art kitchen. Perched atop the roof was an enormous sign with 'Smitty's Backyard Barbeque' spelled out in vintage neon letters and a cartoon pig dressed in a white cook's apron and forage cap. Its arms were crossed triumphantly and in one hand was a pair of barbeque tongs.

Beck pulled into the towering parking garage directly across the street and drove up to the third level. From that vantage point, Nathan would have a commanding view of the front and sides of the restaurant. True to his description, sections of the metal-mesh fencing that ran around the perimeter were woven with bittersweet vines. If anyone at street level bothered to look up, they'd be hard pressed to see him through the knotted thicket.

Beck followed the arrows that directed him around the perimeter of the structure. When he reached the side that faced the restaurant, there were no vacant spaces so he stopped behind a jet-black Toyota Corolla with tinted glass and polished chrome rims.

Kendra arrived several minutes later. The savage look on her face revealed only a fraction of the rage she felt as Gina's words echoed over and over in her mind.

"They take great pleasure in hurting women..."

Beck noticed it at once but said nothing; she was ready for battle and that was all that mattered. Using the truck's tailgate as a makeshift table, he unrolled the map he'd drawn of the property and outlined their plan of attack. "There are only three ways in and out of the building," he said, tapping his fingertip on each one in succession. "The front door, here. A second door here, on the right side of the building facing the parking lot. And a third door here, on the left side, set between a smoker and a wood-fired barbeque pit."

"Nothing along the back side," Kendra noted. "That's good."

"Yes, it is," Beck said. "That limits their options and gives Nathan a clear view of every door."

"Three doors, three goons," Kendra said. "Dollars to donuts they each take a door."

"Agreed," said Beck. "I'm assuming Bolan will go in the front door and send his two buddies around to each side. I'll take the left door, Kendra you take the right. We wait inside until they enter and then give them a warm Smitty's Backyard Barbeque welcome."

"Does that include throwing them in the smoker?" Kendra said.

"Let's see how it goes, but I'm not ruling anything out."

"Hold on," Nathan said. "When Bolan goes inside, Rachel won't be there. Then what?"

"Did you see the parking lot as we drove by?" asked Beck. "It was nearly full, and customers are still pouring in by the carload."

"So what you're saying is, it'll take Bolan some time to look for her."

"That's right. He goes in, he surveys the room. Big crowd. Lots of noise and commotion. He doesn't see her, but he knows she's there somewhere so he scans the crowd for a second time. One of the waitstaff is bound to ask him how many people are in his party. He has to stop looking and answer. Maybe he gets interrupted by customers coming and going. He's sure to see at least one woman with her back to him. He'll wonder if it's her, shift his position and move deeper into the room trying to see her face. By this time a couple of minutes will have passed. Probably more like three or four."

"He might even sit and wait, thinking she's using the bathroom," Kendra said.

"Good point. Either way, we have plenty of time to take down Cafferty and Rodano, leaving just Bolan."

"Two against one. Perfect," Kendra said.

Nathan saw the hint of a smile form on her lips.

Gina walked up the driveway and found her folks in the back yard. They were sitting in plastic Adirondack-style chairs that had been strategically placed beneath an overhanging limb from the neighbor's yard, giving them a small measure of filtered shade.

Gina's mother, Laura, had positioned her phone on the arm of the chair and was busy tapping the screen with her index finger. With her other hand she was plucking seedless red grapes from a zip-lock bag in her lap. Her husband, Bill was sitting beside her, obscured by the Sunday Globe that he was holding open with both hands.

"That must've been some walk," her mother said, glancing up at Gina for a microsecond before looking back down at her phone.

"What was that, dear?" Bill said as he turned to the next page.

"I was talking to your *daughter.*"

Down the came the newspaper with a loud crumpling sound. Bill turned his wrist and glanced at the time on his watch. "Four hours, right?" he said, looking over at Laura for confirmation.

She pursed her lips and nodded. *Yup.*

"Four. Hours," he said, emphasizing each word. "Where could you have possibly gone for that amount of time? And wherever it was, what were you doing there?"

Gina took in a deep breath and then let it out. *Easy now.*

"Well?" her father asked.

"I left you a note," Gina said calmly. "Did you read it? If you did, then you know that I took a walk." She raised both hands in the air, palms up, and looked skyward. "Beautiful day? I figured, why not get out and enjoy it?"

"For four *hours*?" her father bellowed.

Gina calmly slid her backpack off her shoulder. From the center compartment she pulled out her grandmother's book. "I went to the library," she said, holding up the book as proof.

When her mother saw the cover, she spit out the grape in her mouth. "What did I tell you about bringing that trash into our house?" she said.

Gina knew that her mother had a major falling out with *her* mother, the woman known worldwide as famed mystery writer Helen Bainbridge. Was it a professional jealousy? Maybe. But according to Laura's sister, Gina's Aunt Ellie, the fractured relationship had more to do with the dangerous people Helen was associating with in the course of writing her books. The list included known felons, inmates, and a legion of seedy characters from the worst neighborhoods.

"So, what you're telling me" Gina said, "is that you don't want to read it when I'm done."

"Read it?" Laura fired back. "Fat chance of that happening. It belongs at the bottom of a dumpster with all the other garbage."

"Very well then," Gina said, slipping it into her pack, "I'll be sure not to leave it lying around the house."

"See that you don't."

She left them to their Sunday afternoon diversions and went into the house. After grabbing an apple from the refrigerator, she went upstairs to her room, curled up in her beanbag chair, and started to read.

The nature trail that snakes around Grafton Reservoir was one of the most peaceful and serene places in the entire state. Until someone found a dead body. That's exactly what happened on Sunday morning, shortly after 8 a.m.

Twenty seven minutes later, as I was pulling a load of wet clothes out of a machine at that cute little laundromat on Clevenger Avenue, I got the call from my partner, Detective O'Brien. How do I know it was 27 minutes? Because those were the very words he used when he called me.

"Nolan," he said. "Twenty seven minutes ago someone found a dead body out at Grafton Reservoir."

And here I was, looking forward to a day of folding laundry and watching old Veronica Lake movies. Ah, the life of a young police detective—wading through a world of richness and filth. But as a retired patrolman once told me, "You take the caviar with the crud, kid, and just keep going."

So, with a basket of wet clothes in the trunk, I drove out to the reservoir. When I arrived I found O'Brien conferring with the park police next to a utility shed that looked like it had been built by a strapping young Abraham Lincoln in his shirtless, axe-wielding days.

O'Brien made his usual crack about donuts. Where were they? How come I didn't stop and get a dozen? What if we were still there beyond the lunch hour? What was he going to do, chew on a pine cone? I told him I had a KitKat bar in the glove box and he scoffed. Are you kidding me? Who doesn't love a KitKat bar? But enough about food.

I asked him where the body was and he led me down an expertly groomed trail, through a particularly lovely stand of hickory trees, past a gurgling brook, to a large tract of the forest covered with ferns.

"Pteridium aquilinum," he said.

"Really? Is it serious?" I said. "They have a pill for that, you know." Zoology being a secret passion of mine, I knew full well that he was giving me the botanical name for the fern, which is more commonly known as the East-ern Bracken Fern. Sure, I could've explained the false in-dusium, formed by the frond margin, but why confuse the man? He probably thinks frond is Swedish for Frank.

A slender trail cut through the ferns for another 15 feet before coming to a sudden stop. Pointing, I said, "Over there?"

"Yes," O'Brien said. The reluctant tone in his voice told me he had no interest in a second viewing of the corpse, and I decided right then and there to start calling him 'Ol' one-and-done O'Brien.'

"Let's have a look, shall we?" I said with a big smile.

It didn't work. He held his ground and did that thing with his hands that valets do after opening your hotel room door. After you, ma'am.

"Don't mind if I do," I said, then marched through the ferns. "I hope I don't get too much pteridium on my shoes," I shouted over my shoulder.

O'Brien didn't utter a word but I knew he was rolling his eyes.

When I reached the body, I stopped and did a quick visual scan of the surrounding area. The ferns stared back at me and for several seconds we had a serious stare down. The ferns eventually won so I turned my attention to the body.

The victim was female, college age, dressed in college-age clothes that showed the kind of wear that indicated she'd been there for a while. I knelt down for a closer look and that's when I noticed a discoloration on her neck, just below her chin. The rest of the body looked untouched. No cuts. No blood. No other bruising. I stood up and looked back at O'Brien. "Who found the body?"

"Dottie."

"Seriously?" I said. "I had an Aunt Dottie once. She smelled like celery."

"Did she have four legs and a tail?" O'Brien asked.

"No. But you could knit a sweater with her eyebrow hair."

"Well, this Dottie was a Golden Retriever. She slipped her leash and by the time the owner caught up with her, she was right where you're standing."

"Anyone talk to the owner?"

"The park police. They gave me his contact information if we want to talk to him."

"Yeah, we want to talk to him," I said.

"It looks like she took a wicked shot to the throat."

"You noticed that did you?" I said. "What do you wanna bet the cause of death was blunt force to the larynx?"

"Are we talking about a serious wager here?"

"Uh, I think you're forgetting something there pard." He hates when I call him that.

"Oh yeah?" he said. "What's that?"

"You still owe me for the last one."

"Any questions?" Beck asked.

Nathan and Kendra shook their heads in unison. *Nope.*

"Alright then." He rolled up the map and put it in the cab of the truck. From the back seat he grabbed the plastic case filled with two-way radios and set it on the tailgate. "Normally we'd each have a number or a color, signifying who's talking. But since there's just three of us, and I don't anticipate this lasting very long, I think we can skip that. You guys okay with that?"

"Works for me," Nathan said.

"Same," Kendra added.

He handed out the radios and each one was tested. With that done, he put the plastic case back in the truck and then set the scene for what was about to happen. "Kendra, you're going to drive back down to the restaurant. I'll wait here until I see that you've found a parking space in the lot. Try to park as close to the road as possible so they'll see your car right away."

"Will do," Kendra said.

"From there, you'll take a position inside the door on the right. The bathrooms are right there so no one should bother you. Once you're inside, I'll make the call."

"Don't forget…"

"I know, I know. Extra mushrooms."

Not even that could make her smile. She was fully locked in.

"Now, there's no telling how long it'll take the tracker to relay the information to Bolan's crew, so as soon I end the call I'll leave here and park on the street, just past the restaurant. If for any reason Bolan gets away, I'll need to pick up his trail as quickly as possible."

"He's not gonna get away," Kendra said. "Not today. Not ever."

"Atta girl," Beck said. "Oh, that reminds me." He went back to the cab and returned with a handful of black-nylon zip ties. He gave half of them to Kendra and tucked the rest in his back pocket. "Okay, after the call I'll take a position inside the door on the left." He looked at Nathan and said, "You know what you're looking for, right? Three guys in one vehicle?"

"I know their car," Nathan said. "I saw it early this morning on Lafayette Street when they were chasing Kendra and Rachel."

"Okay, that's good," said Beck. "But if for some reason they've changed cars, just look for anyone who shows an unusual interest in Kendra's car. That'll be your first clue that it's Bolan."

"Understood," said Nathan.

"All right. Let's get this done."

They exchanged fist bumps all around and then Kendra got in the Volvo and drove back down to street level. A late model minivan packed with a family of six were pulling out just as she got to the parking lot and she slid into their vacant spot, two spaces from the street.

Beck and Nathan stood at the fence, watching it happen, then Beck took Rachel's phone from his pocket and called Vercelli's. It took several rings before someone answered.

"Vercelli's. Pick up or take out?" The words were fast, the accent heavily Italian.

"Take out," Beck said. "Large pie with extra mushrooms."

"Large pie. Extra mushrooms. Anything else?"

"That's it," Beck said.

"Forty five minutes."

"Perfect. See you then."

Beck ended the call and said, "Let the games begin."

Nathan watched as Beck drove to the exit ramp in the far corner, the growl of the truck's engine echoing across the parking level the whole way. Moments later, he watched through the vine-covered fence as Beck emerged from the parking garage, powered past the restaurant, and drove another 50 feet before parking at the curb.

He took his flip phone from his pocket and checked the time.

1:45 p.m.

The question was: how long would it take Bolan and company to show up?

Thirty minutes?

An hour?

He pocketed his phone and peered through the thicket, watching cars pull in and out of the lot. Kendra's beat-up Volvo was like a flashing road sign that would be impossible for Bolan's crew to miss, which made him wonder if they'd be driving the Chevy Tahoe or something different. He was so consumed by the thought that he never heard the sound of footsteps approaching from directly behind him.

By the time it registered in his ears, it was too late.

9   *Jonath Snrft.*

Get Out of Jail Free

Phillip Roman left the country club and drove to his town-house in Cambridge. It was one of several properties he owned, but unlike the others this one had a state-of-the-art gym—a sanctuary of sorts where he went to work off steam, reflect, and plan. He had just finished an hour-long session of muscle strengthening and was toweling off when his phone rang.

"Tell me you have good news," he said to the caller.

"I found her," Wicks replied

"Where?"

"She's in Somerville, on Webster Ave."

Three minutes later, Magnus' phone dinged with a text from Roman.

Developing situation – hold for further instructions

Nathan was turning from the fence when two hands grabbed his shoulders and flung him sideways into a cement pillar. The impact stunned him momentarily and dislodged his radio and earpiece, sending them falling to the ground with a clatter. He looked up and saw a boy at least five years his senior, dressed in a soiled gray hoodie and ratty blue jeans.

"You keyed my car you little punk," the boy said.

"Huh?" Nathan grunted. He blinked hard, trying to clear his head.

"Right there!" the boy shouted, pointing to a long scratch on the side of the Toyota.

"It wasn't me," Nathan said.

"Oh yeah?" the boy fired back. "It wasn't scratched when I parked there. And you're the only person here."

The haze in Nathan's head lifted but he had no interest in trying to reason with a belligerent moron.

"What? Nothin' to say?" the boy said. "How about I beat the truth out of you?" He advanced, balling his fists and bringing them up to his chest like a prize fighter ready to unleash a flurry of punishing blows.

Nathan stood perfectly still, sizing up his options. He could tuck and roll using Beck's evasion tactic, then hightail it out of there, or he could stick around and practice some of the other things he'd learned.

He chose the latter.

He waited until hoodie boy was two feet away and then juked forward. The boy reacted with a straightaway jab, but Nathan bent his knees, lowering his position, and the jab sailed harmlessly over his right shoulder. At the same time, he pushed off with both feet and drove into the boy's rib cage, forcing him sideways. As the boy tried to regain his balance, Nathan lifted him up and rode him to the ground.

The back of the boy's head bounced off the pavement and his body went limp. Nathan drew his fist back, ready to deliver a jab of his own, when the boy raised his hands in the air, unsteadily, as if feeling his way in the dark. His eyes were glassy and unfocused, staring vacantly at the steel girders overhead.

"Next time try listening," Nathan growled. "It wasn't me." He climbed to his feet and picked up his radio. After pressing the earpiece into his ear he squeezed the PTT button. "Beck, Kendra, can you hear me?"

There was no reply.

He squeezed the button again. "Beck? Kendra?"

The only sound he heard was a loose section of the metal fence clinking softly as it shook in the wind.

Bolan, Cafferty, and Rodano were parked behind a discount tire shop on Charlestown, eating lunch and awaiting instructions. With the inside of the Tahoe reeking of greasy hamburgers and onion rings, each man ate in silence. Knowing Roman the way they did, there would be consequences for their failure to acquire the target.

Bolan had just finished his second burger and was crumpling up the wrapper when his phone rang. He grabbed it from the center console and checked the call screen. "It's Wicks." He tapped the talk button and leaned into the phone. "Yeah?"

"She's in Somerville," Wicks said.

Cafferty and Rodano were jabbering about tracking software and Bolan held his hand up in the air to silence them. *Quiet!*

They stopped talking at once.

"Say again," Bolan said.

"She's in Somerville," Wicks repeated.

Bolan put his hand over the phone. "She's in Somerville," he whispered, then put the phone to his ear again. "Where in Somerville?"

"Webster Ave."

"We're on it," Bolan said.

"I hope so," Wicks told him. "The boss man is not too happy."

Bolan dismissed the comment and ended the call. "Webster Ave," he said. "Either of you know where that is?"

"Yeah, it's not far," Rodano said. "Fifteen minutes tops."

Bolan felt a renewed sense of hope as he drove back out to the street. They'd been handed a get out of jail free card and were now 15 minutes away from erasing their previous failures. He stopped at the entrance, waited for a break in the traffic, then tore out of the lot. As he snaked through traffic, he visualized what he'd do to the woman who had caused them so much aggravation.

Nathan looked at the dead radio in his hand, and then over at the fence. He had no choice. If he was going to observe and report he'd need a new radio, and he knew that Beck had spares in his truck. But to get one, he'd have to move quickly if he was going to be back in position by the time Bolan showed up. This time, however, he'd steer clear of Parking Level #3 and monitor the restaurant from Parking Level #2, which would still offer him an unobstructed view.

He leapt over the boy on the ground and raced across the lot toward the stairwell. Minutes later he reached ground level and darted across the street. He ran past the front door of the restaurant and turned the corner of the building in an all-out sprint. When he came to the smoker and the wood-fired barbeque pit, smoke was emanating from each one, along with the intoxicating aroma of slow-smoked brisket.

He grabbed the handle of the metal door and yanked it open. Inside, he saw an open room with storage racks lining the back wall. Straight ahead, Beck was standing in the doorway that led to the office, engaged in a lighthearted conversation with someone Nathan couldn't see. In the big man's left hand was his eight-sided club, a gruesome weapon that, even from a distance, looked absolutely terrifying.

When Beck saw Nathan, his smile melted away and he hurried over to the door. "What's wrong?"

Nathan held up the 2-way radio. "Radio's dead. I need a new one. I'll explain on the way."

"Go!" Beck said. He followed Nathan along the side of the building to the street where they cut a hard right and bolted up the sidewalk. As they ran, Nathan recounted the assault in the parking garage that had disabled the radio, and then described, blow by blow, his subsequent take down of the boy in the gray hoodie.

When they reached the truck, Beck opened the side door and grabbed the black plastic case. While he was fishing out a new radio, Nathan waited on the sidewalk next to the tailgate, monitoring the flow of traffic passing by in both directions. A moment later, Beck appeared at his side.

"Here you go," he said, handing Nathan a new radio.

Nathan stood frozen in place, his eyes focused on a black Chevy Tahoe that had stopped across from the restaurant parking lot.

"What's wrong?" Beck asked, following Nathan's line of sight.

"They're here."

Gina came to the end of the first chapter and paused. So far, nothing. No cryptic words. No city. And no mention of Jericho. She went back and skimmed the chapter again, just to be sure. The only thing that *might* be a clue was the name Grafton Reservoir. She reached over and pulled her backpack closer, then stuck her hand inside and took out her notepad. At the top of the first blank page, in large letters, she began a new list.

Book Notes

Below that, in smaller letters, she entered the first item.

Grafton Reservoir?

Was it important? She'd have to research the name and see. Maybe it would lead her in a direction, maybe it wouldn't. She set the notepad aside and checked the time. It had been an hour since Kendra dropped her off, which ignited a string of questions. How long would it take for them to implement Nathan's plan? If these men were as bad as Rachel claimed, wouldn't they anticipate such a trap? What if it didn't work? What then? If it backfired, how would she know? Then, thankfully, her voice of reason kicked in and silenced the noise in her head. *More time,* she told herself. *You need to give them more time.*

Her fears appeased for the time being, she picked up the book again. There was something in it that her grandmother wanted Rachel to see. But why? Then, another possibility arose. What if it wasn't something she *wanted* her to see, rather, something she thought Rachel *needed* to see? Want and need were two very different things, especially for a person on the run from a band of murderous thugs.

Unlike Ann DeBartolo, Rachel Goudas didn't need to communicate with anyone. Just the opposite. She wanted to be invisible to the world. And she had been, for a time, which launched another carousel of questions. Why did she foolishly decide to use the cellphone? Why did she even have it? And who was she communicating with? They were all questions she'd ask Rachel the next time she saw her. Until then, there was critical information buried in the book she held in her hands. She just had to find it.

She settled back in the beanbag chair, drew up her knees, and opened to Chapter 2.

> As usual, I won the bet. The medical examiner's report confirmed that the victim of the Grafton Reservoir homicide had died from "blunt laryngeal trauma, resulting in acute traumatic disruption of the trachea." I told O'Brien if he could say that five times fast without messing it up, we'd be square on the bet. He got through two attempts fairly easily before his lips and tongue locked up. It was pretty comical to watch.
>
> O'Brien and I scoured the crime scene for clues but came up with nothing significant. The same for the victim's clothes. When we examined her pocketbook, however, which was buried in the ferns five feet from the body, we discovered that her wallet, stuffed with a dozen credit

cards and over $200 in cash, was intact. Conclusion: this wasn't a mugging. Whoever caved in her throat had a very different agenda in mind.

I opened a case file and spent most of the afternoon documenting every detail, including the physical evidence we found at the scene which was pretty much limited to the contents of the victim's pocketbook. O'Brien brought me a copy of the medical examiner's report as well as a report from the park police. It was nearly five o'clock when I finished, and that's when I got a call from my friend Roxy.

"Hey girl," she said. "You ready to hit it?"

Translation: are you ready for another wild night on the town?

It's what I like to call our weekly "chat and chug."

This week's playground turned out to be a new tap-room called "Primal," which pretty much summed up the male clientele. As we sampled an exquisite selection of IPAs, I couldn't help but notice a certain gleam in Roxy's eyes. And it wasn't the IPA. "Okay," I said. "What is it?"

"What are you talking about?" she said, playing innocent.

It was the subtle grin that confirmed it for me. "You do remember that I'm a detective, right?" I said.

Her grin turned into a full-fledged smirk and her eyes brightened another 500 lumens.

"I joined a book club," she said.

"A book club," I repeated. "Is this a joke?"

"No, I'm totally serious. In fact, you should come. The guy running it is H-O-T hot, hot, hot."

"Define H-O-T hot, hot, hot," I said.

"Oh, let's see. Tall. Blonde hair. Eyes as blue as the

sky on a sunny day."

"Ehh," I said. "I prefer the Johnny Depp types."

She leaned closer like she didn't want anyone else to hear. "He's British."

"British? Really?" I said. "Why didn't you say that earlier?" Yeah, I was kidding.

"Guess what his name is," she said.

There was that grin again.

"Uh, I don't know. Chuck?"

She gave me the Roxy smirk. And yes, it's a thing.

"No, silly," she said. "His name is Nigel."

"Nigel?" I have to research this further but I'm pretty sure Nigel is Brit-speak for 'nerd-like'.

"Uh-huh," she said. "Nigel Hewitt. Is that totally British or what?"

It was totally something but I couldn't decide what.

"Seriously," she said. "You should come with me. We're reading this book by an author named Eula Mae Pitman."

"Pitman? Now that's a name you don't hear every day. This book, is it any good?"

"Yeah, I guess. I mean, it's just a collection of her poetry, but according to Nigel she was considered the best of her generation."

"Wait," I said. "They read poetry in book clubs?"

"They read *everything* in book clubs," Roxy said. "I'm telling you, you gotta come with me. It's very entertaining."

"I think we have differing interpretations of what passes for 'entertainment'."

"You don't believe me?" she said. "Come and see for yourself."

Beck never took his eyes from the black Tahoe parked at the curb. "Are you sure those are the same guys?" he asked.

"Positive," Nathan said. It was the polished snowflake rims that confirmed it. He and Beck watched as a man, who Nathan assumed was either Cafferty or Rodano, climbed out of the car and crossed the street. He crept up on the Volvo, keeping one hand behind his back, gripping the Sig Sauer pistol that was jammed in his belt. When he got close enough, he looked into the car and saw no one inside. But this was the same Volvo they'd chased shortly after midnight; the dents and scratches were unmistakable. He flashed a thumbs up to Bolan and then took out his phone and snapped a picture of the license plate.

Seeing that, Bolan backed up, watching the oncoming traffic in the side mirror. He'd gone 10 feet when he stopped, checked the mirror again, and then shot across the street into the parking lot.

Beck didn't need any more convincing. He squeezed his PTT button and said, "Kendra, they just pulled into the lot."

"Copy that," she said. "Where are *you?*"

"Outside on the sidewalk with Nathan. I'll explain later. Stand by for updates." Then, to Nathan, he said, "Come on, we need to hurry."

As they sprinted down the sidewalk, Nathan pushed the earpiece into his ear. But unlike the last time, he didn't clip the radio to his belt, choosing instead to hold it in his hand.

"I'll take the back-left corner," Beck said. "You take the front right. Hopefully, from there, you'll be able to see what they do. Just make sure they don't see you."

"They won't," Nathan said.

When they came to the restaurant, Beck cut to the left and ran past the barbeque pit and the smoker, then hugged the side of the building, keeping his back to the wall as he inched toward the corner.

Nathan continued straight and slowed as he passed the front door, dodging a middle-aged foursome who were leaving with take-out containers in hand. Once he got past them he veered to his left, passing a huge plate glass window. A young family was seated at a table inside and the kids pointed at him as he crept past.

At the corner of the building he stopped, then leaned forward and scanned the parking lot. At the far end he saw the Tahoe parked in front of a dark green, slant-top dumpster. Directly behind it was a ragged chain-link fence that bordered the back of the property. Standing beside the car were Bolan, Cafferty, and Rodano.

Nathan pressed the PTT button. "They parked in the back corner, in front of the dumpster."

Beck's reply came first. "Copy."

"Yeah, copy that," Kendra said, seconds later. She didn't bother to ask where he was or why he wasn't in the parking garage as they had originally planned.

Nathan watched one of the men, whom he assumed was Bolan, bark an order to one of the others and point at the side door. At that, the man took off running toward the door. Bolan repeated the process with the third man, directing him to check out the back of the building. He had just disappeared from Nathan's view when Bolan began walking back toward the front of the restaurant.

"They spread out," Nathan reported. "One of them is taking the right-side door. Another went behind the building. Bolan is heading back toward the street."

"Right-side door, copy," Kendra said.

"Back of the building, copy," said Beck. "Now find a place to hide where he won't see you."

"On it," Nathan replied. Staying low, he sidled around the corner. Using the parked cars as a shield, he worked his way along the side of the building and stopped in front of a cherry red Honda CR-V.

The right-side door of the restaurant was a code-compliant fire exit positioned directly across from the bathrooms. It had a panic bar running across the middle, and just above it was a green adhesive sticker that read, "PUSH BAR TO OPEN." Because it was locked from the outside, Kendra had eased it open from the inside and used a small rock from the parking lot to keep it from closing.

Moments after Nathan's transmission, she positioned herself to the left of the door with her back to the wall. She held her baseball bat parallel to the floor with her left hand just above the knob and her right hand tight on the barrel. Further up the hallway, she could see the restaurant's open dining area where tables of happy customers were busy devouring platefuls of Smitty's barbequed favorites. They had no idea that 60 feet away, a woman with a baseball bat was about to inflict serious bodily injury on a hired killer.

She heard him before she saw him. His feet made a telltale scuffing sound on the packed gravel as he approached, and the second she heard it she brought the bat up to her chest, cocking it back slightly as an archer would draw back the bowstring. As the door began to move, she kicked it with her foot and it swung all the way open. Startled, Cafferty hesitated for a split second, long enough for Kendra to drive the knob of the bat into his forehead, the select Pennsylvania maple delivering the desired result.

Cafferty's world went dark and he fell backward onto the ground. Kendra was on him in a flash, rolling him over, taking his gun, and securing his hands with a zip tie. Under different circumstances she would've used him for batting practice before turning out his lights completely.

Rodano ran along the back of the building, pistol at the ready, past a haphazard collection of broken chairs and a square metal table with a bent leg. He was almost to the end of the building when he slowed to a walk and moved closer to the wall. As he crept closer toward the corner, he saw a cloud of pale-gray smoke wafting lazily through the air. He paused momentarily to listen, breathing in the pleasing aroma of barbequed brisket, then stepped around the corner.

In a maneuver that spanned all of two seconds, Beck brought the eight-sided club down on Rodano's wrist, knocking his gun to the ground, and threw a vicious elbow that caught Rodano square in the forehead. He buckled and collapsed on the ground, and as he lay unconscious on the pavement, Beck quickly zip-tied his hands. In his ear, he heard Kendra's voice, "One down. It's Cafferty."

"Copy that," Beck said. "Number two is down. I'm assuming it's Rodano."

"Does his head look like used string mop?" Kendra asked.

"Affirmative," Beck replied.

"That's Rodano."

"Copy," said Beck. "That just leaves Bolan."

Nathan looked to his left and saw the fire-exit door swing open. But from his vantage point next to the building, the door blocked his view of Kendra and her lightning-quick takedown of Cafferty. Obscuring his view of the hunter and her prey as she applied the zip tie was a monstrous quad-cab F-350 dually pickup truck.

Moments later, when he heard Kendra's audio confirmation, he rose up slowly and tried to locate Bolan. Across the lot he saw the middle-aged foursome huddled together, talking and laughing. His mind raced. Did Bolan walk past him as he was watching Kendra take out Cafferty? Did Bolan see it happen and go back to investigate? Staying low, he crept along the side of the Honda and stopped at the back bumper, then leaned forward and looked left, then right. No Bolan. In his earpiece he heard a voice. It was Beck.

"Nathan, have you got eyes on Bolan?"

"Negative," Nathan replied, softly. He backed away from the bumper and retraced his steps. When he reached the side of the building, he looked to his right and saw Bolan standing in front of the Honda waiting for him.

His left arm was hanging idly at his side.

In his hand was a jet-black Glock 19 pistol.

10 *Oliver Goldsmith*

The Shadows Grieve

"What are you doin', kid?" Bolan said. His left hand was still hanging at his side.

Nathan nonchalantly pulled the earpiece cable to the side of his body, shielding it from Bolan's view. At the same time he squeezed the PTT button. "Nothing," he said, loudly. "Just waiting for my folks. They'll be out any minute."

"Will they now?" Bolan replied. "What's with the 2-way radio?"

"This?" Nathan said, holding it up. "It was a birthday present."

"Nice try," Bolan said. "I saw you watching me. Who're you talking to?"

"Nobody."

"Like hell," Bolan said. He gestured with his free hand. "Let's have it."

The words had barely left his lips when a shadow fell across the front hood of the Honda. He turned to look when the business end of Kendra's bat connected with the back of his head. His body wilted and he toppled over, dropping the Glock on the packed gravel. Across the parking lot, the foursome had stopped their discussion and were watching in astonishment as Kendra rolled him over and zip-tied his arms and legs.

"What about this?" Nathan asked, picking up the pistol.

"Here, give me that," she said, motioning with her hand. He'd already been mistaken for the known criminal Asher Rickman, based on their nearly identical appearance. If a picture of him brandishing a firearm were to get out, every cop that saw him would arrest him on sight.

He handed her the Glock and she tucked it in the waistband of her jeans, alongside Cafferty's pistol. "Time to take out the trash," she said. She grabbed Bolan under one arm and Nathan did the same with the other arm. As they dragged him towards the dumpster, Kendra shouted to the foursome, "This guy likes to hurt women."

She didn't notice, but both of the women in the group pumped a fist in the air. *You go girl!*

They had just deposited Bolan behind the Tahoe, out of sight from the customers exiting the restaurant, when Beck appeared. "Where's Cafferty?" he asked.

"He's taking a little nap right over there," Kendra said, pointing at the side door.

"You and Nathan get him, I'll go get Rodano."

As he sprinted along the back side of the building, he pulled his cellphone from his pocket and called Jameson. "We've got three packages ready for pickup," he said, his breathing uneven from running.

"Are you all right?" Jameson asked.

"Couldn't be better. I'll fill you in later."

"Very good," Jameson said. "The driver will be there shortly."

Louise Hayden was standing at her office window, taking in the commanding view of the Charles River. From that vantage point, she could monitor the traffic flow on the Cambridge Parkway below as well as on the Longfellow Bridge off to her right.

Sitting on the leather couch positioned along the near wall, Rachel was tapping her foot nervously on the floor and checking the time on her watch with an ever-increasing level of anxiety.

"You need to relax," Louise said, her eyes fixed on the bridge traffic. "Beck is a very capable young man."

"Capable?" Rachel said. "That's not going to cut it. Not with Bolan's crew. I tried to warn them but they wouldn't listen."

Louise offered no reply. She'd been holding her phone in her hand for the past hour awaiting a call from Kendra. When she heard it ring, she checked to see who was calling and answered it at once. "Jameson? This is unexpected. Are you all right?"

"I'm fine," he said. "Are you aware of the situation with Gina and the woman she's trying to protect?"

"Yes."

This came as no revelation to him; he had expected as much.

"Her name is Rachel," Louise said, "and she's here at the office with me."

Of course, he thought. "Please let her know that the three men who have been pursuing her will no longer be a problem. They're on their way to the Repository as we speak."

"Beck called you," she said.

"He did."

"Were there any difficulties?" she asked, a reference to the well-being of Kendra and Nathan.

"No."

"Good," she said, relieved. She flashed Rachel a thumbs up. *It's done!*

Rachel closed her eyes and exhaled, then buried her face in her open palms, fearing the consequences that would follow.

"It would appear that your assessment of Beck was accurate," Louise said.

"Yes, he's very talented," Jameson offered, "although much of the credit for today's events should go to Nathan. According to Beck, he was the one who came up with the plan."

"Also, very talented," Louise said.

"Maybe too much so."

"Does that surprise you?" Louise asked. "Given his bloodline?"

"Not at all."

Louise moved away from the window and walked to the opposite end of the room. "I trust you'll process the packages in the usual manner?" she asked, keeping her voice down.

"Yes. I'll let you know if anything of interest arises."

"Thank you," Louise said. She ended the call and stared out the window, calculating how long it would take until he called her back. She knew his people could be very persuasive and she estimated Jameson's callback would come in less than an hour.

Beck grabbed Rodano's pistol off the ground, then lifted him up and flopped him over his shoulder. Rodano mumbled incoherently but Beck paid it no mind as he carried him over to the dumpster where Kendra and Nathan were waiting. Cafferty was on the ground next to Bolan, both men still unconscious after their run-in with Kendra's bat.

Beck had just dumped Rodano on the ground next to Cafferty when a sleek gray commercial van pulled up to the parking lot entrance. The driver surveyed the scene momentarily, spotted Beck's towering frame at the far end of the lot, then continued past the restaurant before pulling into the narrow lane that skirted the left side of the property.

He circled the building and came to a stop next to the Tahoe, using the van to shield himself and what was to follow from the crowd that had assembled out near the street. "Good day to all," he said, cheerfully, through the open window. "You have a pickup for the Repository?"

"Yes. Those three dirtbags," Kendra said, pointing. "Oh, you might as well take these too," she said, pulling the two pistols from her waistband.

"Don't forget this one," Beck said, handing the driver Rodano's gun.

"Of course," the driver said. He took all three and set them on the passenger seat, then pushed the door open and got out. Just like last time, he was dressed in crisp gray slacks and a dark blue corporate-style polo shirt with a matching ball cap. Nowhere on his clothes, or on the van, was there any branding that indicated who he worked for or the specialized service they provided. If anything,

158

the van looked like it came from the Amazon fleet.

Moving with speed and precision, he slid the side door open and took out three nine-foot Christmas tree storage bags. Beck offered to help, but the driver politely refused and went to the Tahoe to begin securing the three passengers for transport.

"What happens now?" Nathan asked.

"You mean, with those three losers?" Kendra said.

"Yeah. Will they get turned over to the police?"

"Eventually."

"What's that supposed to mean?"

"First, they'll be questioned."

Nathan raised both eyebrows. "Questioned?"

"Well, technically, yes," Kendra said.

Nathan's expression didn't change.

"It's true," Kendra said. "They'll be asked questions…at first."

"At first?"

"Uh-huh. Of course, they'll refuse to talk. It's a code of honor thing. But, with a little convincing…it'll happen."

"And after that they'll be handed over to the police?"

Kendra nodded. "They'll be *begging* to be handed over to the police."

When three o'clock came and went, Roman's patience had reached its limit and he called Wicks. "I thought I told you I wanted updates on the half hour."

"There's nothing to update," Wicks told him.

"Nothing to update?"

He was shouting now.

"That's right," Wicks said, calmly.

"They didn't call you?"

"No. Not yet."

"Did you try—"

"Hold on," Wicks said, cutting him off as his eyes were drawn to a news flash on the television that was mounted on the far wall. In the picture, a woman reporter was standing on the sidewalk in front of Smitty's Backyard Barbeque, the sign prominent in the back of the shot. "Are you seeing this?" he asked.

"Seeing what?" Roman said.

Wicks grabbed the remote and turned up the volume so Roman could hear the newscaster's report.

"Yes, Robin, it was quite a disturbing chain of events that took place less than an hour ago here at Smitty's Backyard Barbeque in Somerville. According to eyewitnesses, a young woman assaulted two men with a baseball bat in the parking lot, knocking each of them unconscious. What prompted the attack is unknown at this time. The patrons I spoke with told me that the woman was joined by a teenage boy who helped her drag both bodies to the back of the property. At that point, witnesses say, an additional body was dragged to that same spot by a third participant, an adult male in his mid 30s. That brings the total count to three. In an equally puzzling development, all three victims were then loaded into an unmarked van and taken away."

Roman listened intently but said nothing. Something wasn't right here. Three men, all expertly trained and fully armed, put down by a woman with a baseball bat? The mention of an adolescent accomplice was equally troubling. Whoever was helping Rachel Goudas clearly had skills, but it appeared that they weren't

160

acting alone.

Wicks lowered the volume as the reporter recapped what had happened. "What would you like me to do? he asked.

"Nothing," Roman said. "I'll take it from here."

He ended the call and texted Magnus.

> The team was ambushed. Last known
> address was Smitty's BBQ on Webster
> Ave in Somerville. Need details.

Seconds later, Magnus replied.

> Leaving now.

Gina set the book down and checked the time as her initial questions about Nathan's trap seeped back into her thoughts. From the far end of the street she heard the familiar growl of Beck's pickup truck. As it grew louder, she marked the page in the book, jumped up, and ran to the window.

Beck's truck turned into Nathan's driveway and came to a stop several feet from the garage. As it sat there, the growl of the engine softening to a warm purr, Beck and Nathan remained in the cab, engaged in conversation. When she saw that, she raced out of her room and hurried downstairs to the living room. Working quickly, she grabbed the wireless extension from the end table and punched in Nathan's phone number. As it connected, she went to the entryway and peeked around the frame, checking to see if her parents were in the kitchen. Seeing neither of them, she pulled back and began to pace in a tight circle.

"Hey, I was just about to call you," Nathan said, forgoing any of his usual wisecracks.

"What happened?" Gina demanded. "Did it work?"

"Like a charm," Nathan said. "They're gone for good."

"Gone? What does that mean, exactly?"

"It means they're not coming back."

Gina said nothing. If Rachel's assessment of the man who had hired Bolan and his crew was accurate, he would bring in another team more experienced and potentially more ruthless.

"Are you still there?" Nathan asked. He tapped the speakerphone button on the phone.

"Yeah, I'm here," Gina said, her voice filling the cab of the truck. "Just thinking of what to do next."

"Well, maybe if you told me—"

"No!" she said, cutting him off. "What did I say about questions? I just need some time to fix this, that's all."

"How much time do you need?" he asked.

"I don't know," she said, vaguely. "A day or two…maybe?" *I hope.*

"Gina."

It was Beck.

"Yeah?"

"If you need time, we'll find a safe place to keep Rachel until you get it done."

"Thank you," Gina said. "I'm open to ideas."

"There are other safehouses," Nathan said to Beck, "but I don't know who would stay with her."

"She can stay with me," Beck said.

"You would do that?" Gina asked.

"If it helps you buy more time, yes. Where is she now?"

"She's with Louise."

"Louise…?"

"The woman in the white Mercedes," Gina said.

Nathan pulled the phone aside. "The one she was screaming at when we were leaving," he said softly.

"I heard that!" Gina said.

"Well, you were," Nathan replied.

"Can you call her?" asked Beck.

"Yes."

"Have her bring Rachel to my house on Braden Street. No, wait. Scratch that. Where did you hand her off to Louise?"

"At the town library."

"Perfect. Have Louise bring her to that same location. I'll meet them there in an hour."

"I will," Gina said. "And again, thank you…for everything. That goes for both of you."

She disconnected and called Louise. Ten minutes later it was arranged. Rachel would stay with Beck while she continued her search. Relieved, she went back upstairs to her room and continued reading, even more determined to find a clue that would help her end this madness.

After the call from Gina, Nathan didn't get out of the truck. He held his flip phone in his hand, staring at it silently with a look of concern on his face.

"What's wrong?" asked Beck.

"This is just like before," Nathan replied.

"What are you talking about?"

"Six months ago, Gina was involved in something. It had her all worked up, maybe even a little bit scared. When Kendra and I tried to help her, she warned us off…wouldn't tell us anything."

"Huh," Beck said, thinking.

"And now it's happening again," Nathan said. "I mean, I want to help her. I really do. But without knowing what's really going on…"

Beck didn't offer a reply.

"By the way," Nathan said. "Why did you change your mind?"

"About what?"

"You were going to have Louise drop Rachel off at your house but then you changed the location to the library."

"That's right," Beck said.

Nathan looked at him, expecting an answer to follow, but Beck just looked back, waiting for him to figure it out on his own.

"What?" Nathan asked.

Beck continued to stare. "Think about it."

Nathan looked down at the footwell as he sorted through a number of possible explanations. Then it came to him. "You don't want Louise coming to your house because you think she might be followed?"

Beck nodded his head, slowly. *Correct.*

"By who?" Nathan asked.

"Replacements."

Nathan's expression darkened. "Replacements? You really think…?"

"Yes," Beck said, before Nathan could finish. "Someone has it out for this woman in a big way. Someone with the money and the means to find her. The way they tracked her phone? That requires a person with access to some extremely well-protected information. Bolan and his crew? They weren't just common street thugs. Judging by the handguns they were carrying, all military grade weapons, they were mercenaries: well-trained and well-paid. And the payroll doesn't stop there. What we witnessed today is just the prelude to something much worse. You can bet the call has already been made. And until we know who's behind this, and how much they know about you or Gina, or any of us, I'm not taking any chances."

The words hit Nathan like a punch in the gut and he looked over at Gina's house, scared for his friend like never before. "Gina," he said quietly, "what have you got yourself into now?"

Like she'd done with the first chapter, Gina read all of Chapter 2 and then went back and scanned it again. Still nothing. But she wasn't deterred. "Something she wanted Rachel to see," she reminded herself, then turned to Chapter 3 and continued reading.

Roxy wouldn't let it rest. In the days that followed, all she could talk about was Nigel, Nigel, Nigel. I think she used the word 'hot' 50 times. That's a serious amount of heat to assign to one human being. By week's end I came to the realization that the only way I was going to get her to stop was to go with her to the next book club meeting, or what I was now calling "Poetry Paradise." But before that happened, we needed to establish some ground rules.

Rule #1: I wasn't going to read an entire book of poetry. I'd listen. I'd smile. But that was it. I have no interest in being pulled into a mind-numbing debate about Atlantic or gigantic, or is it romantic, pentameter? See? I'm not a poetry person. Up until a few years ago, I thought pentameter was a laboratory instrument used by geeks in lab coats who studied particle physics.

Rule #2: matchmaking was strictly forbidden. Hot or not, I wasn't interested in Nigel, the Poetry Prince, or anyone else for that matter. My current dance card is filled quite nicely, thank you very much.

Rule #3: this would be a one-time visit. There was no way she was going to drag me back there week after week. Unless they had a buffet. And I'm not talking about one of those lame continental-breakfast spreads, mind you. You roll out some grilled jerk shrimp and pineapple skewers, or maybe some crab legs with cheddar bay biscuits, and I'm there for the duration.

Roxy quickly agreed to the first two rules and assured me that there would be no buffet. I was almost disappointed, but I let it pass. On Thursday night, we piled into her car and she drove to a small bookshop on Dixon Ave called Biblio.

The bookshop had a decidedly cramped feel. Because it was after normal business hours, the few lights that had been left on made it feel more like the Catacombs of St. Callixtus in Rome. By the time we arrived, the poetry posse, almost all women, was already gathered in a large room in the back, seated in chairs that had been set in a large circle. Standing proudly in the center, looking very pleased with himself, was none other than the stud with English blood, Nigel Hewitt.

I'll give Roxy points for this: her description of the

man was right on the money. He had the bluest eyes I've ever seen. He was on the tall side, with an Olympic swimmer build. I'm guessing his stomach was like a slab of granite. The turtleneck beneath the Harris Tweed sport coat, however, gave him more of the college professor look. Oh well, you can't have everything, right?

"Welcome, welcome, come right in," he said, waving Roxy and I into the circle.

We promptly took our seats, and after looking over the gathering like a shepherd admiring his flock, he raised a small hardcover book in the air and proudly announced, "Let's have a chin wag, then…shall we?"

I tried not to giggle. I mean, seriously, who did this guy think he was? Michael Caine? I'd bet you a dozen bombolini from Fossano's Italian Bakery that Nifty Nigel was from South Jersey. Maybe even Philly.

He waited for everyone to open their copy of the book, then called their attention to a poem on Page 17. "As we've been discussing," he said, eyeing each of us with a smile that could melt plastic, "Eula Mae Pitman produced many fine literary gems in her time, but none, in my humble opinion, as entrancing, nay, bewitching, as this one."

Nay? Did I hear him right? Okay fine. I'll see your nay and raise you a moo.

When Roxy saw me smirking, she elbowed me, then pointed to the poem in question,

"The Shadows Grieve."

Nigel held the book up like a church hymnal, and read aloud with theatrical effect that suggested he had spent time on a Broadway stage. I leaned closer and followed along in Roxy's copy, word for word, hoping that actually reading them might stave off the attack of the giggles that was waiting in the wings.

> Hope forsaken, the shadows grieve,
> Their words a prayer for swift reprieve:
> 'Guide my path as morning stills,
> Oh, Shepherd of the Seven Hills'.

Gina stopped reading, her mind flashing back to what Rachel had told her about the bizarre things Helen said to her just moments before she was handed over to the transporter. She grabbed her notepad and jotted down the entire stanza. It was only four lines, but the imagery was powerful.

Cryptic, even.

Magnus found Smitty's Backyard Barbeque with ease and pulled into one of the few remaining spaces in the side lot. Despite the late hour, it was still nearly filled to capacity. Not knowing the exact details of what had happened almost four hours earlier, he went inside the restaurant to question the staff.

A young girl, college age, was standing at the hostess station just inside the door. When she saw him enter, she smiled and pulled a menu from the stand. "Just one?"

"No," Magnus said, doing a quick sweep of the room with his eyes. There were two other waitresses hard at work delivering trays of food and clearing dishes from the tables. Talking to them would be near impossible. His eyes came back to the hostess. "You had an incident here today."

"Uh, yeah, that's what they told me. I just got here for my shift ten minutes ago and I…"

Magnus turned and walked back outside.

"…wasn't here when it happened," she said softly, to no one.

Magnus wasn't interested in speculation or second-hand information. He needed to find someone who had been there when it happened, someone who had seen it go down or had possibly overheard the attackers talking. It followed that the morning-shift employees who been present had long since punched out and gone home, but he wasn't done. He turned his attention to the outside of the building. With any luck, he might discover a clue that would help identify the team that had taken out Bolan's crew.

From the front door, he walked around the corner, scouring the ground as he made his way along the side of the building. Up ahead he saw a powerfully built man in his late 30s, dressed in a white cook's apron, feeding thick chunks of firewood into a large smoker.

"Help you?" Smitty said, when Magnus appeared at his side.

Magnus said nothing as he surveyed the pavement around their feet.

Smitty closed the woodbox and stood up, getting his first good look at the silent stranger. The man was just over six feet tall with the shoulders of an NHL center. But it was his slightly misshapen nose that implied years spent in a boxing ring, or brawling in bars and dark alleys. "Let me guess," Smitty said. "Middleweight?"

"No," Magnus replied. Just beyond the smoker he spotted a black zip tie lying on the pavement. To the casual observer, the thin piece of nylon might look innocent enough. But to Magnus, it spoke volumes. It told him that the team that ambushed Bolan's crew wasn't just a bunch of local punks, working off their pent-up, alcohol-induced hostility; they had a much higher level of sophistication and training. Possibly military.

"Did you lose something?" Smitty asked.

Magnus shook his head. "No." He moved past Smitty and continued around the back corner of the building, stopping long enough to pick up the zip tie.

As Smitty watched him walk away, he was gripped by an uneasy feeling. He'd encountered plenty of troubling characters in his lifetime, especially during his years in the service. But this guy's vibe was on a whole different level. Behind those dead eyes, lurking beneath a cold and heartless veneer, was a core of pure evil.

Magnus walked as far as the dumpster and was checking the ground around it for any additional clues when a boy walked up behind him. He was high school-aged, carrying a bulging trash bag in each hand.

"If you're looking for the baseball bat, she took it with her," he said.

Magnus turned to face him. "You're talking about the incident that happened earlier today?" he said, playing dumb.

"Yup," the boy said, excitedly. He set the bags down. "It was totally sick."

"How so?"

"This woman came out of nowhere and just went nuts," he said. "She popped one guy with a baseball bat, then took out another guy the same way." He pointed to the side of the building. "It happened right over there."

"This woman," Magnus said. "Can you describe her?"

"Uh…well…" the boy said, thinking. "She was average height, I guess you'd call it, and her hair was cut short like she was in the military."

"Anything else?"

"Yeah, she was built."

"Built?"

"Yeah, you know, strong?"

"Was she alone?" Magnus asked, knowing that she wasn't.

"No. She had a kid with her, and a big guy."

A kid, Magnus thought. That was odd. "Tell me about the big guy."

"He was scary big. Like that actor…you know…the one who plays Thor?"

"Yeah," Magnus said, plainly. He knew the boy was referring to Christopher Hemsworth, but this wasn't the time for an in-depth discussion of the man's movie roles. The boy had firsthand information and he needed to keep him focused on the subject at hand. "What did *he* do?"

"He dragged a third guy right over there, in front of the dumpster."

"Another guy?" Magnus asked, to keep the boy talking.

"Yeah, there were three in all. The two guys who got popped by the woman, plus one more. I'm not sure where the third one came from but they lined 'em up on the ground behind somebody's car."

"Describe the car for me."

"It was black Chevy Tahoe with these awesome rims," the boy

said.

Bolan, Magnus thought. The rims confirmed it. "What happened to it?" he asked.

"The cops went through it and found some weapons. After that, they towed it away."

"What about the bodies?"

"It was freaky," the boy said. "Out of nowhere, this van shows up and hauls them away."

"The van, can you describe it?" Magnus asked.

"Sure. It was gray...shiny..."

"Shiny?"

"Uh-huh. It looked brand new."

Magnus tucked that detail away in the back of his mind. "What about the woman and the big guy? Did they go in the van, too?"

"No, she left in a run-down old Volvo. The big guy...?" he said, pausing as it dawned on him for the first time. "I didn't actually see him leave. He and the boy just sort of vanished."

"How old was the boy?"

"Uh...13 or 14?"

Two adults and a child, Magnus thought. Something didn't fit. Families didn't just go around assaulting people, then hauling their bodies away in a van.

The side door opened and one of the cooks stuck his head outside. "Kyle! What's the holdup?"

Kyle waved him off. *All right, all right...I'm coming.* "I gotta go," he told Magnus, then took hold of the two trash bags and dragged them over to the dumpster.

Magnus waited until he went back inside, then walked over to the side door. Parked to the left of it was a showroom-new Infinity QX80. To the right, a coal-black Dodge Charger. He squatted down between them and examined the gravel, then got down on all fours and searched beneath each vehicle. Under the Infinity he saw a cellphone. He was reaching for it when he heard a voice directly behind him.

"Uh, excuse me! What do you think you're doing?"

He grabbed the phone and stood up, taking care not to touch either vehicle. The voice belonged to an attractive young woman dressed in cowboy boots, blue jeans, and a gathered knit tee shirt. Her center-parted blonde hair was messy with uneven waves that barely grazed the top of shoulders, making her look like a Hollywood actress. In one hand she was holding a Smitty's take-out bag. In the other, a ring of keys with a sterling silver western spur.

"Dropped my phone," he said, acting embarrassed as he brushed the grit off his pants.

The woman eyed him with pity. *Maybe you should be more careful next time.* Without another word she got in the Infinity and backed out, the rear tires spitting gravel as she drove away.

He watched her leave and then went to his car, parked on the opposite side of the lot. Sitting in the front seat, he turned on the cellphone and navigated to the settings menu. At the top of the screen was Cafferty's name along with a small picture of him standing on the back of a large fishing boat, holding an enormous fish in both hands.

When he checked the photo library, one picture stood out: the last one Cafferty had taken. It showed the back end of an old Volvo 240 sedan, dented and scratched, the license plate clearly visible in the shot. He slid the phone in the glove box and then texted Roman. As usual, he kept it brief and to the point.

> Bolan's crew taken by unknown group
> Will have a name for you shortly

11

Vanished

G ina raced downstairs and grabbed the phone from the living room, then sprinted back up the stairs two at a time.
Punching the numbers into the phone as fast as she could,
she called Louise who picked up on the first ring.

"Hello, this Louise," she said. The cheery voice was back again.

"It's Gina. Have you dropped off Rachel yet?"

"Oh, hello Gina. Actually, we're on our way right now."

"I need to talk to her," Gina said, urgently. Before Louise could
respond, there was a knock on the door. "Hold on," Gina said. She
pulled the phone from her ear and held it down by her side. "Yes?"
she called out.

The door opened and her mother stuck her head in the room.
"Who are you talking to?"

Gina showed her the phone. "Uh…a friend?" she said, irritated.

Now if you don't mind...

Her mother considered the phone briefly, then said, "Your father and I are going to the grocery store to get something for dinner. Is there anything in particular you want?"

"No, whatever you choose is fine," Gina said, a little too quickly.

"What's wrong?" her mother asked. "You seem edgy."

"I'm fine. Just hungry, that's all."

"Well, there's fruit in the refrigerator. That should hold you over until dinner is ready."

She watched her mother pull the door shut, then waited, listening to her continue down the hallway. When she was convinced her mother wouldn't make a surprise curtain call, she pressed the phone to her ear again. "You still there?"

"Still here," Louise said. "Is everything all right?"

"Maybe better than all right. There's someone Rachel wants me to find. She said he's the guy my grandmother used to smuggle her out of area."

Louise nodded her head, smiling. "And you think you've found him?" she asked.

"I found *something*. Whether it's important or not remains to be seen. I was hoping Rachel could tell me. Can you meet me on Lafayette Street?"

"Certainly," Louise said. "How will I find you?"

"Look for me on the sidewalk about halfway down the street. Rachel should remember the house."

"Okay," Louise said. "We're not that far away. We should be there in about 10 minutes."

"Perfect," Gina said. She ended the call and grabbed her notepad.

By the time she got downstairs, her parents were just backing out of the driveway. She stood at the living room window and watched them drive away. After they had turned the corner at the far end of the street, she left the house through the back door and sprinted across the lawn toward Nathan's garage. As she snuck past the side door, she glanced through the window and saw him in the far corner, punishing the heavy bag with a series of rapid-fire jabs.

She climbed over the mashed wire fence and ran through the neighbor's yard, past the shed where she and Rachel had stood in the wee hours of the morning. *Was it really just 16 hours ago?* she thought. After everything that had transpired since that time, it felt like it had been two days.

When she reached the sidewalk, Louise was parked at the curb across the street. She ran to the driver's door and spoke to her through the open window. "Thanks for doing this," she said. Her eyes shifted to Rachel who was slouched down in the back seat. She was clutching her backpack, looking more nervous than usual. "We need to make this quick," Gina told her.

Rachel sat up at once. "Why?" she asked. "What's going on?"

Gina ignored the question and ran around the back of the car. When she reached the rear passenger-side door, she pulled it open and motioned for Rachel to get out. "Come on," she said, "I don't have much time."

Rachel kept a hold of her backpack and fumbled her way out of the car.

"Are you all right?" Gina asked, closing the door behind her.

"No comment," Rachel said

Fine, Gina thought. "I need to talk to you," she said, then took

177

Rachel by the arm and walked her down the sidewalk, stopping at the brick-tiled driveway of a giant Tudor-style home.

Rachel looked up and down the street nervously.

"Relax," Gina told her. "They're gone. And they're not coming back."

Rachel eyed Gina, cautiously. "It's not them I'm worried about," she said.

Gina didn't want to open that can of worms; she just wanted to get this ordeal over with as fast as humanly possible. "You said something about what my grandmother told you, the night she dropped you off? Cryptic words?"

"Yeah? What about it?" Rachel said, her apprehension easing.

Gina pulled her notepad from the back pocket of her jeans and flipped to the page with the lines from Eula Mae Pitman's poem. "Does any of this sound familiar?" Reading slowly, she said, "Hope forsaken, the shadows grieve."

"No," Rachel said. Her eyes drifted over to the Tudor house, where a plump black and white cat was sitting at the bottom of the front porch steps, licking a paw.

"Their words a prayer for swift reprieve," Gina said.

"No," Rachel said again, without emotion. The cat had finished its cleaning routine and was slinking along the rose hedge that lined the front of the house.

Gina felt a twinge of doubt.

Was she mistaken?

Maybe this wasn't the clue she thought it was.

Magnus found Kendra's information with a single phone call,

using a well-placed contact who was an expert in unearthing such information, no matter how far down he had to drill to get it. As Magnus wrote down the details, he wondered why a seemingly harmless woman would get involved with the likes of Rachel Goudas. And what would prompt her to spearhead such a vicious attack on Bolan, Cafferty, and Rodano? Were the two women blood relatives? Childhood friends? College roommates? On the surface, the pairing made no sense whatsoever.

He placed a call to Roman, knowing the man was already planning a response to the attack—a counterpunch with an equal measure of force. But what form would it take? Would Roman have him simply take the woman at gunpoint, or have him wait until the pre-dawn hours and pay her a visit at her apartment while she slept?

The call rang twice before Roman answered. "How'd you make out?" he asked.

"I have the name and address of the woman. Nothing on the big guy or the kid."

"Change of plan," Roman told him. "Today's episode has turned into a full-blown media circus. Every news station is running it and there doesn't appear to be any end in sight. We do *not* want to do anything to feed it. If the truth about the target gets out, the press will have a field day with it and that's a risk we simply can't take. The situation demands that we follow another course of action."

"They need to pay for what they've done!" Magnus said, fiercely.

"And they will," Roman said. "Trust me."

Magnus listened carefully as Roman explained how they would proceed.

Unseen.

Unheard.

Like whisper-thin clouds drifting silently across the night sky.

"Start with the woman who's been helping her," Roman said. "She'll be the first domino."

As a kid, Magnus loved dominoes. Especially when he stood them up on end in a giant figure eight and watched them cascade forward with a simple flick of his finger. "What about the big guy and the kid?" he asked.

"All in good time," Roman said. "The woman first, then we'll worry about the other two."

Louise was watching Gina and Rachel in the side mirror when her phone rang. When she saw Jameson's name on the call screen she grinned. *Just as I thought.* "I'd say that was quick, but I think impressive might be a more apt description," she told him.

He let the compliment pass. As a general rule, any accolades for the Repository were best left unspoken. "Where are you right now?" he asked.

"I'm with Rachel and Gina on Lafayette Street," she said, cautiously.

"Lafayette Street?" he repeated.

"Yes. I was on my way to hand Rachel off to Beck at the library when Gina called me. She said she wanted to talk to her. Why do you ask?"

"This business with Rachel is much more serious than Gina knows. I fear for her life, and the lives of everyone involved."

"How so?" Louise asked. She looked up at the rearview mirror. Gina was still reading from her notepad. Rachel was standing across from her, growing more agitated by the second.

"That's what we need to discuss," Jameson said. "I called Beck. He wants you and Rachel to meet us here at Birch Meadow."

"Okay, we're on our way."

Gina kept reading, despite Rachel's exasperated reactions. "Guide my path as morning stills."

Rachel glared at her. "NO!" she groaned, then looked back at the house. The cat had stopped moving and was crouched down, watching a small rodent tunnel through the leaves at the base of the rose hedge.

Gina felt the last bit of hope slipping away. Clearly this wasn't the clue and she scolded herself for being so quick to deem it so. *Next time, don't assume,* she told herself. All she could do was go back and read more of the book. The clue was there, somewhere; she just had to work harder to find it. She looked down at her notepad and read the last line, more to herself than to Rachel. "Oh, Shepherd of the Seven Hills."

Rachel jerked her head back in Gina's direction. "What did you say?"

"Oh, Shepherd of the Seven Hills," Gina repeated, slower. "Is that important?"

"That's what she called him."

Gina's heart raced. "Called who?" she said, her words coming quickly. "The man in the cloak?"

"Yes."

"Are you sure?"

"Positive," Rachel said. "She was staring right at him when she said it. To me it sounded like gibberish. I mean, what does that even mean?"

"That's what I intend to find out," Gina said. She closed the notepad, energized by Rachel's revelation, and was slipping it in her back pocket when she heard the Mercedes backing up. It came to an abrupt stop at the curb next to her and Louise shouted through the open window.

"Rachel! We need to leave. Right now!"

Rachel instinctively checked both ends of the street and then ran to the car and climbed in the back seat. "What happened? Where are you taking me?" she asked, panicked.

Gina appeared at the driver's-side window. "What's wrong?"

"I'll explain later," Louise said. "For now, go home and wait for my call."

"But...my parents..."

"Hold on," Louise said. She reached into her purse and pulled out a cellphone. "Here, take this, and keep it close by."

Gina took the phone and stepped back as the Mercedes sped away. "Now what?" she said.

Following Roman's directive, Magnus found Kendra's coffee shop and parked across the street. It was five o'clock and he watched as one of the staffers, a spindly girl in her mid 20s, locked the door. The home address he had matched the street number of the coffee shop, which told him the apartment on the second floor must belong to Kendra. The entrance was a nondescript metal door, painted clamshell gray, set to the left of the shop's front window.

He waited and watched for 30 minutes. No one matching Kendra's description came out the front door.

No matter. He'd come back later.

When the cover of darkness would be his ally.

Louise pulled into the lot at Birch Meadow and saw Beck and Jameson waiting for her beneath the gabled canopy that extended outward from the front entrance. She pulled up to the curb and was lowering the passenger-side window as they came walking over.

"Did anyone follow you?" Beck asked.

"Not that I noticed," she replied.

Jameson threw a quick glance at Rachel, who was passed out in the back seat, her head tipped back against the window like she'd been staring up at the clouds overhead. To Jameson she appeared innocent enough, but through the years he'd dealt with more than one innocent-looking person who had singlehandedly brought down a firestorm upon those around them.

This woman was no different.

Beck eased the door open and slid his hand inside, grasping her shoulder to keep her from falling out. She flinched, breaking out of her slumber, and slapped his hand away.

"STOP!"

"Easy does it," Beck said, pulling the door all the way open. "You're safe. There's no danger here."

She blinked hard several times as she got her bearings, then surveyed the parking lot to her left and the building to her right. "What is this place?"

"This is where I live," said Jameson, kindly, as if talking to a young child.

183

"And you are…?"

"I'm Jameson. Why don't we all go inside. They're just about to serve dinner."

"It's all right," Louise said. "Go inside. I'll be right in after I park the car."

Rachel clutched her backpack and grabbed the doorframe, using it to pull herself up and out of the car. With everything she'd been through that day, she couldn't remember the last time she'd eaten. She wobbled slightly as she stood and Beck took hold of her arm, steadying her as they made their way up the walkway and into the building.

After Louise joined them, Jameson led the procession through front foyer and into the spacious lobby, decorated with a variety of vintage-style chairs and couches, plush oriental rugs, and an assortment of strategically placed parlour palms, bird's nest ferns, and dracaena plants with sword-shaped leaves. He continued into the adjoining dining room where a large dinner crowd had assembled, filling the room with the usual thrum of voices and the rattle of glasses and silverware.

They sat at a table in the back of the room, next to a pair of glass-paned doors that looked out onto a large stone patio. They weren't there for long when a dining room employee appeared with a pitcher of water and began filling the glasses.

"Good evening sir," he said to Jameson. "I see you have some guests with you tonight."

"Yes, Jared, these are friends of mine. I would ask you to treat them as you would me, but I suspect that was already your plan."

"Right you are, sir," Jared replied. He finished filling the glasses and addressed the group as one. "We have a choice of two entrees tonight. The first is a braised lamb shank in a red wine sauce, with rosemary, garlic, and tomatoes, served with garlic-mashed potatoes."

That brought a soft murmur from the group.

"The second is a crab-stuffed haddock filet with lemon butter sauce, served with oven-roasted vegetables picked from our very own garden." He paused momentarily, then looked at Louise. "Ma'am, would you like go first?"

"How can I say no?" she replied. "I'll have the haddock."

"Very good," Jared said. He went around the table and took the remaining orders, storing them in his memory without the need to write them down. When he was done taking everyone's order he promptly walked back to the kitchen.

Rachel looked around the room, amazed. This wasn't like any assisted living facility she'd ever seen; it felt more like The Plaza in New York City. "You *live* here?" she asked.

"Yes. For some time now," Jameson replied. "You, on the other hand, gave up your residence rather abruptly as I understand it. North Carolina, correct?"

"Didn't have much choice," she mumbled, fidgeting with the cloth napkin next to her water glass.

Beck and Jameson shared a brief look, knowing full well that she *did* have a choice, one that she foolishly squandered away by means of an old company-issued cellphone.

"We'll talk about that," Jameson said. "But for now, let's enjoy a delightful dinner."

Rachel looked past him, through the glass doors. The sky, once sapphire blue, had grown dark with gray clouds that were dotted with pockets of black—a troubling reminder of the tenuous situation she was in ever since Bolan and his crew had been removed from the equation.

The thought faded away when Jared appeared at her side and set a plate on the table in front of her. She leaned in, closed her eyes, and inhaled deeply, letting the tantalizing aroma of the red wine sauce wash away her every worry.

As the rest of the plates were being brought to the table, Beck's phone pinged. He stood up at once and stepped outside to take the call.

"This is Beck," he said, glancing up at the ominous clouds overhead.

"Beck, it's Smitty."

"I thought I might hear from you," Beck said. "Thanks again for letting us use your place to grab those lowlifes. Sorry if it upset any of your customers."

"No worries, I'm happy to help," Smitty said. "Hey, I thought you should know. Late this afternoon I got a visit from a pretty rough-looking character. The guy was bad news and I got the feeling he was tight with those three clowns you nabbed."

"What'd he look like?"

"Big guy. Broad shoulders. Had a nose that's been reset a few times."

"Did he say anything?" Beck asked.

"Nope. Barely spoke at all. He was too busy checking the pavement. I asked him if he lost something and he didn't answer; he just kept moving, searching the ground."

"Where was this?" asked Beck.

"The side of the building, near the smoker. I saw him stop to pick up something off the ground. It looked like a zip tie."

That's exactly what it was, Beck thought, silently cursing himself. It wasn't in his nature to be so careless. "Smitty, do me a favor. If you see this guy again, call me right away."

"Will do."

With the first drops of rain starting to fall, Beck ended the call and went back inside. As he took a seat at the table, Jameson couldn't help but notice the concerned look on his face.

"Problem?"

Beck picked up his silverware and attacked his lamb shank. "Smitty got a visit from Bolan's replacement," he said.

Rachel stopped chewing.

"What makes you think it was a replacement?" Jameson asked.

"From the way Smitty described him, and by the way he was acting, it has to be," Beck said. "Smitty said the guy looked like a pro boxer. Huge frame. Bent nose."

Magnus! Rachel thought. She reached for the water glass with a trembling hand and took a sip, nearly spilling water in her lap.

"Smitty said he was nosing around, asking people about what had happened earlier in the day."

Through the rest of dinner, they didn't speak of it again. But once they were finished with dessert, Jameson folded his napkin, laid it on the table, and said, "Let's go back to my room. There's much we need to discuss."

One by one they each stood and followed him back through the lobby and down the long hallway to his room. They had just stepped inside when Rachel spotted an English Victorian easy chair positioned near the large window on the far wall. The rain had begun in earnest and was streaking down the glass, turning the once-clear view of the lawn and expertly maintained flowerbeds into a velvety smear of muted colors that resembled a Claude Monet painting.

She went to the chair and sat down, setting her backpack on the floor near her feet. "I need to close my eyes for a little while," she said, defiantly. "If anyone has a problem with that, well, I'm sorry. After the day I've had, I'm sure you can understand why."

"Here, why don't you stretch out on the bed," Jameson said, making his way across the room. "It'll be much more comfortable." He plumped the pillows and then stood back as she removed her shoes and slowly eased herself down atop the bedspread. "We'll step out for a bit and give you some peace and quiet." On the way out of the room he turned off the lights, leaving behind a gloomy haze, the only illumination coming from the rain-drenched window.

He led Beck and Louise back up the hallway, nodding politely to the residents they passed. They were almost to the front lobby when he stopped at a pair of French doors that opened into an elegant sitting room with a stacked-stone fireplace and built-in bookcases. Positioned around a large mahogany coffee table were four Chesterfield wingback armchairs, made with tufted oxblood leather and dark walnut cabriole legs. He gestured for Beck and Louise to enter, then stepped inside and closed the doors.

"We need to talk before any other action is taken on Rachel's behalf," he said. Normally, he would invite his guests to sit before indulging them in conversation, but this matter was so troubling that he felt the need to stand.

Louise watched him walk to the fireplace, turn, and walk back, his expression vague, like a man who was grasping for words that were hovering just beyond his mental reach. "What's wrong?" she asked.

He rested both hands on one of the wingback chairs and let out a troubled breath. "Despite her innocent appearance, Rachel Goudas is extremely dangerous—more dangerous than any of us could've suspected." The tone of his words bordered on sinister. "And now she's put us in a very perilous situation."

Louise and Beck listened in stunned silence as he recounted what his team at the Repository had learned following the interrogation of Bolan, Cafferty, and Rodano, including how long they had been pursuing Rachel Goudas and how they had managed to track her cellphone. "A man named Phillip Roman is running the crew," Jameson explained. "It's the man who hired him that worries me. He's ruthless, well-funded, and has the muscle and the firepower to get whatever he wants. Those who cross him have a way of disappearing…permanently."

"What's his interest in Rachel Goudas?" Beck asked.

"Roman's men claim she has something he wants, and he won't let anyone stand in his way until he gets it back. According to Bolan, she had it with her when she vanished seven years ago."

Louise looked away, thinking back to what Helen had told her about Rachel's plight. Nowhere in her memory did she remember any mention of an item Rachel had in her possession, notably, one that a man like Phillip Roman's boss would want back.

"Our mandate is simple," Jameson said. "We need to steer clear of Roman's musclemen and concentrate on freeing ourselves of Rachel Goudas."

189

"These 'musclemen' as you call them. What happens to them now?" asked Beck.

"They've been put on ice, so to speak."

"Okay, I need to stop you right there," Beck said.

"Speak your mind," Jameson told him.

"I get it. Rachel has something Roman's boss wants. He enlisted Roman and his team to get it back. Bolan, Cafferty and Rodano failed. Now Roman has enlisted the help of someone else, a very serious player who got Smitty rattled—and trust me when I tell you that Smitty isn't the type who gets easily rattled. What I want to know is how Gina got mixed up in all this. Earlier today, at my house, she begged us not to ask any questions about Rachel. All she would say was that there were 'things at work' here. So, I ask you: what 'things' could pull a 13-year-old girl into such a dangerous predicament?"

Jameson and Louise exchanged a cautious look that didn't escape Beck's watchful eye.

"What is it?" he said.

"Do I tell him?" Louise asked Jameson.

"I think you have to."

"Very well." She looked at Beck and said, "What I'm about to tell you stays in this room, is that understood?"

"Of course," Beck replied.

"I'm not sure if you know this but I'm a literary agent. Gina's grandmother was my client. Her name was Helen Bainbridge. Perhaps you've heard of her?"

"Helen Bainbridge? Who *hasn't* heard of her," Beck said. "I like her mystery series, the one with the woman detective...Nikki Nolan?"

"So do each of the women who came to her seeking her help."

"Her help? With what, writing?"

"No," Louise said. "Helen secretly helped women who were being pursued by the most evil, the most vile men imaginable."

"Helped them how?"

"She made them disappear, effectively blotted out their existence which, in each case, saved their lives."

"That sounds a lot like what Nathan's grandfather did."

"Yes," Jameson said. "They worked in a similar fashion, albeit with different tools at their disposal."

"You're saying Gina's grandmother helped Rachel Goudas escape?"

"Not just escape, she erased her, permanently."

"And the evil men pursuing her were…?"

"Bolan, Cafferty, and Rodano," Jameson said. "All hired by Phillip Roman to retrieve this unnamed thing she has."

"Fearing what they would do to her if they caught her, Rachel approached Helen, seeking her protection," Louise said. "Helen agreed and Rachel subsequently vanished."

"But something happened," said Beck. "Otherwise, she wouldn't be here right now."

"Yes," Jameson said. "Five days ago, she began texting with her old company-issued cellphone, the one you used to lure Bolan, Cafferty and Rodano to Webster Ave. According to Bolan, they already had the number and were tracking it before she disappeared. Once she started using it again, she popped up on their radar."

"That still doesn't answer my original question. Why Gina?"

"Yes, why Gina?" Louise said. "Before I continue, let me reiterate

191

that this information cannot be shared with anyone."

"You have my word," said Beck.

She paused briefly, then said, "Before she died, Helen named Gina as the legal owner of the mystery series, including its highly sensitive book notes."

"Book notes? I don't understand."

"In addition to being a very popular series, each book contains information, carefully hidden within the text, designed to help or communicate in some way with the woman Helen was helping at the time. Think of it as a secret communication network."

Beck nodded his head slowly, searching his memory. He had read the books. He had any number of favorite parts—sections he could recite from memory. But he was hard pressed to remember any words that seemed coded.

"With Bolan, Cafferty, and Rodano closing in on her again, Rachel called me," Louise said. "I was the one who gave her Gina's information."

"Why?" Beck asked, stunned that she'd do such a reckless thing. "Because she owns the series and the book notes?" *That's crazy!*

"No," Louise said. "Because along with her notes, the quest that Helen Bainbridge was on has been handed down to Gina. This Rachel Goudas business is just an aberration, but Gina has already begun the necessary steps to reconcile it."

"What steps?"

"She's trying to find the person Helen used to relocate Rachel seven years ago."

"Relocate? You mean, like a transporter?"

"Yes. He has no formal name. He's a ghost. His existence is based on rumor and speculation. But he's very real and extremely good at what he does, which is why Helen used him. Gina may have found a way to locate him. If she succeeds, we'll be free of Rachel Goudas for good."

"But first, she has to find him," Beck said.

"Yes."

"And we're going to help her," Jameson stated, matter-of-factly. "The quicker we deliver Rachel to this transporter, the faster this nightmare will end. Louise, I need you to convey that to Gina. She needs to move with extreme haste on this."

"I'm prepared to help her with anything she needs," Louise said.

"Okay, good. Beck? I need you to talk to Kendra and relay what we've discussed here. As I'm sure you understand, it's best if you do that as soon as possible."

"I'll talk to her tonight."

"Thank you. In the meantime, we need to find a way to sequester Rachel."

"She can stay with me," Beck said. "I have an extra room and it'll be easier than hiding her in a safehouse."

"Agreed," Jameson said. He looked at Louise. "Time is of the essence. Gina needs to hurry before this Rachel Goudas inferno consumes us all."

They left the sitting room and fell in with a string of residents ambling down the hallway, chatting about the dinner entrées and the equally delicious dessert. The storm outside had intensified, and when Jameson opened the door to his room, the diffused light filtering in through the window was painting the entire space in a mist-like wash. He took several steps forward and stopped short.

"What's wrong?" Louise asked. When he didn't answer, she stepped around him and saw that Jameson's bed was empty, the bedspread uncreased.

Rachel was gone.

wordsworth   **12**

Hints And Insinuations

All through dinner, six words consumed Gina's every thought: *Oh, Shepherd of the Seven Hills.* Not only was it the first confirmed clue from *The Crown Killer*, it revealed the literary device her grandmother had used to disguise her secret message. And while the line sounded almost biblical, her gut told her that the word 'Shepherd' was a veiled reference to the person she was trying to find.

The only way to be sure was to scour the internet, but she knew that sitting at the computer, scrolling through page after page, would only attract her parents' attention and unleash a barrage of questions.

Why are you spending so much time on the computer?

You never use the computer.

And what interest do you have in shepherds?

Does this have something to do with Nathan Cole?

Are the two of you up to something?

Making matters worse was the way Louise had whisked Rachel away in a panic. Clearly something had happened. Was it related to what Nathan and Beck and Kendra had done at the restaurant? If so, why would Rachel be in danger?

At nine o'clock her parents went upstairs. She waited a half hour then went up and stood outside her bedroom door, listening. Down the hall she could hear the sound of the television in her parents' room. Whatever they were watching had lots of screeching tires and sirens. She knew, given the hour, that they would eventually nod off, if they hadn't done so already.

It was computer time.

She went in her room to get her notepad when she heard the cellphone Louise had given her emit a tinny *plink-plunk* sound, like something out of deep-space movie. She hurried over to her back-pack that was hanging on her desk chair and pulled out the phone. After thumbing the "Accept" button at the bottom of the screen, she pressed it to her ear. "Hello?" she said. "Louise?"

"Yes, it's me," Louise said. "I'm sorry to be calling so late."

"Is everything all right?" Gina asked, keeping her voice low.

"No," Louise said. "You and I need to talk and I'm afraid it can't wait."

Gina pulled the phone from her ear and looked over at the alarm clock on her bedside table. 10:40 p.m. She was raising the phone to her ear again when she realized the time was displayed right there at the top of the phone's call screen. *Duh.* "Do you want to meet now?" she asked.

"Yes, but only if you can leave the house without arousing suspicion."

"I can do that," Gina said. "Where can we meet?"

"Look out your window."

Gina went to the window and pulled back the curtain. Two houses down the street, parked at the curb, a car flashed its headlights.

Once.

Twice.

"Wait there," she said. "I'll come to you."

She tiptoed out into the hallway and paused to listen. The
screeching tires and sirens were gone, replaced by dialogue and dramatic music. She continued down the hall and went downstairs.
When she opened the front door and stepped outside, the heavy
rains had passed, leaving in their wake a cool thin mist that hung in
the air and gently brushed her face as she hurried down the sidewalk.

After the news broke about the assault on Bolan, Cafferty, and
Rodano, Roman kept his cellphone within arm's reach, waiting for
the call that he knew would eventually come. The Red Sox/Yankees
game had just gone into extra innings when he heard the telltale
ringtone that stabbed at his relaxed composure like an ice pick. He
muted the television and grabbed the phone off the coffee table.
"Good evening," he said.

"Did I not make myself clear?" came the heated reply. "I distinctly remember saying I wanted this matter tied up quickly and without
any complications."

"Yes, you did."

"Then perhaps you can tell me what the hell happened this afternoon in Somerville, and why it's been running on every news sta-

tion ever since."

"That was… unexpected," Roman said, choosing his words carefully.

"Unexpected? That's not the word I'd use."

Roman remained calm. "I can assure you that it won't happen again."

"Is that a promise? Because by the way this thing is spinning out of control, it sounds more like a pipedream."

Roman stemmed the tirade with five words: "There's been a positive development."

"I'm all ears."

"Late this afternoon we acquired a significant lead, one that will deliver us the target and avoid any unwanted attention from the media."

"Then get it done."

"It's in process as we speak."

He waited for a reply but the connection had already ended.

Gina slid into the front seat of the Mercedes and pulled the door shut. From where Louise had parked, she had a clear view of her parents' bedroom window at the back corner of the second floor. The glow from their television was illuminating the break in the curtains in short, sporadic bursts.

"Thank you for meeting me on such short notice," Louise said. "I apologize for the late hour."

"It's fine," Gina said. "What's going on? You sounded worried on the phone."

"I just came from Birch Meadow. Rachel, Beck and I had dinner with Jameson and the situation with Rachel is much more dangerous than we first thought."

"But, how can that be? Nathan told me his plan worked. They caught those three men who were chasing her."

"Not only caught them, they were questioned by some of Jameson's people."

Gina didn't ask which people. "And…?" she said.

Louise shared what Jameson told them about the interrogation, explaining that Bolan, Cafferty, and Rodano were being directed by a man named Phillip Roman, whose boss was intent on retrieving something in Rachel's possession, which had ignited his pursuit of her in the first place.

"Hold on," Gina said. "She said something about that, but she denied that it was true."

"Well, from what Jameson said, Roman's boss is merciless. Not only does he have the money and the firepower to get whatever he wants, he won't stop coming after her until he gets it. And if anyone gets in his way? It won't end well for them either. Bolan, Cafferty, and Rodano may be out of the picture, but Beck has since learned that they were only the first wave. It would appear that Roman has already brought in someone else to replace them."

"Rachel warned me that might happen."

"There's something else, too," Louise said.

Gina gave her a look. *There's more?*

"She's gone."

"Who? Rachel? Gone where?" Gina exclaimed.

"We don't know. After dinner, we left her in Jameson's room to rest and when we returned she was gone."

"Do you think someone…" Gina began, unable to voice the rest.

"No. There were too many residents and staffers in the building. If anyone tried to do her harm, someone would've seen it…or heard it."

"Why would she run?" Gina asked. "We've done nothing but protect her since she showed up."

"Good question," Louise said. "You can ask her when you see her again."

"What makes you think I'll see her again?"

"You're the closest thing she has to your grandmother—the one person who can return her to a life of obscurity, far away from Roman's boss. Plus, you're the only person she trusts."

"I think you're right," Gina said. "Why else would she tell me about how my grandmother helped her, and the person they met on the night she vanished."

"The courier," Louise said.

Gina stared at her, awestruck. "Excuse me?"

"Your grandmother called him 'the courier'."

"You *knew* about him!" Gina exclaimed. "And you didn't say anything?"

"I knew him only by title and reputation," Louise said. "Your grandmother used him because he's extremely proficient at his job: careful to a fault; his movements covert; operating in the dark for the safety of those he's charged with transporting. That's all she told me. If there was anything else, she kept it to herself."

"Please!" Gina groaned. "She told you things. How else would you know about James Donnelly?"

"Yes, from time to time she would share things with me, but they were mostly just hints and insinuations. I think she was trying to protect me by limiting the amount of information she shared about her shadows."

"Her what?"

"Shadows," Louise said. "That's what she called the women she was helping."

"Of course," Gina said, just above a whisper. "The shadows grieve. Their words a prayer for quick reprieve."

"I'm sorry, what was that?"

"It's a passage from her book, *The Crown Killer*. I read a portion of it to Rachel today when we were on the sidewalk. I thought it might be a clue about this *courier* person. But..." she said, then paused.

"What?" Louise asked.

"Why would my grandmother hide information about the courier in the book? Once Rachel was gone she'd never need him again... unless..."

"Go on."

"Maybe it wasn't just for Rachel. She could've put it there for any of the women she helped."

"It's possible," Louise said, "but if you're right about the hidden message, I think she definitely put it there for Rachel, as a safeguard."

"Safeguard? What are you talking about?"

"Rachel Goudas is a runner. By the time she made first contact with your grandmother she'd already been on the run for several weeks. The woman is very elusive. It turned what should've been a seamless three-day process into a two-week headache. She trusted no one. She was never in the same place twice. Getting in touch with her was problematic at best, which frustrated Helen to no end."

"Well, clue or not, she definitely recognized it. She said my grandmother uttered the words the night she dropped her off."

"Keep looking," Louise said. There was an audible tension in her voice, "Your grandmother never discussed the particulars of the courier with me but it's imperative that we find him."

"Understood."

"And if Rachel contacts you, you know what to say, right?"

"Yeah. Stop running!" Gina said, forcefully, as if Rachel was sitting there in the car with them. "You wanted me to find this guy, remember? If I do, you need to be here so we can take you to him."

"That's perfect," Louise said. "Knowing that you've got a line on the courier may be the only thing that keeps her from fleeing again."

"Well, now that I know what I'm looking for, it shouldn't take long."

"Good. Call me if you get stuck. I made an agreement with your grandmother and I intend to honor it."

"Excuse me?"

"Before she died, I made a promise to your grandmother that I'd help you if you ever needed it."

"You mean, like Jameson did with Nathan's grandfather?"

"Exactly."

"I'm going to hold you to that," Gina said. She looked through the windshield at her house. The window in her parent's bedroom was dark, the drapes nothing but a fuzzy black rectangle in the pale gray night. With her parents asleep, she knew she could read to her heart's content without fear of them barging into the room. She was reaching for the door handle when she stopped and pulled Louise's cellphone from her pocket. "Almost forgot," she said, "here's your phone." She handed it across the center console but Louise pushed it away.

"You keep that," she said.

"Wait, what?"

"If we're going to talk to each other, we can't have you using your house phone, now, can we? Not with your parents lurking around every corner."

"Uh, no, but…I mean…it's just that…"

"It's yours," Louise said. "The phone number is listed under Dilly Dallyer. The only calls you'll get will be from me, or possibly Jameson. Share the number with Nathan if you like. Come to think of it, you should give it to Kendra and Beck too."

"Dilly *Dallyer*?" Gina said, with a smirk.

"That was my pet turtle when I was 10 years old."

Gina stared at the phone, awestruck. *My own cellphone? Are you SERIOUS?*

"Whatever you do, don't let your parent's find it," Louise said.

"They won't," Gina replied, firmly. "But…shouldn't I pay you for it? I mean, there's a monthly charge, right?"

"Don't worry about it. That's all been taken care of."

"Huh?"

"The monthly bill is being paid courtesy of your grandmother."

Gina eyed her suspiciously. "What do you mean?"

"Years ago, your grandmother set up a private bank account for you." *More than enough to cover a thousand monthly phone bills*, she didn't say.

"And when were you planning on telling me this?" Gina asked.

"I was waiting until the time was right."

"Well, I think this certainly fits that criteria," Gina said, unable to take her eyes from the phone.

"You and I are the only ones who know about that," Louise said, "so let's just keep it between us, shall we?"

"Sure," Gina said, her mind reeling. Suddenly it felt like Christmas morning.

"Right now, I need you to focus all your attention on the clues Helen put in the book. I can't stress this enough: we have to find the courier and we have to do it as quickly as possible. We want no part of Phillip Roman's boss, or whoever they bring in to find Rachel."

"I'll call you as soon as I figure it out," Gina said. She climbed out of the car and walked home, moving faster with every step, Louise's directive foremost in her mind.

As she walked away, Louise phoned Jameson with an update.

"You told her everything?" he asked.

"Yes."

"And she's fully onboard?"

"What choice does she have?"

After sneaking out of Birch Meadow, Rachel hid in the trees across from the parking lot for nearly an hour before spotting a young couple leaving the building through the front entrance. She intercepted them as they walked to their car and concocted a hard-luck story about needing a ride after she'd had an argument with her boyfriend, who had left her stranded there to fend for herself. They immediately took pity on her and gave her a ride as far as Mount Auburn Street in Watertown.

With her wet clothes clinging to her body like a hard candy shell, she found a 24-hour laundromat, one she knew from her college days. In the back was a huge cardboard box filled with random clothes that the owner had found over the years. She pawed through the jumble and found a ghastly pair of plaid slacks and an oversized man's white dress shirt, then went to the restroom and put them on.

As she waited for her wet clothes to dry, she sat in one of the cheap plastic stacking chairs along the side wall, keeping an eye on the front windows. The only other person there at that hour was a middle-aged woman who was busy folding clothes on the long table that ran down the middle of the room. Behind her, only Rachel's dryer was turning, emitting a high-pitched whirring sound that was oddly hypnotic.

The woman was halfway through the pile of clothes on the table when she reached down and pulled a cellphone from her purse that sat in an empty basket on the floor near her feet. After a brief conversation, she ended the call, muttered something under her breath, and then dropped the phone back in her purse.

Several minutes later, she finished folding and went to the restroom. When Rachel saw that, she jumped up from the chair and hurried over to the basket. She dug through the woman's purse until she found the cellphone, then carried it over to the pay phone that was mounted on the wall in the front corner of the room.

Years earlier, someone had etched the pay phone number on the coin vault. She typed it into a text and hit send.

Call 617-640-1583

Rachel

As the text was being delivered, she ran back to the table and dropped the woman's phone in her purse. By the time she got back to the payphone it was already ringing. She grabbed the handset and faced the wall as she spoke. "We need to keep this short," she said.

That was fine with Rios. He was busy enough as it was and it showed in his tone. "Is it done?" he asked, impatiently.

"Not yet," she told him.

"What happened to your plan?"

"My plan is fine," she lied, "but there were some developments."

"What are you talking about?"

"Bolan, Cafferty and Rodano, that's what I'm talking about. But they're gone now. Oh, by the way, you need to trash your phone."

"And why would I do that?"

"Because someone may be tracking it."

"Impossible. I only use burner phones. Where *are* you?"

"At a laundromat in Watertown. Don't worry. No one knows I'm here. Call me at this same number tomorrow at 10 o'clock and I'll give you an update."

"Tomorrow, 10 o'clock," he said, making a mental note. "You'll be there?"

"If I say I'm going to be here, I'm going to be here," she said, her patience waning.

"You also told me this was going to be a piece of cake."

"And it will be. The person helping me is making progress. It won't be long now."

"The person helping you," Rios said. "You mean the 10-year-old girl?"

"She's not 10, she's 13."

Rios said nothing and ended the call.

Gina attacked the rest of the book with a whole new focus. No longer was she interested in the twists and turns of Nikki Nolan's murder investigation; she focused her full attention on any mention of Roxy's book club, especially if it included passages from Eula Mae Pittman's poetry that were being read aloud by Nigel Hewitt or, in some cases, by one of the book club's quirky participants.

We had just sat down at the bar when Roxy launched into another enthusiastic tale about "Nifty Nigel." Apparently, things at the book club weren't so chipper. One of the regulars, a frumpy woman name Darlene, who looked like a catalog model for billowy, tent-like clothing, had been plucking Nigel's strings by challenging his interpretations of Pittman's poetic verses.

"I thought poetry was supposed to be calming," I said. "You know, brew a cup of tea, kick back in your favorite chair, read some poetry, take a nap?"

"Someone forgot to explain that to Darlene," Roxy said.

Two pints of IPA appeared on the bar in front of us and we attacked them like we'd been crawling across the Mohave Desert for the past month with nothing to drink.

"So, this week," Roxy said, pausing to take a breath, "Darlene, Darlene, The Poetry Queen, as some of us are calling her, goes off on him about this one stanza. She told him he had the meaning all wrong. You should've seen the look on his face. I thought he was going to throw his book at her."

"You say tomato, I say to-mah-to," I joked.

"Yeah, right?" Roxy said. "Tell you what. You read it and tell me what you think it means." She reached into her purse and pulled out the book of Pittman poetry. When she

found the words in question, she handed me the book and
I read them silently. Then I read them again.
The gentle wind, so mild and meek,
will guide us toward the path we seek.
And fearing not the darkened sky:
Phoebe's brightest shining eye.

Gina stopped reading. "The path we seek," she said aloud. That sounded suspiciously like a clue. It certainly fit with Rachel's plight: seeking a path to safety, and with it, an entirely new life. The next two lines held her attention for several minutes. She knew "the darkened sky" was a time reference, but "Phoebe's brightest eye" made no sense at all. She wrote the four-line stanza in her notepad just below the first one. If her hunch was right, the words were meant to sound like poetic verse, but to any of the women who had sought Helen Bainbridge's protection they were a veiled set of instructions.

With midnight closing in, and fatigue sapping what little energy she had left, she closed her notepad and got ready for bed. Outside her window, the night sky had cleared, leaving a dazzling canopy of stars. She was pulling the curtains closed when the moon caught her eye and she froze. As she stared at it, two of the lines she'd scribbled in her notepad flashed in her memory. *And fearing not the darkened sky, Phoebe's brightest shining eye.* Could that mean what she thought it did?

Feeling a bolt of renewed energy, she let go of the curtain and hurried downstairs to the living room. With the glow from the computer monitor illuminating the room, she did a quick search of the word 'Phoebe'. Five minutes later her hunch was confirmed. She quickly exited the page and did another search—this one taking less than 30 seconds. What she saw on the screen made her gasp. "No!"

Time was no longer her friend.

She shut down the computer and raced back upstairs to her room to call Louise.

"Gina?" Louise asked, sounding half asleep.

"I'm sorry to call so late but I figured out when the courier is going to appear again. It was in the book, in a passage that mentions Phoebe's brightest eye."

"Phoebe? You lost me."

"Phoebe is another name for Selene, the Goddess of the Moon."

"O-kay," Louise said, still not grasping the meaning.

"Phoebe's brightest shining eye would be the full moon. According to the moon-phase calendar, that's tomorrow night."

"This is astounding," Louise said. "Do you know *where* he'll appear?"

"Not yet, but I'll call you back as soon as I do."

"If you're right about this, then we don't have much time," Louise said.

"I'll find it. Don't you worry about that."

This girl is remarkable! Louise thought. She clicked off the call and sent Jameson and Beck a quick text.

> The courier appears tomorrow night
> Gina should have the location soon

Much to her surprise, it was Jameson who replied first.

> Call me as soon as you know

Beck's reply followed moments later.

209

Standing by to help

When Rachel's dryer completed its cycle, she changed out of the hideous plaid slacks and oversized dress shirt and tossed them back into the box of abandoned garments. The warmth of her own clothes was a soothing relief and helped to settle her thoughts. She pulled the hood of her pink sweatshirt over her head as she left the laundromat and walked around the corner to a 24-hour convenience store to buy a pre-paid phone. Inexpensive and untraceable, it would allow her to communicate freely without the possibility of being detected by Roman or any of the gorillas he sent after her.

She loaded up on minutes and left the store. It was late and she was tired. She knew that checking into a local hotel was out of the question because, by now, Magnus would've alerted every front-desk manager in the greater Boston area to be on the lookout for a young woman travelling alone with no luggage, paying cash for a one-night stay. But there was another option open to her, someone she could call without risk. And while their communications had dropped off seven years earlier, their previous business dealings had forged an unbreakable bond that no amount of time could break.

She moved down the sidewalk, away from the harsh neon glow emanating from the storefront windows, and pulled her address book from her backpack. She quickly found the number she wanted and made the call, hoping the phone was still in service. Halfway through the first ring she got the answer.

"Hello?"

"Allison?"

"Yes, this is Allison."

"It's Harper," Rachel said, using her real name, the only one

Allison knew.

"Harper?" Allison said, sounding relieved. "Oh my God. You're alive!"

"Alive and on Mt. Auburn Street in Watertown if you can believe that. I need a place to crash for the night and I was hoping you might—"

"Say no more," Allison cut in. Whereabouts on Mt. Auburn Street are you?"

"I'm at the 24-hour convenience store near Bigelow Ave."

"I know it well. You sit tight. I'll be there in 15 minutes."

Magnus returned to Kendra's coffee shop just after 11 o'clock. Parked across the street, he could see that the windows in the upstairs apartment were all dark. Either Kendra wasn't home, or he'd returned too late and she had already turned in for the night.

He got out of the car and walked the street for two blocks in both directions, looking for her Volvo. When that search came up empty, he went back to his car and continued his vigil. Twenty minutes later the Volvo cruised past him, slowed, and turned into the small alley next to the coffee shop. Not long after that Kendra emerged. She stepped around the front corner of the building dressed in a baseball uniform and stopped in front of the door to her apartment. In one hand she was carrying a baseball bat. In the other, her baseball glove.

As she fumbled with both, attempting to dig her keys out of her pocket, he eased the door open and stepped out of the car.

Nothing more than a shadow.

Moving silently in the dark.

211

ALFRED M. STRUTHERS

13

Another One of Those Things

Kendra was sliding her apartment key into the lock when she heard Beck's Dodge Ram rumbling up the street. Seconds later it came to a stop at the curb and he climbed out of the cab, his long legs reaching the pavement with ease.

"I've been calling you," he said, as he stepped up onto the sidewalk.

She held up her baseball glove. "Had a game."

"Did you win?"

"What kind of question is that?" she said, smirking. "Of course, we won."

In the reflection of the shop window, Beck detected movement across the street. It was very subtle, but it was enough to make him turn and look.

"What's wrong?" Kendra asked, following his gaze.

Magnus stood perfectly still, his silhouette masked by the thick stand of arborvitae directly behind him.

"Wait here," Beck said.

He stepped off the curb, his eyes trained on the sedan parked across the street. In the meager light it was hard to tell the exact shade, but it was definitely somewhere in the brown palette. Directly behind it he saw the outline of a very large person.

Cars were speeding past, keeping him from crossing the street, when the light at the intersection 90 feet to his right turned red. As traffic slowed to a halt, an outbound MBTA bus stopped directly in front of him, blocking his view. By the time he made his way around it, the sedan was gone.

"You done playing in traffic?" Kendra shouted.

Beck made a mental note of the car and then went back to the sidewalk and followed her inside.

"I'd offer you coffee but it'll keep you up all night," Kendra said, as they climbed the steps to her apartment.

"Don't bother," Beck said. "I won't be here that long."

She unlocked the door and let him in, then set her bat and glove on a wooden bench in the small foyer. "I need water," she said, gesturing for him to follow her into the kitchen. From the refrigerator she pulled out two bottles of spring water and offered one to him.

"No thanks, I'm good," he said.

She twisted the cap off the first bottle and drained every last drop.

"Remind me not to challenge you to a chugging contest," he told her.

"It was a long game." She bumped her fist against her chest, burped, then sat down at the table and emptied the second bottle. "So, what brings you to my humble abode at such a late hour?" she asked.

"Jameson told us about the interrogation of Bolan, Cafferty, and Rodano."

"Oh? And how did that go? Not so good for the bad guys, I'm guessing?"

"It was worse than bad," Beck said.

"Ooh, tell me what happened, and don't leave anything out."

He walked over to the window and parted the bamboo shade with his finger, checking the street below.

For Kendra, that was red flag #1.

After scanning the street in both directions, he let go of the shade and took a seat across from her.

That was red flag #2

In all the time she'd known him, Beck wasn't the sit around-and-chat type of guy. He preferred to stand like a sentry, armed and ready to face whatever threat might come at him.

He relayed everything Jameson had shared in the front room at Birch Meadow, putting special emphasis on Phillip Roman and the ruthlessness of his boss. From there, the conversation shifted to how they were going to deal with Rachel.

That was red flag #3.

Allison arrived as promised, 15 minutes after Rachel's call. They exchanged a warm hug in the front seat, then Allison pulled away from the curb and looped around in the middle of the street, heading back to Chestnut Hill.

"It's been a long time," Rachel said, breaking the silence.

"Yes, it has," Allison replied. "I wasn't sure I'd ever see you again."

"I meant to call you, after, you know…"

"Forget about it," Allison said. "You did what you had to do."

"Yeah, I know…but still…"

An empty silence followed.

"You're not… still *active* in the real estate market…are you?" Allison asked, cautiously.

"No, but I'm planning to get back into it again, once I get settled."

"What are you saying?" Allison asked. "They found you?"

"Yes, but—"

"Wait," Allison cut in. She cut across the left lane and pulled into the parking lot of a large medical professional building. She drove to the back corner and turned off the engine, her jet-black Audi S8 nothing more than a hazy silhouette in the darkness.

"What's wrong?" Rachel asked.

Allison looked over at her, stone-faced. Gone was the chummy old-friend. In its place was the intent, laser-focused stare she wore as the CEO at Reed & Croft Financial Group. "How did they find you?" she asked.

"They tracked my phone signal," Rachel said, angry at herself for the mindless blunder she'd made. "And before you say it, yes, I know, it was stupid of me to use it."

"That's *it?*" Allison said. "They tracked your phone?"

Rachel nodded.

"Then you've got nothing to worry about."

"That's easy for you to say," Rachel muttered.

"I'm serious," Allison said. "If your phone number is all they've got, just get a new phone." She paused for a beat. "Tell me you did that."

"I did," Rachel said, regretting the ease with which she'd surrendered her old work phone to Beck. Looking back at how things unfolded, she realized she should've worked harder to hide it from him. Nathan's plan of using it to lure Bolan, Cafferty, and Rodano into an ambush had blown the lid off a whole new level of anxiety, and had endangered her chances of escaping to a place where no one would ever find her.

Allison saw the look of regret on her face and rested her hand on Rachel's shoulder. "Hey, don't worry about it. Without a way to track you, you can just vanish. I mean, you did it before, you can do it again, right?"

"That was the plan," Rachel said. Ever since dinner she'd been contemplating the safest way to proceed.

"What is it?" Allison asked. "What are you thinking?"

"There's someone I need to go see."

"Now?" Allison asked, checking the time on the dash.

"No, it can wait until morning, but I need to do it without being seen."

"No problem," Allison said.

"You don't mind driving me?"

"Do I mind? I'm sorry, I don't think we were properly introduced. My name is Allison Reed? Reed & Croft Financial Services? We provide 24-hour service, 365 days a year."

Rachel smiled.

Her chummy old friend was back.

Monday, 6:00 a.m.

Shortly before six o'clock, with the day's first light spilling over the window sill in her bedroom, Gina's eyes opened and she sat up, ignoring the lingering haze of sleep that gripped her. She reached over and grabbed *The Crown Killer* from her bedside table as if her brain had been secretly plotting such a move while she slept.

Propped up against the headboard, the book open on her lap, she ran her finger across each line of text like a speed reader, skimming each page in rapid succession for any mention of Eula Mae Pittman's poetry. Even though she wasn't focused on the main plot of the story, it still managed to seep into her subconscious.

There had been another discovery at Grafton Reservoir—a male victim this time. Nikki Nolan was obsessed with his clothing and personal effects. The severe bruising on his throat was eerily similar to that on the first victim, which meant they had a serial killer on the loose. And of course, there was the ongoing saga of Roxy. She was mentioned regularly, mostly in after-hour social settings, where she and Nikki compared notes on a variety of topics, mainly the various men they had dated, could have dated, or wished they'd dated.

Gina made it through two chapters and was starting on a third when she found another poetry reference.

What was one shall soon be two,
Our journey long, with hope renewed
Ever moving, coursing on,
To freedom's shore, at mercy's dawn

One shall be two, at mercy's dawn, she thought. It sounded completely arbitrary, but wasn't that what her grandmother had intended? Words that had a random meaning to the casual reader but carried a concealed message to her intended target? If her suspicion was correct, this was a specific time reference—the exact hour when the courier would return.

She grabbed her notepad from the bedside table and added the stanza to her growing list of clues. She now had four: three poetry clues, as she was calling them, and Ann DeBartolo's perplexing reference to something called Jericho.

Just after 7:30, she stood at her bedroom window and watched through the break in the curtains as her parents backed down the driveway and drove to work. Once they were out of sight, she went downstairs and got right to work on the computer. Other than the rush of early morning commuters speeding past the house, the only sound to be heard was the soft clacking of the keys on the keyboard as she typed.

She started with the first poetry clue, the line Rachel had recognized from the night Helen delivered her to the courier. "Shepherd of the Seven Hills," she said aloud as she typed it. Seconds later a divergent list of links appeared on the screen, each one different than the next. There was a documentary, "Shepherd of the Seven Hills," released in 1933. Next was the Shepherd of the Hills Lutheran Church in California, followed by a novel by Harold Bell Wright, entitled *Shepherd of the Hills*, written in 1907. Other than that, there was nothing even remotely substantial.

She exited the page and was beginning a new search when she heard a knock on the kitchen door. Unsure who it could be, she went to the window and looked out at the driveway, expecting to see a

UPS truck, or maybe FedEx. The driveway was empty.

She heard another knock.

Louder.

She left the room and hurried down the hallway to the kitchen. Standing on the porch, visible through the glass-paned door that led into the house, was Rachel. She was dressed in a pink sweatshirt with the hood pulled up over her head.

Gina yanked the door open. "Where have you been?" she said, annoyed.

Rachel didn't move. She held her ground, studying Gina's face and looking like she might turn and run at any moment.

"Are you all right?" Gina asked. "I was worried about you."

"Were you?" Rachel asked, her expression rigid.

"Yes!" Gina said, excitedly, like two schoolgirls meeting up after a long summer apart. "I have so much to tell you."

"Like, what?"

"The man in the cloak?" Gina said. "He's called 'the courier'."

"Go on," Rachel said, her icy expression starting to melt.

"He's going to appear sometime after midnight *tonight*."

"And just how do you know that?"

"My grandmother laid it all out in her book."

"You mean, in those lines of nonsense you were asking me about?"

"They're not nonsense," Gina said. "I'm still working on the exact location but I should have it in another hour." *I hope.*

Rachel nodded slowly as she evaluated what Gina was telling her. "Tonight," she said.

"Yes. Sometime after midnight."

"And you're sure about this," Rachel said.

"Absolutely," Gina said. "That's why you can't just run away and hide. We're *so* close now!"

"You have no idea how bad these men are," Rachel said. *Especially Magnus.*

"All the more reason why you need to stay close by, somewhere safe where I can find you when it's time to leave."

Rachel looked away, thinking, then looked back. "You say you'll know soon?"

"An hour. Two at the most."

"And you're convinced that he can do what he did before and get me away from these butchers?"

"Yes!"

"Okay, fine. But there's an errand I have to run. As soon as I'm done I'll call for a ride."

"An errand?" Gina repeated. She tried to imagine what errand a woman who was running for her life could possibly have to do. The only thing she needed to do was to stay invisible to the people pursuing her.

"Who do I call?" Rachel asked, sidestepping Gina's question. "You?"

"Yes, but not on the house phone," Gina said. "Call my cellphone. Hold on, I'll get the number." She left the kitchen and hurried down the hallway to the living room. Moments later she returned, phone in hand. In the settings menu she found the number and read it aloud.

Rachel entered it in her phone, then said, "I'll be in touch. Should be in about two hours."

After she left, Gina went to the window expecting to see her

221

darting across the lawn or sneaking down the driveway toward the street. But she was nowhere to be seen. Once again, the woman had simply vanished. She pushed the thought from her mind and hurried back to the living room to continue her search.

By her estimation they had a little over 17 hours until the courier would return. Ordinarily, that block of time would seem like an eternity, but she knew almost nothing about the man. Where would he appear? How long would he wait around? Louise was preparing a destination for Rachel, but who would relay that information? Her? Louise? Rachel herself? As the questions mounted, she felt the walls of time closing in on her.

She sat down at the computer and typed in two words from the passage Rachel had recognized: seven hills. The list of links that appeared was massive. There was the Seven Hills Foundation in New Hampshire; a real estate investment firm in Newton; the stately Seven Hills Inn located in the Berkshires; The Seven Hills School in Ohio; a preparatory academy in Minnesota, a winery in Washington state, and an animal hospital in Virginia. She scrolled down further and found a listing for The Church on Seven Hills in Worcester. At first glance it didn't strike her as relevant, until she read the description:

Worcester is known by a few different names. One of them is The City on Seven Hills, which is where we get our name.

"The City on Seven Hills," she said slowly, seeing a possible connection. Working quickly, she brought up Google Maps and typed in Worcester, Massachusetts. In the "Directions" box she entered her home town of Arlington.

The two cities were 52 miles apart.

She flashed back to what Rachel had said about the night she'd been passed off to the courier; how Helen had driven her to an undisclosed location, never telling her where they were going. Was it Worcester? Less than an hour away?

Feeling the need to move, to think, to process each of the clues, she got up from the computer and began to pace. "She told me she was exhausted and fell asleep in the car. When she awoke, she had no idea where they were, but she said she was fully awake."

She stopped pacing.

"Fully awake…that's it! She wasn't exhausted anymore, which means she'd been sleeping for some time. If they'd only gone a short distance, she still would've been wiped out when they arrived." The location where the courier would surface again was Worcester—she was sure of it.

On a hunch, she went back to the computer and brought up the homepage for the city of Worcester. As the bottom, she clicked on the History tab and followed a series of links that brought her to a timeline chronicling Worcester's industrial boom.

It started in the early 1800s, when wealthy local investors who had an eye on innovation and diversity built numerous factories and textile mills that quickly crowded the landscape. One businessman in particular caught Gina's eye, his story jumping right off the page.

Perhaps one of the most notable industrialists to shape the landscape of Worcester was a wealthy investor from Boston names Asa Mothram. Following the opening of

223

the Worcester and Boston Railroad in 1835, Mothram built a sprawling mill complex along Jericho Street that consisted of eight separate factory buildings arranged in a grid-like pattern. Originally called "The Mothan Block", over time it earned the nickname "The Mothram Maze," due to it's labryinth of narrow, interconnecting alleyways.

Thunderstruck by the revelation, she called Louise.

"Well, good morning," Louise said, brightly.

"Worcester," Gina blurted out.

"Excuse me?"

"The location, it's Worcester."

"And you're sure?"

"Positive. I even know the street."

"Incredible," Louise murmured quietly, once again marveling at Gina's proficiency with unearthing critical information. "We've got to move quickly," she said. "The courier won't take her unless he has an address, someplace where he can hide her."

"You mean, like a safehouse?"

"Yes."

"And you know of such a place?" Gina asked.

"Several, actually. There's a network of them spread across the country. Your grandmother referred to them as 'safe havens'."

"This sounds like another one of those things," Gina said.

"What are you talking about?"

"One of those things? You know, that you should've *told me* about my grandmother?"

"I'll add it to the list," Louise said. "In the meantime, since you know the time and place, I'll let you work out the logistics: when to leave, what route to take, and so on. Let me know as soon as you get it all worked out, okay?"

"Will do."

"I'm assuming Rachel will insist on you accompanying her?" Louise asked.

"I would think so," Gina said. "By the way, you were right about her. She paid me a visit."

Of course, she did, Louise thought. "When?"

"Less than an hour ago."

"What did you tell her?"

"I told her that sometime today I'd know the exact location of the courier's return and that she needed to be someplace where I could reach her."

"Did it work?"

"Yes. At least I think it did."

"What do you mean?"

"She stayed for a few minutes, then left. She told me she had something to do."

"Did she say what it was?"

"No, but she promised to call me when she's done. Said it would be…" she said, pausing to check the time on her phone, "about an hour and a half from now."

"Time will tell if she holds true to that promise," Louise replied.

"I guess, but she sounded pretty sincere. She said she'd need someone to pick her up."

"Call Kendra. Do you have her number?"

225

"Uh…no," Gina replied, "I haven't put it in my phone yet." *My phone,* she thought, smiling. Were there two more exquisite words in the English language? If so, she couldn't imagine what they were.

Louise read off Kendra's number, then said, "Check with Nathan. See if he can arrange a place where we can stash Rachel until it's time to leave for Worcester. This ordeal is almost over and we can't have her wandering around on her own all day."

Gina walked over to the window and pulled back the curtain. Beck's truck was sitting in Nathan's driveway. How it got there without her hearing it was a mystery. Then she saw Nathan and Beck in the backyard, locked in a bizarre embrace. They were either wrestling or dancing, she couldn't be sure. "Uh, Louise, about Nathan?" she said, watching them romp and tumble on the grass. "Let me get back to you on that."

After the call from Gina, Louise immediately dialed Jameson. The call found him sitting in the spacious and mostly empty dining room at Birch Meadow, feasting on the Monday morning edition of the Boston Globe.

"Good morning," he said, sitting back in the chair. "Any news?"

"Yes," Louise told him. "Gina has all the information. The courier will appear in Worcester after midnight tonight. As we speak, she's working out the timing and the best route to get to the drop spot."

Jameson breathed a sigh of relief. "Call me the minute you know the details."

"That was my plan."

Allison was parked on Lafayette Street in front of a shingled cottage-style home that looked like it had been trucked in from Hyannis. Rachel had directed Allison to that specific location because directly behind it, shielded by a swath of leafy maple trees, was Gina's house.

"How did it go?" Allison asked, after Rachel got back in the car.

"Better than I expected," she said, imagining how the next 48 hours would play out. She was almost home free. All she had to do was lay low until she connected with the courier. After that she'd be free to resume the good life, the one she'd enjoyed before everything came crashing down around her.

Allison started the car and drove to the end of the street. As she eyed the line of traffic racing past in both directions on Mass Ave, she voiced the concern that had been drumming a slow and steady beat in the back of her mind since breakfast. "About the real estate thing…" she said.

"What about it?" Rachel asked.

"Were you serious about that?"

"Very serious," Rachel said. "Why?"

"I just…" Allison said, then paused, wanting to phrase it right. "I want you to be safe, that's all. I'd hate to see anything bad happen."

"Relax," Rachel said, free and easy. "Nothing bad is going to happen."

"I hope you're right," Allison countered. She saw her chance to pull out and took it, sliding seamlessly into the flow of traffic.

"I appreciate your concern," Rachel said, "but do you know what I've been doing for the past seven years?"

"No. What's that?"

227

"My homework."

14

Just Today

Beck stood directly across from Nathan, less than three feet of lawn separating them. In his left hand was a thick wooden stick roughly eight inches long, meant to resemble a weapon. He pointed it at Nathan and said, "I'm coming at you with a gun, what do you do?"

Nathan looked to Beck's left, then right, contemplating the "tuck and roll" evasion technique he'd been taught. "You didn't leave me much room," he griped.

"That's right," said Beck. "And neither will someone who wants to do you harm."

"I guess I could run."

"Yes, you could do that," Beck said. "But can you outrun a bullet?"

Nathan shook his head.

"What about a knife? If you turn your back on someone with

229

advanced knife skills, you'll never see the blade when they throw it at you. Do you really want to take that chance?"

"Not especially," Nathan said.

"I didn't think so. You need to disarm the weapon hand of your attacker, separating him from his weapon, *before* you run."

"And you can do that without getting shot?"

"Yes. What I'm going to show you is a Judo technique that uses your hand, your leg, and your hip to neutralize an armed attacker. For this demonstration you'll be the bad guy and this stick is a knife." He handed it to Nathan and said, "I want you to extend the stick like you're trying to cut me."

Nathan gripped the stick tightly and jabbed it in Beck's direction. Beck, in turn, swatted Nathan's hand to the side, then quickly hooked his arm around Nathan's forearm, clamping it tightly in the crook of his elbow. "See how I did that?" he asked, releasing Nathan's arm. "I swiped your hand aside, then I hooked your arm."

Nathan nodded his understanding.

"Say it," said Beck.

"Swipe the hand, hook the arm."

"Good. Let's try it again. A little faster this time."

Nathan raised the stick again, but this time he charged forward. In a blur, Beck swatted his hand away and hooked his forearm, hard, causing Nathan to drop the stick on the ground.

"Your turn," Beck said. He picked up the stick and they repeated the process. Slowly at first, then faster. One time. Two times. And a third for good measure. Each time, Nathan got more proficient at it.

"All right, you've trapped your attacker's weapon hand without getting cut, or shot," Beck said. "Now you need to finish the job by disabling *him*."

They went through it again, in slow motion, with Nathan playing the role of the knife-wielding villain. When Beck had Nathan's arm hooked, he paused. "After you hook the arm, you pivot and plant your left foot outside your attacker's left foot. At the same time, you plant your open palm on his chest and push." Beck did it slowly, calling out each part. "Pivot, step, hand to chest. Got it?"

"Got it."

"All right, time to finish the job. With your weapon hand trapped, my left foot in place, and my open palm on your chest, I'm going to turn and push."

Nathan knew what was coming next. It was that inelegant moment when he'd get thrown to the ground as if being jettisoned off the back of a 1,500 lb. rodeo bull.

"Ready?" said Beck.

Nathan nodded his head. *Giddy-up.*

Beck completed the move just as he'd described: thrusting his hand forward as he twisted his upper torso, flipping Nathan backward over his leg and depositing him on the ground.

Nathan sat there for several seconds, blinking hard, then climbed to his feet.

"I want you to practice it every day," Beck told him. He called out each of the steps as he repeated them in a slow, continuous motion. "Swipe…hook…step…turn and push."

Nathan set himself, then ran through the sequence, reciting each move just as Beck had done. "Swipe…hook…step…turn and push."

"Again," said Beck.

Nathan repeated it once, then again.

"Okay, ready to try it for real?"

"Let's do it," Nathan said.

Beck raised the stick and advanced. Five seconds later, he was on the ground.

As Nathan stood over him, his jaw partially open in disbelief, he looked at his hands, then down at Beck. "That was crazy," he said.

"Crazy?" Beck asked.

"Crazy easy!"

"If you do it right, yeah…it's pretty easy."

"Can we do it again?"

Gina got dressed and hurried downstairs. She stopped in the kitchen to grab a piece of fruit from the refrigerator, then dialed Kendra's number.

Kendra answered on the third ring, her voice barely audible over the sound of coffee beans spilling out of the roaster and into the cooling tray like so many coins from a casino slot machine. "Yeah?" she said, nearly shouting.

"Kendra, it's Gina."

"Hold on." There was a brief pause, then Kendra came back on the line again, the sound of the coffee roaster muted by the walls of her office. "Hey, Gina," she said. "What's up?"

"I need a ride," Gina said. "Actually, Rachel does."

"Rachel? She showed up again?"

"About an hour ago," Gina said. "She left to run some kind of errand and said she'd call when she was done."

"For a ride," Kendra confirmed.

"That's right. Can you do it?"

"Yeah, no problem."

"There's one more thing," Gina said "We need to stash her some-place until later tonight when we deliver her to the courier."

"To the what?"

"Not a what…a who," Gina said. "The person she wanted me to find. The one who's going to take her off our hands for good. Louise suggested I ask Nathan."

"Let me do that."

"Fine by me," Gina said. "Rachel said she'd call me sometime after 10 o'clock. By the way, I have a cellphone now."

Kendra could just see her grinning from ear to ear. "Congratulations," she said. "What's the number?"

Gina read it off to her, then said, "I'll call you when I hear from Rachel."

"Don't bother," Kendra told her. "When I'm done here I'll head over to your house. Do me a favor and don't say anything to Nathan until I get there."

"Why? Do you think he'll have a problem with it?"

"No, it's not that. There's a related matter I need to discuss with him."

"Sounds important," Gina said.

"Important? Yeah, you might say that. If he doesn't want to get both of his arms ripped off, that is."

"You wouldn't…" Gina said.

"That's right, but I'm not talking about me."

At 9:30, Magnus returned to Kendra's coffee shop. He parked at the curb three doors down, then got out of the car and walked up the sidewalk, breathing in the fresh morning air and tilting his face toward the sky, savored the feel of the warm sun on his skin.

Dressed in a black turtleneck and black jeans, with a crisp gray sport coat, he appeared to be just another professor from nearby Tufts University, taking a leisurely walk between classes.

When he came to the narrow alleyway next to the shop, he turned down it and kept walking. It led to a small rectangular parking lot big enough to accommodate about a half dozen cars. He counted five. One of them was Kendra's faded blue Volvo.

Logic dictated that she was at work in the coffee shop, but there was only one way to be sure. He was walking back up the alley toward the street when he heard the sound of a car engine starting up. When he turned around and saw Kendra backing out of her parking space, he sprinted back to his car. He had just climbed in behind the wheel when she tore past him.

He wheeled around in the street, tires squealing, and gave chase. As he sped down the street his cellphone rang. He held it up to see who was calling, then peered over it at the road ahead and pressed the speakerphone button. "Yeah," he said.

Roman sensed a note of anxiety. "Everything okay?" he asked.

"Yeah, I found the helper," Magnus said. "She's a slippery one."

"You know what to do," Roman said.

"Uh-huh."

"Make sure you do it quietly."

After Beck left, Nathan stayed outside in the backyard to practice the moves he'd been shown. He broke them into two parts: the hand-swipe/arm-hook, and the left foot step/left hand thrust. After

234

doing 10 reps of each, he strung them together in a sequence that resembled the graceful moves of a Tai Chi master.

As he worked through the progression, the sound of Kendra's Volvo chugging up the driveway made him stop and look. She came to a grinding halt in front of the garage and called to him through the open window. "Yoga? Really?"

Before he could respond, he heard the back-porch door at Gina's house slam shut. He looked in that direction and saw her sprinting across the wide strip of grass that separated their two driveways. Something was amiss. He walked over to the Volvo just as Kendra was closing the door. "You want to tell me what's going on?" he said.

Gina raced around the back end of the car and nearly toppled over as she skidded to a stop next to Kendra.

"We need to hide Rachel in one of the safehouses," Kendra said.

"For how long?"

"Just…today," Gina managed to say, trying to catch her breath.

"Just today," he confirmed. *What am I running, a daycare center?*

"Yes. Just after midnight…we're…dropping her off…with the guy…" Gina said, her words spilling out of her mouth in broken clusters that were punctured by her erratic breathing.

"The guy? You mean the one you were trying to find?"

Gina nodded her head. *Yeah, him.*

"You found him? With no name or address?"

Again, Gina just nodded.

"Wow, I mean…not wow…more like, amazing, or, awesome, or—"

"Nathan!" Kendra yelled. "The safehouse?"

"Oh, yeah, right. Uh…sure, no problem. Which one?"

"Canton."

"I'm not familiar with that one."

"I know," Kendra said. "That's why you're coming with us."

"Huh?"

"You need to familiarize yourself with each of the safehouses," she said.

"Because?"

"You need to see their layouts and learn their secrets."

"Their secrets?" he said, with a dubious look.

"Yes. If you learn their secrets, you might just survive them."

At 9:45, Allison pulled into a vacant parking space in front of the laundromat. Rachel thanked her for the overnight accommodations and told her she'd be in touch once she had successfully relocated. If it was anything like last time, it wouldn't take more than a couple of days, a week at the most.

"And you're sure about this?" Allison asked. "The girl, the courier...?"

"Will you stop?" Rachel groaned. "It's going to be fine."

Allison looked away, overcome with doubt.

"You need to trust me on this," Rachel said. "It's like you told me last night. If I vanished once, I can do it again."

"You promise you'll call me?" Allison said.

"Yes. I promise."

They exchanged a long hug, then Rachel got out of the car and ducked into the laundromat. There was only one person there, a middle-aged man dressed in a coffee-colored work shirt and dark blue pants. He was pulling clothes out of a canvas duffle bag and dropping them into one of the washing machines. There was a company patch sewn on the breast pocket of his shirt but from where she was standing she couldn't read what it said.

She walked over to the phone and set her backpack on the floor. While she waited for Rios' call she went to the window and watched the street. Cars lined the curb on both sides and pedestrians were passing by on the sidewalk, each one walking with purpose to their chosen destination. Not a single one looked her way or seemed the least bit suspicious.

The payphone rang at precisely 10 o'clock. The man with the duffle bag looked her way briefly, then finished feeding the machine with quarters. She raced back to the phone and grabbed the handset before the second ring.

"Hello?"

"It's me," Rios said.

He sounded distracted.

"This is your burner?" she asked.

"Yes."

"Hold on," she said, realizing she should have gotten the number from him during their previous phone call. She clamped the handset against the side of her face and pulled her cellphone from her pocket. "Okay, what's the number?" As he read it off, she entered it into her phone and then gave him her new number. "So much for them tracking us," she muttered as she stuffed the cellphone back in her pocket.

"Them? Last night you told me Bolan, Cafferty and Rodano are gone."

"They are," she replied.

"Gone where?"

She had no idea of their current whereabouts, but she wasn't about to tell him that. "Does it matter?" she said, dodging the question.

"Of course, it does," he shot back. "If they're not still chasing you, it means that Roman has brought in someone else to finish the job."

Rachel said nothing, leaving an awkward gap in their conversation.

"All right, who is it?" he asked. "Who did he send?"

The mechanical thrum of a washing machine starting its wash cycle filled the room.

"Magnus," she said, meekly.

"Speak up, I can't hear you."

"He sent Magnus," she said, louder.

Rios pulled the phone from his ear, blew out an angry breath, then pressed the phone to his ear again. "You need to leave the area immediately," he said. "Not tonight. Not tomorrow. Right now!"

"But…"

"Now!"

"Okay, fine. I'll grab a taxi and—"

"No!" he barked, cutting her off mid-sentence. "A taxi driver will remember your face, especially if Magnus shows him your picture. Take a bus to the South Station Greyhound terminal and mix in with the crowd. Take the earliest bus available, preferably an express to the furthest location. Call me when you arrive."

"I will."

She hung up the phone and picked up her backpack. Standing at the window, she took out her cellphone and called Gina.

238

"Hi, Gina? It's Rachel. I'm ready for that ride now."

Fifteen minutes later, Kendra pulled up to the curb across the street. Nathan was sitting in the front seat while Gina sat directly behind him, clinging tightly to the arm rest with both hands, relieved that she'd survived another pulse-pounding ride with Kendra at the wheel.

Rachel was pacing back and forth at the front window of the laundromat, but when she saw the Volvo she pulled the hood of her sweatshirt up over her head and hurried outside. She was halfway across the street when she paused to let an MBTA bus pass, leaving her standing in a cloud of thin gray exhaust.

When she finally made it into the backseat of the car, she clutched her backpack to her chest and looked out the window, surveying the line of parked cars across the street. She still hadn't acknowledged Kendra or Nathan.

"Laundry?" Gina groaned. "*That* was the errand you had to run?"

"Yup," Rachel said, turning her attention on the pedestrians filing past on the sidewalk.

Gina looked up at the rearview mirror and saw Kendra looking back at her. For several seconds the two shared a wary look.

"Are we just going to sit here?" Rachel asked. She turned from the window and eyed Gina, then Nathan, and then Kendra, trying to get a read on them. No one was talking, which tweaked her paranoia. She slid her hand off the backpack and reached for the door handle just as Kendra stabbed her foot down on the gas pedal and the Volvo shot away from the curb and rocketed down the street.

Nathan and Gina had anticipated it and were already holding

onto something. Rachel wasn't so fortunate. She was thrown backward and her head bounced off the headrest.

Kendra glanced up at the rearview mirror and saw her grimacing as she rubbed the back of her head. *You were saying?*

Three storefronts down from the laundromat, Scottie Rios was parked at the curb in his dark blue Mustang GT Coupe. He watched Rachel exit and make her way across the street, her pink sweatshirt like a lighthouse beacon cutting through the dark of night.

After their phone conversation, he expected to see her wait on the sidewalk for the next inbound bus, one of that would take her to the Red Line, and from there to South Station. But when she climbed into Kendra's beat-up Volvo, his mood grew dark.

Why had she ignored his directive? Had the driver of the Volvo offered to take her to South Station directly? That seemed like a stretch, unless they were already planning on going there. Again, what were the odds of such a chance encounter? As the Volvo drove away, he started the car and fell in with the Monday morning traffic, keeping far enough back to blend in. He was so busy watching the Volvo that he didn't notice the metallic brown sedan three cars back. Or the massive build of the driver.

Kendra had gone a quarter of a mile when she first noticed the Mustang in the line of cars behind her. *Nice!* she thought, although, given the choice she would've gone with the Race Red. *Yeah, definitely the red,* she told herself.

A half mile later it was still there, which wasn't a big deal; Mt. Auburn Street was a busy road, especially on Monday mornings. But after another mile she noticed it again. The driver was maintaining a constant four-car buffer, and that was a very big deal.

They had just crossed the Newton town line when Nathan noticed her checking and re-checking the rearview mirror. "What's wrong?" he asked.

"We have company," she said.

"Are you sure?" he asked, glancing at the side mirror.

"Let's find out."

She changed lanes and veered right onto Washington Street, bypassing the Centre Street intersection and the short connector that would put them on Rt. 90 West.

Rios did the same.

Three traffic lights later, Kendra swerved left onto Church Street just as the traffic signal turned red.

"What are you doing?" Rachel shouted as she was thrown sideways in the seat.

"Saving your life," Kendra fired back. "You can thank me later."

15   *John Keats*

Button, Button, Who's Got The Button?

Rios had no intention of stopping at the light. As Kendra disappeared from view, he pulled into the right lane and accelerated past the three cars at the front of the line. He had just cleared the last one when he cut back across the intersection and shot down Church Street amidst a chorus of blaring horns.

Waiting in line several cars back, Magnus saw Kendra turn left, followed by the dark blue Mustang that had been tailing her all the way from the laundromat. "Who do we have here?" he said aloud as the line of traffic began to inch forward. He made the turn onto Church Street and picked up speed, hoping not to lose sight of the Mustang, which seemed to be tethered to the Volvo for reasons he couldn't imagine. With his free hand he thumbed Roman's number and waited for the call to connect.

"You have an update for me?" Roman asked, straightaway.

"Yeah," Magnus said. "I'm following the helper. She has the target with her."

"Well what do you know?" Roman said, upbeat. "You hit the daily double."

Church Street crossed Rt. 90 and then bent to the left. After that, it was a straight shot all the way to Centre Street. When Kendra hit the open stretch of road, she leaned on the gas pedal and doubled the posted limit, checking the rearview mirror every few seconds.

Rachel twisted around in the seat and looked out the back window. "Who's chasing us?"

"Someone in a blue Mustang," Kendra said. "You know anyone who drives one?"

Rachel searched her memory but no one came to mind. "No."

There were approaching the Centre Street traffic light when the Mustang came into view a quarter mile back. Kendra took a right, then another onto Wesley Street, which turned out to be nothing more than a small rectangular loop. She made the first turn and then slowed to a crawl, buying as much time as she could.

Magnus reached the straightaway and saw the Mustang at the far end, waiting at the Centre Street intersection. It was there for a split second before it turned right and disappeared from view.

He drove faster.

As Kendra came around the second turn, she eyed the far end of the street and saw traffic streaming by on Centre Street. She continued on slowly, taking note of every vehicle. So far she hadn't seen anything with a dark blue paint job manufactured by the Ford Motor Company. It wasn't until she reached the stop sign that she saw the Mustang fly past in a blur.

"*That* blue Mustang?" Nathan asked, tracking it with his index finger.

"That's the one," Kendra said.

Suddenly, its brake lights flared.

"Uh…Kendra?"

"Yeah, I saw it."

She muttered something under her breath and then shot straight across onto Hollis Street.

"Do you know where you're going?" Rachel asked.

"Nope," Kendra said. "Just makin' it up as I go."

Rachel sat back in the seat and nibbled the edge of her lip. Her plan, so perfect in its planning, was suddenly crumbling before her very eyes. She turned to Gina and asked, "Did you find the rest of the information?"

Gina was leaning forward, watching the road ahead. "Uh-huh."

"And?" Rachel said, exasperated. Getting information out of a 13-year-old was like trying to pry a rusty spike from a railroad tie.

"Worcester," Gina said.

Rachel's expression brightened. "Are you sure?"

"Yes."

Rachel breathed a sigh of relief. In a matter of days, this nightmare would be a distant memory. She'd be free of Roman's boss and his merry band of mercenaries and she could start reconstructing her previous life of luxury. This time, however, she'd do it differently. She'd be smarter and more careful—two safeguards that would make her untouchable.

Rios only saw Kendra's Volvo for a split second as he drove past, but his rearview mirror confirmed that it was her. He jammed his foot on the brake and came to a stop at the next street, Franklin Avenue, cursing as he had to wait for a line of oncoming cars to pass. When he finally saw an opening, he shot through the turn, the Mustang's tires scorching the pavement yet again.

He drove past the giant beehive of condos on the corner, then pulled into the driveway and reversed direction. As he waited to pull back out onto Centre Street, he took his phone from the illuminated cupholder and punched in a number that was rooted in his memory like a weed.

It took several rings but Shawn Quinlan finally answered. He and his brother Derrick were sitting at the bar in their favorite pub on Harvard Ave in Allston. They had just returned from a week-long hunting trip in Maine and were still dressed in their customary woodland attire of green, army-issue, commando sweaters and camo pants.

"Scottie! You missed a helluva trip," Shawn bellowed, his voice barely audible over the sound of the jukebox blasting a ZZ Top song in the background. Something about cheap sunglasses.

"Where are you guys?" Rios asked, keeping his eyes glued to the seemingly endless line of traffic.

"We're skimmin' the foam off a couple of pints. Care to join us?"

"Can't," Rios said. "I need your help. Are you boys still in the hunting mood?"

"Always," Shawn replied. "Why, what'cha got?"

"A varmint," Rios said.

Derrick elbowed his brother. "Who are you talking to?"

Shawn leaned away from the phone and said, "It's Scottie. He's got a pest problem he needs help with."

"Well, what are we waiting for?" Derrick shouted. He slammed his empty mug on the bar. "Let's go help the man!"

After making the turn onto Centre Street, Magnus searched the traffic ahead but saw no sign of the Mustang. Just then, he saw Kendra's battered blue Volvo streak across the road from right to left, cutting through a break in the traffic before disappearing down a side street. He drove past it then pulled over to the curb to ponder his next move. He hadn't been there long when he spotted the Mustang driving straight toward him. As it passed him, he got a brief look at the driver. "Was that?...no, it couldn't be," he said out loud.

Hollis Street was another loop. It was larger than Wesley Street and shaped like an elephant's ear. Kendra made the first turn and then pulled to the curb, stopping next to a row of towering ash trees that were bathing the street in shade.

The neighborhood looked like a Norman Rockwell painting. Anytown, U.S.A. The houses were solid 1960s construction, each one painted a pleasing pastel color. The lawns were neatly mowed and every shrub was expertly maintained. The only thing missing was a group of skinny kids playing stickball, chasing a Labrador Retriever that had stolen first base.

"What are we doing?" Rachel asked, nervously.

"Waiting," Kendra told her.

"For what?"

"The ice cream man...what do you *think* we're waiting for?"

Rachel closed her eyes and flopped her head forward, resigned to the fact that her plan was circling the drain.

They sat there for another minute before Kendra finally drove to the next turn in the road. From there, it was a straight shot all the way to Centre Street. She eased around the corner and picked up speed, keeping her eyes trained on the road ahead when she detected a low rumbling sound. It grew steadily louder until, suddenly, the Mustang appeared on her left side. Rios pulled ahead and then angled to the right, forcing her off the road. She missed a telephone pole by less than six inches before skidding to a stop on the lawn of a large multi-apartment dwelling.

Rios was out of the car in a flash. His black tee shirt and thin black-leather jacket made him look like he'd just climbed off a Harley, but the gun he was holding down by his side painted a very different picture.

When Rachel saw him, she slid down in the seat. *What's he doing here?*

Kendra had no intention of sticking around to find out. "Everybody hold on," she said, then shifted into reverse and mashed her foot down on the gas pedal. The Volvo's tires bit into the lawn and sent the car shooting backward. By the time Rios climbed back into his car, she had already reached the stop sign at the end of the street.

She turned left onto Centre Street, pulling out ahead of a long line of cars, then drove south toward Rt. 9, a road that would take her west to Rt. 95, and from there, south to Canton. In the rearview mirror she saw Rios waiting to pull out, and with every car that delayed him she was that much closer to losing him for good. But she wasn't about to leave it to chance.

As they passed the Newton Country Day School, she saw an opening and cut into the left lane, ignoring the double-yellow line as she sped past a service van. At the Boston College Law Library, she did it again, this time powering past a trio of cars.

Rachel sat like a granite statue in the back seat, struggling to understand Rios' sudden appearance and his aggressive behavior. *Was he spying on me? He must be. Why else would he be following us? If he was so bent on me leaving the area, why didn't he just take me to South Station himself? Is he just being paranoid or does he know something I don't? And what was with the gun?*

They had just crossed Commonwealth Ave when Kendra said, "Did you recognize that guy?"

"I'm sorry, what?" Rachel said, snapping back into the moment.

"The guy in the Mustang. Have you ever seen him before?"

"No," Rachel lied. In truth, she'd seen him plenty of times. They'd met years ago at Metro in Boston and several dates followed. After that things got much more serious. But that was more than seven years ago. Other than their phone communications, she hadn't seen him in person since that time.

Rios waited at the stop sign, cursing the line of cars slogging past. He finally saw an opening and shot out onto Centre Street. As he blasted by one car after another, zipping in and out of the left lane just as Kendra had done, he got a call from Shawn Quinlan.

"Hey buddy, where's the fire?" Quinlan said.

The roar of the Mustang's engine made it difficult for Rios to hear. "What was that?" he shouted. He sailed around a mail delivery truck and then swerved back into the right lane, narrowly missing an oncoming car.

"You still want our help?" Quinlan said.

"Yes," Rios said. "Where are you?"

"Look in your rearview mirror."

Traffic slowed to a crawl as Kendra approached Newton Centre. She'd been checking her mirror repeatedly and was yet to see any sign of the Mustang. Nathan was monitoring the side mirror and Gina was turned around with her elbow resting on the rear deck, offering yet another set of eyes on the long string of traffic behind them. Rachel was still sitting motionless, her mind trapped in a void that was free of logic or reason.

The plan she'd made with Scottie was simple: let me do this my way and everything will work out fine. And so far, it had. She'd managed to elude Bolan and his cronies, Magnus had yet to get within five feet of her, and Gina had found the critical information that would ensure a clean getaway into a life without worry. So, what changed?

They had just passed Crystal Lake when Kendra spotted the Mustang. By some miracle of driving, or traffic, or speed, it seemed to appear out of nowhere and was now less than 10 cars back.

"I see him!" Nathan exclaimed.

Rachel spun around in the seat and looked back just as Rios sped past another car that was making a leisurely turn onto a side street.

He was eight cars back.

"He's getting closer!" Rachel exclaimed. "Can't you go any

faster?"

"It's too late for that," Kendra said, as they were approaching Rt. 9. "Now that he caught up to us, there's no way we can outrun him; his car is too fast. But there might be another way to lose him."

"And how do you plan to do that?" Rachel snipped.

Two cars in front of Rios turned off on Walnut street.

Now he was just six cars back.

"How?" Kendra said. She veered right onto the Boylston Street, a short connector to Rt. 9. "You ever hear of the game called Button, Button Who's Got the Button?"

Ten seconds later, Rios made the same turn. Following right behind him were the Quinlan brothers in their dark brown Chevy Silverado. The body was encrusted with a thick layer of dirt from their week-long romp in the Maine woods and it was difficult to tell what was the original factory paint job and what was Oxford County mud.

The Monday morning lunch surge had begun in earnest and traffic on Rt. 9 was bunching up, stopping and starting in surges. When Rios got to the top of the ramp, he drove down the shoulder and bullied his way into the next lane seconds before traffic came to a halt at the Woodward Street traffic light. Three cars ahead of him, sitting at the front of the line, was the battered blue Volvo.

Kendra took note of Rios in her rearview mirror, then surveyed the intersection. For her plan to work, timing would be critical. She looked at the car next to her in the left-turn lane—a ragged Toyota Corolla with a magnetic Papa John's Pizza sign stuck to the roof.

The driver was a teenage kid with spikey hair that looked like a variegated spider plant. One arm was draped over the steering wheel and he was bobbing his head to the sound of Bob Marley's "Three Little Birds" blasting from the car's speakers.

She looked to her right, at the traffic light support pole. From where they sat she had a perfect view of the three-light stack that regulated the traffic crossing from the left and right. The light was green but would change at any moment. "You guys might want to grab a hold of something," she said, watching the light.

The words had barely left her lips when the light changed from green to yellow. With only seconds at her disposal, she punched the gas and the Volvo shot forward into the empty intersection. She cranked the steering wheel hard to the left and fishtailed, then yanked the wheel back to the right to stop the skid and stepped on the gas pedal, sending the Volvo speeding down Rt. 9 in the opposite direction.

Rios saw her jump the light and immediately tried to squeeze into the left-turn lane. He edged the nose of the Mustang across the line but no one could move and he was forced to wait yet again. When the traffic light changed, he cut into the line of cars that were slowly crawling forward behind Pizza Boy, who was bobbing his head to the loud Rastafarian beat as he made an unhurried U-turn.

Kendra went a short distance and turned sharply into the parking lot of a modern, two-story professional building. "Get ready to jump out," she said, as she drove around to the back.

"Jump *out?*" Rachel shouted.

"Yes," Kendra said. "You guys hide here while I lure the Mustang guy away. After I lose him, I'll circle back and pick you up. Wait for my call, then meet me here behind the building."

Suddenly, Rachel understood Kendra's cryptic button-game reference: she'd drop them off before Rios could see her do it, then lure him away making him think they were still in the car with her. "What if he doesn't fall for it?" she asked.

"Make sure you're someplace where he can't find you," Kendra said. She came to an abrupt stop at the back entrance and shouted, "GO!"

After they piled out of the car, she made a tight U-turn and left the way she'd come in. When she got to the street, she looked left and saw Pizza Boy leading a procession of cars like it was a parade through the streets of Venice during Carnival. She waited until Rios made the turn then pulled out onto Rt.9 and sped away, watching him in her rearview mirror as he took the bait.

Magnus saw the whole thing unfold from across the median strip as he sat in the line of traffic that had once again stalled at the light. When the Mustang screamed past, he got another look at the driver's face. It was brief, but enough to confirm his suspicion. He grabbed his phone and called Roman.

"Hey," he said, after Roman answered. "You remember that punk we ruffed up a few years ago? Scottie Rios?"

"Rios? Yeah, I remember that lowlife. Why do you ask?"

"He seems to have taken an interest in our target."

"And why would he do that?" Roman asked.

"Beats me."

"You keep him away from her!" Roman said, loudly. "She's ours!"

"Understood."

"Under no circumstances is he to go near her!"

"I'll take care of it," Magnus said.

"You do that. And feel free to use whatever means necessary."

Click!

Kendra maintained a constant speed for a quarter mile before turning down Walnut Street. The road went straight for a short distance before bending to the right. She cruised through the turn in the road and picked up speed, racing through the thickly settled residential neighborhood faster than she would ordinarily drive. "Sorry folks," she said aloud, "I have an armed crazy man chasing me."

When she came to the junction of Dedham Street, she slowed and made a rolling stop at the stop sign, then continued straight in hopes of drawing Rios further away.

Rachel, Nathan, and Gina rushed through the back door and found themselves in a small entryway. Directly ahead of them was a hallway that led to the front of the building. On the wall to their right was a large directory that listed every business in the building, which floor it was on, and the suite number. To their left was a narrow stairway that led to the second floor.

"This way," Nathan said, starting down the hallway. They followed it to the front foyer, a cavernous space tiled in white marble that had been buffed to a glossy sheen. A wide marble stairway led up to the second floor, and directly across from it, through the front doors, they could see traffic racing past in both directions on Rt. 9. To the left and right, matching hallways stretched to either end of the building.

"What now?" Rachel asked.

"It's like Kendra said, we need to find a place to hide in case her plan doesn't work." He looked left, then right, surveying each of the hallways. Unlike a conventional office building with solid walls decorated with stylish artwork, these offices were a modern design with large plate-glass façades and glass doors stenciled with the name of the business. He knew they could just duck into any one of them and give the receptionist a hard-luck story about having to wait for a ride, but the glass would make them completely visible to anyone passing by in the hallway.

"You two wait here while I go look around. Rachel, you watch the front door. Gina, you watch the back. If either of you see a dark blue Mustang, call me."

"Call you?" Rachel asked. "On your phone?"

"No," Nathan said. "Shout."

He hurried down the hallway, his eyes darting from side to side as he assessed their options. He had passed several offices when he came to one that was undergoing renovations. It had been completely gutted and the overhead lights were turned off. The only illumination came from the windows that faced the street. He tried the door, found it unlocked, and stepped inside.

Several step ladders were positioned around the room, set directly beneath large openings in the ceiling. A wooden pallet parked just inside the door was loaded with boxes of new lighting fixtures. He walked the perimeter of the room, looking for a place that would hide three people who didn't want to be seen, but he found nothing.

No bathroom.

No break room.

Not even a supply closet.

Kendra continued down Dedham Street at a steady clip. When she reached the Charles River Country Club, she pulled down a side street and made a quick three-point turn, then parked at the curb and dialed Gina's number.

As the call connected, Gina was in the ladies' room just off the front foyer. She was standing at the sink drying her hands with a paper towel when her phone rang. She pulled it from her pocket and checked the call screen, then tapped the talk button. "Tell me you lost him," she said.

"I lost him," Kendra replied. "I'm going to head back your way now. Should be there in less than ten minutes."

"All right, see you then."

Gina ended the call and left the bathroom. When she walked back into the front foyer, Rachel was gone. "Now where did she go?" she groaned. She scanned the hallway in each direction, saw no one, then climbed the stairs to the second floor.

Nathan stepped back out into the hallway and hurried back to the foyer. When he reached the front door, he stopped and did a slow 360° turn. "Where did they go?" he mumbled. "They were right here."

He sprinted up the center stairway, to a tiled landing that was roughly 10' square, and saw Gina standing at a large window that overlooked the parking lot below. "What are you doing?" he asked.

"I'm watching for Kendra. She'll be here any minute now."

"How do you know that?"

"I spoke with her."

"You *spoke* with her?" Nathan asked, perplexed. "How?"

"I'll explain later."

Nathan let it go. "Where's Rachel?" he asked.

Gina spun around to face him. "She's not with you?"

"With me? The last time I saw her she was in the foyer with *you*."

"She was. I used the bathroom and when I came out she was gone. I figured she went off to find you."

Before Nathan could respond, the sound of shuffling feet erupted from the first floor as someone exploded through the front entrance, followed by a second person, then a third. He edged over toward the stairway and looked down into the foyer. The driver of the Mustang was standing ten feet inside the front door, flanked by two men clad in olive-green commando sweaters and baggy camo pants. Each man was holding a handgun.

He backed away from the top step and hurried back to Gina. "They found us," he whispered. He looked to his left and saw a hallway that extended past a row of offices. To his right, the same. Tucked in the corner was a gray metal door with a small square window. He ran to it, peered through the glass, and saw a narrow stairway that led back downstairs.

Rios' voice thundered up the stairs. "You!" he barked at Shawn. "Check that end of the building." Then, to Derrick, "You check that end. I'll look upstairs."

Nathan pushed the metal door open with one hand and motioned frantically to Gina with the other. *This way, hurry!*

She ran to the door and paused. "What about Rachel?"

The sound of heavy boots scuffing the polished marble was

growing louder.

"For all we know, she could be back outside. Now, go!"

As Gina disappeared down the back stairway, he sprinted down the opposite hallway, passing the same style of glass-front offices that he'd seen on the first floor. He came to the end of the hall, where it took a 90° turn to the left, when Rachel stepped around the corner. The resulting collision stunned them both and sent them tumbling to the floor just as Rios reached the top of the marble stairs. When he looked down the hallway and saw Nathan and Rachel laying in a heap on the floor, he turned toward the stairway and shouted, "UP HERE!"

Nathan, groggy from the collision, sat up and shook Rachel's shoulder. "Hey!"

She didn't move.

He shook her shoulder again, harder. "Get up!"

Behind him, the sound of footsteps, running.

Rachel made a soft murmuring sound, as if lost in a dream, but her eyes didn't open.

Nathan shook her again when the sound of footsteps stopped.

In the silence that followed, he turned and saw a Beretta M9 pistol pointed directly at his head.

16 *R.w. Emerson*

Sebastian and Leopold

Rios jammed the barrel of the gun into Nathan's neck. "Get your hands off her," he snarled.

Nathan let go of her and held his hands up in the air as a show of surrender. *So much for Kendra's button plan,* he thought.

"That was a nifty trick your friend pulled," Rios said. "Too bad it didn't work. Now, stand up." He flicked the barrel of the gun upward as if Nathan had no idea what 'up' meant.

Using his right hand for support, Nathan brought his left knee up and placed his foot squarely on the floor, followed by his right, mimicking the three-point stance of a pro football center.

"Slow!" Rios said, keeping the gun pointed at Nathan's head.

As Nathan slowly stood up, he kept his eyes glued on Rios' left arm and gun hand.

"Over there," Rios said, waving the gun toward the far wall.

Nathan held both hands up at shoulder height. "Okay, okay, relax…I'm going."

Rachel stirred, making a painful groaning sound as she brought her hand up to her aching head.

Rios looked down at her for a brief second and that was the opening Nathan needed. He swatted Rios' gun hand aside and then hooked his arm. As Rios struggled to break free, the gun went off with a deafening roar and the glass wall behind Nathan shattered into a thousand pieces.

Just as he'd practiced, he stepped forward and placed his left foot outside of Rios' left foot, then thrust his open palm into Rios' chest. Rios wasn't big by any means and when Nathan pushed him, his wiry frame tumbled over with ease and he dropped the gun. But as he fell he grabbed hold of Nathan's shirt, just as Beck had done in the backyard.

As Nathan rode him down, he slid his hand up to Rios' throat and slammed his head against the hard tile. Rios blacked out and Nathan quickly scrambled to his feet. He helped Rachel up and she leaned on him for support as they made their way up the hallway. They reached the landing and pushed through the metal door just as the Quinlan brothers came rushing up the center stairway. The sound of their boots on the marble steps was like the pounding hooves of a buffalo stampede.

Kendra was on Winchester Street, racing back toward Rt. 9, when her phone rang. She had yet to see any sign of the blue Mustang and when she saw Gina's name on the call screen she got a bad feeling in her gut. "Gina, what's up? Are you guys okay?"

"Uh...no," Gina said, pointedly. "The Mustang guy showed up, along with two goons."

Kendra clenched her fist in anger. Somehow, Rios had seen through her ruse and had doubled back without her knowing it. "Where are you now?" she asked.

"I'm outside, hiding behind a dumpster."

"What about Nathan and Rachel?"

"He's still inside, looking for her."

"*What?*" Kendra shouted.

"She disappeared just before the three guys showed up. Nathan sent me outside while he went to...wait...I see them. They just came out of the building."

"What about Mustang Man?"

"I haven't seen him." The words had barely left her lips when she saw two hulk-like figures in the picture window that overlooked the parking lot—the exact same spot where she'd been standing just moments earlier. "Uh...Kendra? I think we have another problem."

"Why, what's wrong?" Kendra asked. She pressed on the accelerator, nearly doubling the speed limit.

"Those two goons that came in with the Mustang guy are on the second floor, watching the parking lot through the window."

Kendra swerved around an SUV backing out of a driveway. "Did they see you?"

"I think so."

"Okay, good. Here's what I want you to do."

As Gina listened, she leaned around the corner of the dumpster and motioned to Nathan, who was standing with Rachel at the back door, scanning the parking lot. They started across the lot when she jumped out from behind the dumpster and rushed over to meet them. "Wave," she said.

"Do what?" Nathan asked.

"Wave. Up there," she said, nodding at the second story window.

Nathan turned and looked up. Rios was standing at the window between the Quinlan brothers, leaning on them for support and looking ragged and unsteady.

"Don't forget to smile," Gina said, waving.

Nathan raised his arm and gave a tentative wave. "And why are we doing this?" he asked, keeping his eyes trained on Rios.

"Watch."

Kendra was passing beneath the Rt. 9 overpass when her phone rang again. It was Louise this time. She thumbed the talk button with one hand as she palmed the wheel with the other, cutting a sharp left onto Boylston Street, the same route she'd taken less than an hour earlier. "Hey," she said.

"Did Gina call you for a ride?" Louise asked, ignoring the screech of squealing tires in the background. It was a sound she'd grown accustomed to whenever she spoke with Kendra on the phone.

"Already done," Kendra said. "I was taking Rachel to one of the safehouses when we picked up a tail. Some guy with a serious attitude driving a dark blue Mustang."

"Did you do something to make him mad?"

"No!" Kendra said, offended by the question. Not that angering other motorists hadn't become a staple of her driving.

"Just checking," Louise said. "Are you okay?"

"Me? I'm fine. Rachel and the kids? That's yet to be determined."

"Get ready to run," Gina said, watching the window. Rios was pointing at Rachel, as if casting a magical spell with his finger that would make her freeze in place.

She stared up at him, confused. *What are you doing?* she mouthed.

"Now!" Gina said. She sprinted to her right with Nathan and Rachel doing their best to keep up. When they were out of sight of the window, she circled back and crept past the back door, staying close to the wall to avoid being seen from overhead. They had just ducked around the far end of the building when the Quinlan brothers burst through the back door and ran in the opposite direction.

Rios wasn't with them.

"This way," Gina said. She darted across the narrow street that ran behind the building, then continued into a nearby strip-mall parking lot. They had just stepped up on the sidewalk in front of a large CVS store when Kendra's Volvo came to a screeching stop at the curb behind them.

"Everyone okay?" she shouted, through the open window.

"Just barely," Gina said.

They climbed into the car and 15 minutes later they were speeding down Rt. 95 toward Canton. As they drove, Nathan told Kendra about their run-in on the second floor with the driver of the Mustang.

"He pulled a *gun* on you?" she exclaimed.

"Uh-huh," Nathan said, realizing how close he'd come to getting shot.

Kendra looked at Gina in the rearview mirror. "Beck and I are coming with you tonight," she said, matter-of-factly.

"Can I come too?" Nathan asked.

"YES!" Kendra and Gina blurted out at the same time.

Magnus was a dozen cars back. Four cars in front of him, Rios was tailgating a 17' U-Haul moving truck, using its size to obscure his car as he tracked the Volvo south. Magnus had been following his every move, starting from when he took off after Kendra on Rt. 9, to his sudden decision to turn back and return to the professional building. Parked in an adjoining lot, Magnus watched Rios enter the building with two other men dressed in matching camo gear. A short time later Rios pushed through the front door, walking erratically like the ground was shifting beneath his feet.

At nearly the same time, the two men with him exited the back door. They ran for a short distance before stopping and turning around, just in time to see Rachel, Nathan, and Gina sprinting toward the strip mall parking lot.

He waited and watched as Rios and his two associates fell in line behind Kendra after she pulled out onto Rt. 9, headed for Rt. 95. As he tailed them down the highway, he once again wondered what interest Rios could possibly have with Rachel Goudas. Whatever it was, he needed to find a way to erase Rios from the equation without Kendra or Rachel seeing him do it.

The Canton safehouse was an old farm-style home on Pleasant Street, directly across from the Pequit Brook Conservation Area. It was set well back from the road and the wrap-around porch gave it a decidedly old-timey appearance. Behind the house, set at a 90° angle, was a three-bay post & beam carriage house with single-pane transom windows, dark wooden siding and a louvered cupola.

The entire parcel was fenced in by a tall spear-topped wrought iron fence. The only access was through an arched gate at the mouth of the driveway, which required visitors to identify themselves before they were allowed access to the property.

"Okay, a couple of ground rules," Kendra said, as they passed Reservoir Pond. "Once we're at the house, no one gets out of the car. Understood?"

"So, we're just going to *sit* there?" Rachel sniped.

"That's right," Kendra said. "Do not open your door. Sebastian and Leopold take that as a sign of aggression."

"Who?" Rachel asked.

"You'll see," Kendra said as she slowed and then turned into the driveway. It went for several feet before stopping at the locked gate. She rolled up to the intercom that was mounted on a gooseneck post and lowered her window. From the far side of the yard came the low-pitched growl of two large dogs. It was faint at first but grew steadily louder with each passing second.

"I see you're still driving that infernal death trap," Burgess said through the intercom speaker.

Right on cue, Kendra said, "You don't like my baby? She's a classic."

Hearing the code word that indicated everything was fine, Burgess opened the gate. If it were otherwise, Kendra would have uttered a very different response.

As they drove onto the property, Rachel watched the dogs running along either side of the car. They were Bullmastiffs, over 100 lbs. each, and muscular, with smooth, almost silky, caramel-colored fur. "Let me guess," she said. "Sebastian and Leopold?"

"Yup," Kendra said. "Don't talk to them. Don't make any sudden moves in their direction. And whatever you do, don't even think about petting them, unless you don't care about getting your hand back."

"Lovely," Rachel muttered to herself.

Kendra followed the driveway around to the back of the house where they couldn't be seen from the street. After she turned off the car, she twisted around in the seat and spoke directly to Gina. "Let's talk about the schedule."

"Rachel stays here this afternoon," Gina said. "Later tonight, Louise and I will come back and pick her up, then drive straight to Worcester."

Rachel sat quietly, eyeing the back of the house. Her attention was drawn to the narrow flower garden that ran along the base of the porch. It was packed with Astilbes, Shasta Daisies, Salvia, Asters and Peonies set between spidery tufts of Hakone Grass. *This isn't so bad,* she told herself. It was certainly an upgrade from some of the rat-infested dumps she'd hidden in after she'd fled North Carolina.

As they waited, Sebastian and Leopold circled the Volvo, sniffing frantically at the doors and whining. The back door of the house opened and Burgess stepped out onto the porch. He was dressed in a gray tee shirt beneath an untucked blue-denim work shirt. That, and his rugged Carhartt pants, gave him the look of a man about to do some serious yardwork. He walked as far as the top step and shouted, "DOWN!"

Sebastian and Leopold stopped their inspection of the Volvo at once and laid down on the ground, their tongues hanging out of their mouths as they panted in the midday sun.

265

Kendra lowered the window and watched Burgess walk down the steps, work gloves in hand. He looked exactly like she remembered him: ruggedly built, with stylishly long salt and pepper hair that was combed back, and a well-groomed moustache and goatee. "You're not going to ask me to mow the lawn are you?" she quipped.

"I remember a time when you'd *offer* to do it," Burgess said, smirking.

Kendra climbed out of the car and they exchanged a warm hug.

"How's your dad?" he asked.

"Oh, you know Jameson," she replied. "He never changes."

"I see you brought company," Burgess said, leaning down to peer through the window at Nathan, Gina, and Rachel.

"Guys! It's okay," Kendra said, motioning for them to join her. One by one they got out of the car, each of them cutting a wide berth around Sebastian and Leopold. When they were all assembled next to her, she began the introductions. "Burgess, this is Nathan Cole."

"Nathan Cole," Burgess said, smiling as he extended his hand. "I've heard quite a bit about you. All good. When your schedule allows, there are things we need to discuss. I imagine you'll enjoy hearing about some of the adventures your grandfather and I went on."

"Went on?" Kendra said, with a wary look. "Don't you mean, barely survived?"

Burgess gave her a wink.

"Yes, absolutely" Nathan replied, his curiosity spiking.

"And this is Gina McDermott," Kendra said, gesturing toward her with a sweep of her hand.

"Ah, yes, Ms. McDermott," Burgess said. Again, he offered his hand and they shook. "Your fame precedes you."

She smiled and looked over at Nathan. "Hear that?" she said. "My fame."

He rolled his eyes. *Spare me.*

"And your guest for the rest of the day," Kendra said, motioning toward Rachel, "is Rachel Goudas."

"Rachel, a pleasure," Burgess said, with a curt nod.

Kendra took him by the arm and gently ushered him away from the others. "There are two people chasing her, that we know of. I doubt they'll find her here, but it wouldn't hurt to keep a close eye on the yard. We'll be back at midnight to pick her up. Until then, watch her. She has a nasty habit of disappearing."

"Sebastian and Leopold will keep her in check," Burgess said, confidently. "Of course, if the house isn't to her liking, we have other accommodations."

"Let's hope it doesn't come to that," Kendra said, knowing full well what accommodations he was referring to.

Dark and dreary.

Windowless.

Buried in the ground several feet below where they were standing.

Rios slowed as he drove past the safehouse, taking note of the perimeter fencing and the locked gate. He continued to the next side street, drove a short way, then parked on the shoulder. As he sat there considering his options, a bright flash of light made him look up at his rearview mirror.

A metallic brown sedan had turned onto the street, the sunlight bouncing off its windshield. But instead of driving past, it pulled up directly behind him. He continued staring at the rearview mirror, trying to see the driver through the glare of the sun, when Magnus suddenly appeared at the window, his giant frame covering it like a drape.

He pulled the door open and grabbed Rios with both hands, then yanked him out of the car like he was a straw doll. He slammed him up against the side of the car and said, "Hey there Scottie. Remember me?" His ominous tone suggested that Rios' day was about to take a very bad turn.

"Yeah, I remember you, now let go of me!" Rios shouted, struggling to break free. "I got no beef with you."

The growl of a truck engine broke the tension of the moment as the Quinlan brothers came to a stop behind Magnus' sedan. They jumped out of the truck and took tactical positions behind him, leaving him no clear path of escape.

"You wanna take your hands off my friend?" Shawn said.

"I'd do as he says," Derrick added.

Rios shook his head to warn them off. *NO!...DON'T!*

Too late.

Magnus' fist flew with blinding speed in a reverse lateral swipe that smashed Shawn's nose with the force of a sledgehammer. He staggered backward, stunned, blood gushing from his nose, and Derrick grabbed him to keep him from collapsing on the pavement.

Magnus kept a firm grasp of Rios' throat as he turned and looked at the Quinlan brothers for the first time. "Leave. Now. Or you'll get worse than that," he told them.

Derrick stood Shawn upright and helped him stumble back to the truck. Neither one bothered to look back as they drove away.

Magnus watched them go, then turned back to Rios. "You've been following Rachel Goudas," he said. "Why?"

"Who?" Rios said.

Magnus tightened his grip. "I won't ask again."

Rios gagged. "We were…together," he gasped, unable to speak louder than a whisper.

"What do you mean, together?"

"Years ago…she was my girlfriend."

Magnus loosened his grip, but only a little. "And what?" he said. "You think you're going to get her back again? Is that it?"

Rios' only play was to nod. *Yes.*

"Ain't gonna happen," Magnus said. "Not now. Not ever." He leaned in. "Listen to me and listen good. She doesn't exist. As far as you're concerned, she's nothing but a distant memory." He tightened his grip again. "You hearing me Scottie?"

Rios made a choking sound that Magnus took as a 'yes'.

"If I see you anywhere near her again, you'll be fish food in Buzzard's Bay. Nod your head if you understand."

Rios nodded.

Magnus released his grip and Rios buckled over and sucked in a huge gulp of air.

"Now, get the hell outta here," Magnus growled. He watched Rios leave the way he'd come in, then climbed in his car and drove back toward the safehouse. As he was approaching it, he saw Kendra's Volvo cruise through the open gate and pull out onto the main road. He slowed, putting distance between them, but he still managed to count all three passengers: Kendra behind the wheel, and the two kids. No Rachel Goudas. He pulled to the side of the road at once and called Roman, who answered right away.

"What's up?" he asked, hoping to hear good news.

"Rios is out of the picture," Magnus said.

"Did he explain his sudden interest in our friend?"

"He gave me some garbage about her being an old girlfriend."

"Huh," Roman said, thinking back to their initial run-in with Rios years earlier. The question was, why did he surface again now, after all these years? The thought hung in his mind for several seconds and then he let it go. "Where are you now?" he asked.

"Canton," Magnus said. "The helper stashed our target in a house near Reservoir Pond and then took off. The place looks like a fortress. Completely fenced in. Locked gate. A pair of serious guard dogs."

"Guard dogs? Nice touch," Roman said. "Stay close by and keep an eye on things. Someone will come back for her. When they do, that's when we make our move."

"I'm looking forward to it," Magnus said. He reversed direction and took a position in a driveway diagonally across the street. The house appeared to be in good condition but the yard was in dire need of mowing. The owners were either slobs or currently away on vacation. Given the upscale neighborhood, he went with the latter.

After his scuffle with Magnus, Rios flew past the safehouse, drove another half mile, then turned into the driveway of Pequitside Farm. He ignored the parking area on the right and continued past the historical Lynch House to the facilities barn set behind it. With his car safely hidden from view, he sprinted across the lawn to a thick stand of trees 50 feet from the road where he could monitor the street while he considered his next move.

He hadn't been there long when he saw Kendra's battered blue Volvo racing up the street toward him. He was expecting to see the same four people inside, but as the car drove past, he counted only three. Rachel wasn't one of them. "What did they do, leave her there?" he said. He exhaled loudly then took out his cellphone and sent her a text message.

Urgent - call me as soon as you get this message

Burgess watched Kendra leave, then walked Rachel up the stairs onto the back porch. "It looks like you're going to be here for a bit, why don't I show you around?" He looked down at Sebastian and Leopold and let out a sharp, shrill whistle that carried all the way across the yard. They sat up at once and he gave them another one-word command. "SCOUT!"

Hearing that, they took off running toward the back edge of the property and began working their way along the perimeter fence, noses to the ground, sniffing frantically.

"What are they doing?" Rachel asked.

"Hunting," Burgess replied.

"For what?"

"Intruders."

Good, she thought. She'd worked too hard to get to this moment in time, suffered too many close calls and benefitted from too many lucky breaks. Her days of running were just hours away from ending for good. Now wasn't the time for any surprises.

Burgess escorted her into the house and began the tour in the kitchen. She was standing at the long center island, feeling the silky

271

sheen of the black-quartz countertop, when she heard the muffled ping of her cellphone coming from the front pocket of her backpack. She'd received a text message, and there was only one person who knew her cellphone number. "Uh, could I use your bathroom?" she asked.

"Why, certainly. It's down that hall, first door on the right," Burgess said, pointing.

She hurried down the hallway and ducked into the bathroom. After she read the message from Rios, she moved away from the door and called him.

"What's going on?" he barked, answering after the first ring. "I just saw your friend in the Volvo drive by and you weren't with her."

"Where *are* you? And why are you following me?" she asked. "I can't believe you brought the Quinlan brothers with you. I mean, seriously, the *Quinlan brothers?*"

"They're not the ones you should be worried about. I just had a very nasty run-in with your old pal Magnus."

"You saw Magnus? Here?" Rachel said, panicked.

"That's right. He warned me to stay away from you...or else. Now why do you suppose he did that?"

"You're asking *me?* What am I, a shrink?" she shot back. "I have no idea what goes on in the pea-sized brain of that psycho. You need to let it go. I have a plan and it's working. Later tonight, I'm meeting with the one person who can take me to a place where they'll never find me."

"And you trust these people helping you?" Rios asked, "because I don't."

"Well, you're just going to have to live with it because I'm following this through to the end. Once I get settled, I'll reach out to you. Trust me, everything is going to be fine."

"Rachel? Is everything all right in there?" Burgess asked from the hallway.

His voice startled her and she nearly dropped the phone. "Uh… yeah…no worries," she called back. Then, whispering into the phone, "Look, I gotta go. I'll call you in a few days."

The line went dead before Rios could respond and he gripped the phone tightly in his hand, fighting the urge to smash it against the nearest tree.

As they drove back up Rt. 95, Gina called Louise to give her an update. She had finished dialing and was pressing the phone to her ear when Nathan spun around in the seat to face her.

"You never told me where you got that," he said.

"Got what?" she asked, listening to the call connect.

He gave her a tired look. "The phone?" *What did you think I mean?*

Louise picked up right away. "Gina? How'd you make out?" She sounded concerned.

"Well, it's been an interesting morning, I'll say that much," Gina said.

"Is Rachel safe?"

Nathan pointed at the phone. *Well?*

"Very much so," Gina said, frowning at him as she waved him off. *Go away!*

"Just tell me," he said.

Kendra backhanded him upside the head. "Leave her alone."

273

He turned back around, rubbing his sore ear. "This is the thanks I get?"

"Your thanks will come later," she said. Then, in a quieter voice, "If we manage to pull this off."

"What's that supposed to mean?" Nathan asked.

"It means leave Gina alone and let her work. For crying out loud, do 13-year-old boys take special classes on how to be annoying?"

"Yes!" Gina blurted out.

"How are you coming with the logistics?" Louise asked.

"I need to spend some time with a map of Worcester, but that won't take long." She pulled the phone from her ear and checked the time. They were 45 minutes from Arlington. "I'll be home by two o'clock," she said. "I'll call you at 2:15."

"Perfect," Louise said. "You understand how this has to go, right?"

"I'm already on it."

17

Night Moves

Magnus shifted in the driver's seat and stretched the calf muscle in his right leg as it began to cramp. So far, no one had returned for Rachel as Roman had foretold would happen. The only movement he saw was the two Bullmastiffs making regular patrols along the perimeter fence. At one point they stopped and looked over at him, sniffing the air in his direction, before continuing their vigil.

He was massaging his lower leg when his phone rang. It was Roman. "Yeah," he said, feeling the pain in his leg start to ease.

"Text me your address," Roman said. "I'm sending someone to relieve you."

"O-kay," Magnus said. "What's up?"

"Scottie Rios."

"What about him?"

"Where is he?" Roman asked.

"I ran him off, just like you told me to."

"Find him," Roman said.

"You want me to *find* him?" Magnus asked, blindsided by the directive.

"Yes. Do whatever it takes, but find him and bring him to me... still breathing."

"Whatever you say," Magnus replied. He texted Roman the address and then waited, knowing that every second he delayed, Rios was getting farther and farther away. Fortunately, he didn't have to wait long. Ten minutes after Roman's call, a silver Ford Taurus slowed to a stop in the street and then backed in next to his passenger-side door. The driver, a 30's-ish Brockton gym rat named Sisson, lowered the window and nodded. *Hey.*

Magnus lowered his window. "Fenced-in property across the street," he said, without pointing.

Sisson's eyes flashed in that direction momentarily, then back at Magnus.

"They dropped her off about an hour ago and then left," Magnus said. "Blue Volvo 240 sedan. Beat to crap."

"Yeah, I heard."

Without another word, Magnus raised the window and pulled out of the driveway.

He was done talking.

It was time to hunt.

Rios crouched down behind the maple tree and took note of each car that passed, wondering where Magnus had gone. It had been a half hour and still nothing. *What is he doing?* he wondered. Then a disturbing scenario came to him. What if he was going to sneak onto the property, wrought-iron fence, guard dogs and all, and take Rachel by force? The man was just crazy enough to try it, and he wouldn't think twice about eliminating anyone who got in his way, including dogs of any size or temperament.

A less troubling possibility was that he followed Pleasant Street to the opposite end and then cut through town to get back to Rt. 95. But if he knew Rachel was hiding in that house, why would he leave? There was only one way to be sure. He left the patch of trees and hurried back across the lawn to his car. As he drove slowly down the driveway to the main road, he scanned the traffic passing by in both directions.

No Magnus.

He came to the tar road and stopped, waiting for the right time to pull out. A local plumbing-service van approached and he fell in behind it, using it as a moving screen that would block him from the view of the oncoming cars. He rode its bumper for a quarter mile when the driver suddenly hit the brakes and made a painfully slow turn into a residential driveway. As Rios swerved around him, he looked up and saw Magnus' sedan directly ahead.

Both men locked eyes for a split second before Rios cut back into his own lane and tore down the street. Magnus checked the side mirror, saw no cars within 500 feet of him, and slammed on the brakes as he cranked the steering wheel hard to the left. The back end of the car swung around in a tire-squealing fishtail, painting the road with a ribbon of black rubber that resembled a calligraphy swirl.

Kendra pulled into Nathan's driveway and roared up to the garage, coming to a jarring stop just inches from the door. Without a word, Gina hopped out and ran across the yard to her house. The clock was ticking now and she didn't have a second to spare.

Nathan watched her sprint across the lawn, then turned to Kendra and asked the question that had been festering in the back of his mind ever since they left Canton.

"What did Burgess mean, 'there are things we need to discuss'?"

Kendra turned off the car. "Do you remember what I told you this morning?" she said, "about visiting each of the safehouses, seeing their layouts and learning their secrets?"

"Yeah?"

"The Canton safehouse is at the top of the list."

"Because…?" Nathan prompted.

"It's not the cozy cottage it appears to be. Once we're done helping Gina extinguish this Rachel Goudas dumpster fire, we'll set up a time for you and Burgess to sit down and chat."

"He said something about going on adventures with my grandfather."

"Adventures? Yeah, right," she snickered.

Nathan stared at her, waiting for her to continue.

"What?" she said. "You want me to tell you about them?"

"Well, yeah," Nathan said, shrugging. "Why not?"

"Because you wouldn't believe a word I said."

Sitting at the computer in the living room, Gina brought up a map of Worcester and plotted the best route to Jericho Street, jotting down times and distances in her notepad. Ten minutes later, she called Louise.

"Ready?" she asked, after Louise answered.

"I am," Louise said. "What's the plan?"

"At 11:00, we meet on Lafayette Street. You, me, Kendra and Beck."

"Okay, what about Nathan?"

"Oh, right, I forgot. Nathan, too. From there, we drive to Canton, arriving a little before midnight. We pick up Rachel and drive straight to Worcester, which puts us at Jericho Street at around 1 a.m. That's a little early but I don't think we should take any chances."

"Smart," Louise said.

"Once we get to Jericho Street, Kendra, Beck, and Nathan will hang back, out of sight, and watch for any unwanted visitors."

"Are you expecting trouble?"

"Not really, but after what happened today I'm not ruling anything out. Do you have the safe haven information?"

"I do," Louise said. "I'll give it to Rachel when we arrive at Jericho Street and she'll hand it to the courier."

"Like she did the first time," Gina noted.

"Exactly. 'No paper, no ride' as your grandmother used to say."

There it was again, another anecdote about her grandmother. "We are so going to have that talk," Gina said.

"Oh, we're going to talk, trust me. A lot. As I told you before, I made a promise to your grandmother to help you whenever you need it. And if this Rachel Goudas debacle has taught me anything, it's that you're ready to hear everything that I have to tell you."

They spoke for another few minutes and then she called Jameson with an update.

"And you're satisfied with the location and timing?" he asked, after she'd laid it out for him.

"Very much so," she said. "As you know by now, Gina is a wizard at piecing together seemingly random clues to find the truth."

"Agreed. It's just that..."

He paused.

"What is it?" she asked.

"We can't afford any slip-ups with this," he said, solemnly. "Rachel Goudas needs to be gone, permanently, for the well-being of everyone involved, and that goes double for Gina."

"I wouldn't worry," Louise said, calmly. "Her plan is solid, and we'll have Kendra, Beck and Nathan set up around the perimeter to make sure there are no unwanted surprises, not that we're expecting any. But...better to be safe than sorry, right?

"Absolutely," Jameson said. "You'll give me regular updates?"

"I will."

"Okay, then. Good luck, and please be safe."

As Magnus raced down Pleasant Street, he eventually caught sight of Rios' Mustang in the distance. But just as quickly, it disappeared around the next turn in the road. A half mile later, when he reached the Pleasant-Bolivar Street roundabout, the Mustang was long gone. With three streets to choose from, each one branching out from the rotary in a different direction, catching Rios would come down to chance or dumb luck—and Magnus believed in neither. He knew that how things ended were a direct result of how they were managed from the start. "You pays your money and you takes your choice," his father used to tell him.

For whatever reason, Rios had ignored his warning. Instead of leaving town and forgetting about Rachel Goudas as he'd been instructed to do, he'd chosen to stick around. Maybe he was stupid, or maybe he had a death wish. Either way, it got Magnus thinking. *He wants Rachel Goudas and he's willing to risk his life to get her. Why that is doesn't matter. He'll be back for her.*

It was a startling epiphany.

Instead of chasing Rios all over town in a high-speed game of catch-me-if-you-can, he'd sit back and let Rios come to him.

He circled the rotary and drove back up Pleasant Street. After relieving Sisson of watch duty, he opened a map program on his phone and studied the layout of the safehouse property and the surrounding neighborhood. As he navigated the map, he imagined Rios: young, fearless, determined to get into the house without being detected no matter what it took. Looking at the geography of the area, there was only one logical way to do it. It was certainly what *he* would do if he were in Rios' shoes.

Smiling, he closed the app.

Nothing to do now but sit and wait.

Rios followed Bolivar Street into town. When he got there, he parked in a back lot off of Revere Street where Magnus wouldn't think to look for him. A plan of action was taking shape in the back of his mind and he needed time to think it through and evaluate what equipment or materials he'd need. The biggest consideration was time, and by his estimation he had at least six hours, maybe more, before he could make his move.

He got out of the car and cut between the buildings onto Washington Street, then ducked into C.F. McCarthy's. Sitting at the end of the bar with a pint of locally brewed amber ale in hand, he worked through his plan, one step at a time. When he was done, he realized he had everything he needed for the job. Most important of all was the Dead Air "Wolfman" suppressor that he kept in a gun safe in the trunk.

Kendra and Nathan were still sitting in the car when Beck's truck came charging up the driveway. She was already out the door by the time he came to a stop, and the look on her face told him something bad had happened.

"What is it?" he asked, through the open window.

"We have a new player in the Rachel Goudas sweepstakes," she said. "Some squirrely guy in a dark blue Mustang. Earlier today he pulled a gun on Nathan and nearly shot him. The way Nathan described it, Rachel almost got clipped too."

Beck grit his teeth, angry, then pushed the door open and climbed out of the truck. He brushed past Kendra and met Nathan just as he was getting out of the car. "Are you all right?" he asked.

"I'm fine," Nathan replied. Then, with a grin, "More than fine, actually."

"Tell me what happened," said Beck. "Better yet, show me."

They went into the backyard and Nathan recreated his takedown of Rios. He started with the collision with Rachel that stunned them both and sent them falling to the floor, and ended with Rios' head hitting the floor.

"Good," Beck said, nodding his approval.

"Wait!" Kendra exclaimed. "You think that's *good?*"

"Yes. Good that no one got shot."

"Well, there is *that,*" she mumbled.

"I'm going to show you another method for disarming an armed assailant," Beck told Nathan. "It's much quicker and it decreases your chance of accidentally catching a bullet." He went to the truck and dug out a molded-rubber training pistol from the zippered sports bag he kept behind the driver's seat. Other than its featherlight weight, the fake gun was realistic enough to pass as the real thing.

"Take this," he said, handing it to Nathan, "and approach me with it like you intend to shoot me."

Nathan raised the gun and aimed it directly at Beck's chest. "Give me all your money," he said in a low voice, trying to sound ominous.

Beck raised his hands in surrender. "Please don't shoot me," he said. Then, in a blur, his hands flew through the air, each one attacking the gun from opposite directions. Three seconds later he was pointing it at Nathan's head.

"Wow," Nathan said. He flexed his hand back and forth, working out the dull pain in his wrist—the result of having it nearly ripped off.

"Wow, indeed," Beck said. He handed Nathan the gun and they went through it again in slow motion. "First, show the gunman your hands and plead with him not to shoot you. Tell him you're just a kid, tell him you have a sick younger sister who depends on you to take care of her. Tell him anything to make him believe you're harmless, you're surrendering, and you're not a threat."

"And then...?"

"And then you strike. You move your head to the side, off the center line, and grab the barrel of the gun and turn it away from you." Beck stopped to demonstrate, in slow motion. "Lean and grab."

"Lean and grab," Nathan repeated.

"At the same time, you're going to chop at his wrist with your other hand, forcing the tip of the gun back toward him." Again, Beck showed Nathan what he meant. "Most times," he said, "with the barrel suddenly facing him, a shooter will let go of the gun." *Most times.*

He took the gun from Nathan and had him practice the move. It took several tries, but Nathan eventually got a feel for the speed and the power needed to make it work, especially with a giant like Beck, who had hands the size of catchers' mitts.

Kendra sat on the picnic table watching them. When they finished, she said to Beck, "Did you get the word about tonight?"

"I got a text message from Louise. All she said was that tonight was when the courier would appear."

"That's right," Kendra said. "And we're going to be there to make sure it all goes down without a hitch."

The discussion ended abruptly when they heard three simultaneous beeping sounds, each a unique metallic ringtone. They checked their phones and saw the identical text message from Louise laying out the schedule Gina had constructed, including where and when they would meet, the drive to Canton to pick up Rachel, and the ensuing convoy to Jericho Street in Worcester. There was also a reminder that the three of them would stay out of sight and observe, ready to assist should the need arise. They read the information in silence, then put their phones away.

"We need a map of Worcester," Beck said. "We can't just show up and hope to find a good place to hide."

"I have an atlas," Nathan said.

"Too old," Beck said. "We need something more current." He walked back to the truck and pulled a tablet from the center console. Seated at the picnic table, he brought up a Google Maps image of Worcester and zoomed in on Jericho Street. Kendra and Nathan sat on the opposite bench, watching him zoom in and out and side to side, examining every square foot of the street.

When he was done, he spun the tablet around and tapped his finger on four different locations. "Take your pick," he said.

Kendra leaned closer, eyeing each of the choices. "We should spread out," she said. "It'll give us better coverage."

"Agreed."

"Are we going to have radios, like before?" Nathan asked.

"Yes," said Beck. "And this time, try not to drop it, okay?"

Nathan flashed him a phony smile. *Ha, ha…very funny.*

They agreed on who would be positioned where, then Beck and Kendra left. Nathan went into the garage and ran through his usual routine on the heavy bag, using the memory of Rios' pistol jammed into his neck as fuel for his punches.

With the schedule confirmed and delivered to everyone involved, Gina sat on the couch in the living room, puzzle book in hand, staring at a troubling cryptogram. That lasted all of five minutes. She set it aside and went out to the back porch where she plopped down on the wicker couch and pawed through a gardening magazine she found on the end table. That was good for only two minutes. It was a beautiful afternoon and she went outside and sat down in one of the Adirondack chairs in the back corner of the yard. With her eyes closed, she took slow, measured breaths and listened to a bumblebee hovering over a blossom on the climbing honeysuckle vine growing nearby.

Despite her best efforts, she couldn't corral the stampede of questions that were running wild in her mind; questions about the impending meeting with the courier. Would she speak to him? *Should* she speak to him? What would his reaction be when he saw her? Would he simply vanish before her eyes? Someone needed to tell him that she was now the keeper of her grandmother's book notes, and with them, the fate of the women she'd saved—women he had whisked away to safety. Maybe Louise should do it. Then again, did he even know who she was? Would it be better if she and Louise just hung back and let Rachel approach him? After all, he had definitely seen *her* before. But with all the years that had passed since their one and only meeting, would he still remember her?

With her thoughts ricocheting from one uncertainty to the next, she went back inside the house and gave the puzzle book another try. This time, as the minutes ticked by, the cryptogram gently washed away all of the questions for which she had no answers. It was as if her analytical mind was waving the white flag of surrender, saying qué será, será, whatever will be, will be.

For the moment, anyway.

Little did she know that in a matter of hours, questions would be answered, lives would change direction, and she'd achieve a level of clarity that would guide her for the rest of her days.

Magnus and Sisson traded alternating two-hour shifts. Thus far, it was more of the same: no one came, no one went. Even the dogs had suspended their relentless patrol of the yard and were sprawled out beneath the back porch, taking refuge from the blistering afternoon heat.

At six o'clock, Roman called Magnus for an update.

"Where are we with Rios?" he asked.

"It's being handled," Magnus said.

"Meaning?"

"I'll have him in another three or four hours. Five, tops."

"Okay," Roman said, calmly, taking Magnus at his word. "What about our friend? Any movement there?"

"Nothing yet."

"There will be," Roman assured him. "And I want you to contact me the minute it happens."

"Will do."

The call ended just as Sisson arrived with dinner, which consisted of teriyaki beef sticks and garlic green beans. Beef and vegetables—standard gym-rat food.

At nine o'clock, with the dark of evening gently descended on the neighborhood, Magnus changed into a black hoodie and low-cut climbing boots. His SIG Sauer pistol was tucked in a pocket holster for easy access should he need it. But it was hard to imagine he would need it; Rios was no match for him physically and he had no intention of letting the man see him before he got the jump on him. He brought it anyway. Just in case.

Despite the hour, there was still a moderate flow of traffic on Pleasant Street. The air was alive with a medley of random sounds: people laughing; music playing, the clinking of horseshoes, dogs barking, and an occasional car horn. And the dogs were back, resuming their policing of the yard—a stern warning for any would-be intruders. *Enter these grounds at your own peril.*

By 10 o'clock all of that changed. The road was deserted, the guard dogs had been summoned inside, and an eerie silence had settled over the street. The only thing that stood out was the full moon overhead.

At 10:15, Magnus gave Sisson some last minute instructions and then crossed the street. He cut through the side yard of a brick-and-mortar Cape Cod-style home, staying in the shadows of the tall arborvitae that marked the property line. When he reached the back of the lot, he scaled a low chain-link fence and followed it through the woods to the corner of the safehouse lot next door.

From that vantage point the house was two hundred feet away. Every light was on, which was fine with him since he had no intention of going anywhere near the building, let alone step foot on the property. In his mind he envisioned the map he'd studied on his phone, the details of which were locked securely in his memory.

Running parallel to Pleasant Street was Prospect Street, a narrow road that dead-ended in the middle of the deep woods that abutted the back of the safehouse land. He was convinced that Rios would park there at the end of the road, unseen by anyone, and make the 1,000 foot trek through the woods.

Magnus continued along the wrought-iron fence until he reached the imaginary line he'd constructed in his mind, connecting the back door of the safehouse to the end of Prospect Street. Unless Rios was some kind of woodland enthusiast who enjoyed traipsing around a dark forest in the middle of the night, it was the logical line of approach he would follow. It was the shortest and most direct, which meant it was the quickest. And Rios would want to be quick.

Get in.

Get Rachel.

Get out.

He turned around and followed the line deeper into the woods for 20 feet, then ducked down behind a boulder the size of a 19th century cast iron bathtub. He checked his watch. The luminous numbers on the dial told him it was 10:45.

All around him, the air had grown noticeably cooler. The treetops were splintered by beams of moonlight that cut through the canopy at odd angles like shards of glass. The only sound to be heard was an owl making its territorial claim somewhere deep in the woods.

An hour later, Magnus heard the faint rumble of a car engine coming from the direction of Prospect Street. It grew steadily louder before cutting out completely. The woods grew quiet again. Several minutes later he heard a twig snap. He shifted his body into a crouching position: knees bent, weight slightly forward, with one hand on the ground to steady himself.

Another snap.

Closer this time.

He took a long deep breath. *Ready…*

And blew it out slowly. *Set…*

Out of the shadows, Rios emerged. *Go!*

He exploded out of his stance and drove his shoulder into Rios' midsection, knocking him off his feet and down onto the ground. The Beretta in Rios' hand, heavier with the Wolfman silencer, landed several feet away—well out of reach to be of any use to him.

They wrestled momentarily but Magnus was too big and too

strong. He had just climbed atop Rios, pinning him to the ground, when wide beam of light swept through the trees, briefly washing over both men. He turned to look and saw three vehicles passing through the front gate, making their way down the driveway toward the house.

The lead car was a battered Volvo 240 sedan.

Harry W. Longfellow.   **18**

Jericho Street

Monday 11:50 p.m.

Magnus scrambled to his feet, then bent and grabbed the front of Rios's shirt. Rios instinctively swatted his arms and kicked his legs in a vain attempt to ward off his attacker—all to no avail. With hands like pneumatic grippers, Magnus grabbed him and lifted him off the ground with the ease of hoisting a small child.

"Walk," he said, through clenched teeth.

Rios didn't move.

"Fine, we'll do it the hard way." He twisted Rios' left arm around like a pretzel, making him cry out in pain, then clamped his meaty fingers onto the back of his neck and marched him deeper into the forest. When they reached Prospect Street, the Mustang was parked there just as Magnus had forecast—the metallic blue finish gleaming like neon in the bright moonlight.

"Keys," he barked.

When Rios didn't comply, Magnus slammed him down on the hood, face-first. "Give-me, the-keys," he said in two-word bursts.

Rios pawed at his front pocket, then pulled his keys out and held them up for Magnus to see. "You want 'em? Go get 'em," he said, then flicked his wrist and flung them into the woods.

Kendra, Louise, and Beck pulled in behind the house and parked three abreast in front of the carriage house. The powerful motion-activated flood lights had come on and were bathing the entire area in bright light.

Kendra had driven alone, Gina was riding with Louise, and Nathan was with Beck.

"Don't get out yet," Gina told Louise.

Louise looked left at Kendra, then right at Beck, and saw them just sitting in their vehicles. "Am I missing something?" she asked.

"Just wait," Gina told her.

The back door to the house swung open and Sebastian and Leopold came charging out, growling, their claws making a staccato ticking sound on the wood as they galloped down the stairs.

"Sebastian and Leopold," Gina said.

"Cute," Louise said, "in an oddly disturbing way."

Burgess stepped out onto the porch, eyed all three vehicles briefly, then called out a single-word command. "PORCH!"

Sebastian and Leopold gave up their inspection of the vehicles and ran back up on the porch where they sat down obediently on either side of the door.

Kendra was already out of the car as Burgess made his way down the stairs. "How's our girl?" she asked. "She give you any trouble?"

"No trouble at all," Burgess said. "She laid down for a nap about two hours ago." He looked over at Louise's white Mercedes and then at Beck's pickup truck. "More friends?"

"Some friends and some muscle," Kendra said. The others joined her next to the Volvo and she introduced Louise and Beck.

"Louise," Burgess said, warmly, as he took her hand in his. "Very nice to meet you." He turned to Beck. "And you, sir, may be the largest human being to ever step foot on this property."

They exchanged a hearty handshake, then Gina held up her wrist and tapped her watch. "We gotta go."

"Yes," Kendra said. "We need to wake up the princess. We're on a tight schedule."

Magnus yanked Rios up off the hood of the car and spun him around. "Bad move, Scottie." He punched him in the forehead so hard that Rios' eyes rolled back in his head and he passed out. Magnus let him drop to the ground and then took the small flashlight from the pocket of his hoodie and quickly scoured the woods for the keys. Fortunately, Rios wasn't the Hall of Fame pitcher he thought he was and the keys were lying in a patch of loose gravel that skirted the tree line.

Working quickly, he opened the trunk and rifled through the contents. Stuffed in a small gym bag, along with a random collection of hand tools, he found exactly what he needed.

Duct tape.

He dragged Rios to the back of the car and secured his hands and feet with generous lengths of tape. He wrapped another strip around his head, covering his mouth, making it impossible for him to cry out for help. Not that there was anyone around to hear him.

Rios was just regaining consciousness when Magnus picked him up and dropped him in the trunk. "You be a good boy, now, until I get back," he said, then slammed the trunk shut and quickly retraced his steps through the woods.

He walked until the safehouse came into view, then paused. A small crowd had gathered next to the vehicles in the driveway. On the porch, the two dogs were sitting up, sniffing the air in alternate directions. He pulled out his phone and called Roman.

"Talk to me," Roman said.

"I have Rios safely tucked away. He won't be going anywhere for a while."

"Excellent. What about our friend?"

"Three vehicles just showed up at the house. The Volvo and two others."

"Three vehicles? Interesting," Roman said. "Let me know the minute they leave. And whatever you do, don't lose them. Tonight they're all going to pay for what they did to Bolan, Cafferty and Rodano."

Burgess led the group into the house and offered them coffee for the road, which they all politely refused. Gina was awarded the task of reviving Rachel, who awoke fully rested and eager to get on the road.

At 12:15, they loaded into the vehicles: Kendra riding solo in the Volvo, Gina and Rachel in Louise's Mercedes, and Nathan and

Beck in the truck. Like a presidential motorcade they drove down the driveway with Kendra in front, followed by Louise, then Beck in the third spot. The plan was for Kendra and Beck to create a protective buffer that would shield the Mercedes should anyone try and impede their trip.

"How long will it take to get there?" Rachel asked, after they pulled out onto Pleasant Street.

"An hour," Gina said.

"And you're sure about the address?"

"Positive."

"Let's talk about what's going to happen when we get there," Louise said.

"You guys aren't going to just drop me off and leave me there, are you?" Rachel asked.

"No, but Gina and I will keep our distance while you approach the courier."

Rachel flashed back to her first meeting with the man in the cloak, trying desperately to remember what words were exchanged. So much time had passed and she'd endured so much since that night that, at best, her memories were nothing more than hazy fragments.

"You'll need this," Louise said, handing a plain white envelope over the seat.

"Oh, right," Rachel said, turning it over in her hands. "I remember Helen gave me an envelope just like this."

"The courier doesn't know me and he doesn't know Gina," Louise said, "but when he sees you with that envelope, he'll know why you're there. It contains the information he needs to get you to your first stop."

"And after that?" Rachel asked.

"You leave that up to me. There are still some details to work out, but everything will be set by the time you reach your initial destination. Once you're there, I'll contact you. Do you prefer sunny and warm, or someplace decidedly cooler?"

"I prefer sunny and warm," Rachel said, sliding the envelope into her backpack.

"Okay, sunny and warm it is."

Travelling in separate cars, Magnus and Sisson followed the convoy at a safe distance as it snaked through town on the way to the interstate. They had just turned onto Rt. 95 when Magnus called Roman, as instructed

"Where are you?" Roman asked.

"Just got on Rt. 95 in Norwood."

"North or south?"

"South."

"Huh," Roman said, thinking. He pondered it momentarily, then said, "Stay with them. And call me with regular updates."

"Will do," Magnus replied. He clicked off the call and smiled, thinking about how much he was going to enjoy this.

Payback was at hand.

At last.

Beck maintained a steady distance from the Mercedes—not quite a car length, but close enough so that no one would attempt to pull in between them.

Nathan was sitting in the front seat, examining the radio he'd be wearing once they arrived at Jericho Street. "Why did you give me that spot," he asked.

"The one directly across the street?" asked Beck, surprised by the question. He thought Nathan knew. "You're the scout, just like at Smitty's," he said. "If things go sideways, you'll report it immediately. Kendra and I will be in flanker positions, ready to move in from either end of the street."

"Sideways," Nathan repeated. "I like that." He paused several seconds, then said, "Do you think it will? Go sideways?"

"My gut tells me no," Beck said. "But my gut also told me to order the barbequed monkey meat at a restaurant in the Philippines."

Nathan made a sour face. "Was it bad?"

"I wouldn't recommend it."

"Thanks," Nathan said. "I'll keep that in mind the next time I'm in the Philippines."

Beck's phone emitted a soft ping and he picked it up at once. "It's Jameson," he said, then tapped the talk button. "Jameson, I was just about to call you."

"You're on your way?" Jameson asked.

"We are."

"Any sign of trouble?"

"Nothing so far."

Jameson breathed a sigh of relief. "I don't think this is what Helen Bainbridge envisioned when she helped that woman disappear," he said, referring to Rachel with an air of contempt.

"Louise mentioned there were others?" Beck said.

"There were five others. Six in all. Gina's grandmother saved

297

their lives by giving them a brand new start, far away from their oppressors. As Louise said, that information is not to be shared with anyone."

"Understood. Let's hope each of them stays hidden."

"I always entertain great hopes," Jameson said. "Those are Robert Frost's words, by the way, not mine."

"And it was Nietzsche who said 'Hope is the worst of all evils because it prolongs the torments of man."

"Torments, indeed," Jameson replied. "You'll let me know when it's done?"

"You'll be my first call," said Beck. He was putting his phone back in the center console when he noticed Nathan staring at him. "What's wrong?" he asked.

"Who were you talking about?"

"What do you mean?"

"Just now, you said, 'Let's hope each of them stays hidden'. Them, who?"

Beck kept his eyes focused on the road ahead, remembering his promise not to discuss Helen Bainbridge's secret crusade with anyone.

"That's it? Nothing?" Nathan griped. "Okay, fine. Let's see if I have this right. *You* know. *Jameson* knows. You mentioned Louise, so *she* knows. That means Kendra probably knows. Does Gina know?"

Still, Beck said nothing.

"I'll take that as a yes," Nathan said, "which leaves…hmm…only me. I'm the only one who got left out. Why is that…do you think?"

"Drop it," Beck said.

"Sure. No problem. Wait, I have another idea. How about you

just—"

"Drop it!" Beck barked, louder.

Nathan pulled back, surprised by the ferocity of Beck's outburst.

"Do you remember what Gina told us at my house?" Beck asked.

"She said lots of things."

"Yes, she did. Let's run through them, shall we? What was the first thing?"

"The first thing?

"Yeah, what was the very first thing she said?"

"Uh…" Nathan said, fumbling for the answer.

"Think," said Beck.

"She said there were things at work…"

"That's right. Her exact words were, 'There-are-things-at-work-here'. What else?"

"Don't ask questions," Nathan muttered, his words barely audible.

"What was that?"

"She said don't ask any questions."

"She didn't *say* it, she *pleaded:* 'I beg you please don't ask'. Do you know what that means? It means *drop it!* Your best friend begged you not ask any questions. So don't!"

Nathan couldn't think of a suitable reply. Beck was right. Gina was his best friend. She had made an impassioned plea and it was time to honor that request and let "it" go. Whatever "it" was. If, in the future, she chose to tell him…wonderful. If not, oh well, he had plenty of other things to think about, like Burgess' assertion that there where things they needed to discuss, and Kendra's curious comment that the Canton safehouse wasn't "the cozy cottage" it appeared to be.

"When we get to Jericho Street, I need your head in the game," Beck said, breaking the strained silence.

Nathan pushed aside his questions about Burgess and the Canton safehouse. "It will be," he said. *For Gina.*

At 12:45, Magnus called Roman with another update. "They're on 495 north," he said. "We just passed Franklin State Forest." As he'd done every few miles since they'd gotten on the highway, he fell back and let Sisson pull into the lead. By alternating the positions, they were making it that much harder to be spotted by Beck, or any of the others, if they were monitoring the traffic behind them.

"You're sure they haven't seen you?" Roman asked.

"Positive," Magnus said.

"Okay, good. Stay with them."

Twenty minutes later, Magnus called him again.

"They're on Rt. 290 now, headed for Worcester."

"Stay sharp," Roman said. "They could pull off and head into town or they could blow right past it and continue south."

"Don't worry," Magnus said. "I won't lose them."

With Gina's directions stitched into her memory, Kendra turned off the highway at the Vernon Street exit, then took a series of rights and lefts to Southington Ave, once the main corridor through the old mill district. Running down the right side were industrial buildings, storehouses, and old brick mills that had been gutted and converted to businesses. Jericho Street was halfway down on the right.

She drove a short distance and pulled over to call Louise who had come to a stop behind her. "Everybody ready?" she asked.

"We're ready," Louise said. "How much time do you need to get into position?"

"Give us five minutes. We're going to park one block over and then work our way back."

"Understood. We'll wait here for five minutes before we leave."

"Actually, let's make it 10, just to be safe," Kendra said.

Louise pulled the phone away and looked over at Gina. "How are we on time?"

"We're good," Gina said.

"Okay," Louise told Kendra. "Ten minutes it is."

Kendra lowered her window and signaled to Beck with a sweep of her hand. *GO!*

When he saw that, he eased away from the curb and crept slowly down the street, the Ram's engine purring softly like a night predator slinking through the jungle. One block past Jericho Street he turned down a narrow service road with uneven pavement and streetlights standing unlit, their bulbs long-since shot out.

A row of single-story concrete buildings lined the right side, their windows boarded up and their cinderblock walls covered with elaborate graffiti. Running between each one was a narrow alley that led back to Jericho Street.

He drove past three of them and stopped the truck. "This is you," he told Nathan. "Now remember to stay hidden at all times. And let us know the second anything looks peculiar."

"Will do," Nathan said. Moving quickly and quietly, he climbed down from the truck and disappeared down the alley.

In the rearview mirror, Beck saw Kendra turn in, kill her headlights, and park behind the first building. He continued on until he came to the last building and did the same, parking the truck next to an overturned dumpster.

After a quick check of the time, he clipped a two-way radio to his belt and pressed the wired earpiece into his ear. He tapped the PTT button and said, "Radio check. Talk to me, guys."

"In position," said Kendra.

"In position," said Nathan.

"Copy on both."

He slid out of the truck and worked his way down the alley. When he came to the end he pressed his back up against the building, leaned sideways, and looked around the corner. All clear. He waited and watched, looking for any uninvited guests. Thirty seconds later, he saw Louise's Mercedes turn the corner. He tapped his PTT button again.

"Okay, folks. It's showtime."

19

Payback

A tense silence filled the car as Louise drove slowly down Jericho Street, past the historic Mothram Block with its tall brick structures looming high overhead. Through the years, a number of them had been converted to office space and at the current hour their windows were dark.

Antique-style streetlamps with tapered globes, set atop decorative pillars, were spaced at intervals along the right side of the street. The left side, with its abandoned storefronts that would eventually be knocked down to make way for further development, had no such amenities. The ragged buildings were lit only by the raw moonlight.

They were approaching the second mill building when Gina pointed. "Right there."

Louise rolled to a stop in front of the narrow cobblestone alley that divided the second and third building.

Gina checked the time. It was nearing 1:15 a.m. They were right on schedule. "Let's park there," she said, pointing at the vacant curb on the opposite side of the street.

Louise did a quick three-point turn, parked at the curb, and turned off the car.

"What now?" Rachel asked. Her backpack was in her lap and she was holding the white envelope with one hand, her other hand resting on the door handle.

"Do you think he's in the alley but we can't see him?" Gina asked Louise.

"Maybe. Your grandmother wasn't very forthcoming about this part of the process."

"What if I just show myself?" Rachel asked. "I mean, if he's in the alley like you say, he'll see me, right?"

Gina gave Louise a tentative look. *What do you think?*

Louise shrugged. *Sure…couldn't hurt, right?*

"All right," Gina said. "Go stand in front of the alley. Don't go *in*…let him come to you. Louise and I will wait back here by the car."

"Okay, I got it," Rachel said. She opened the door and then paused. "Gina, I want to thank you…for everything you've done…"

"No thanks required," Gina said. "I'm just glad we were able to get you here in one piece. Now you have the rest of your life to look forward to."

"I won't forget you," Rachel said. "Ever."

She climbed out of the car and made her way across the street, her backpack in one hand and the white envelope in the other, held close to her chest in plain sight.

Louise and Gina got out of the car and stood in front of the grill, neither of them talking.

They were sure they were in the right place.

On the right day.

At the right time.

All they could do now was wait, and watch, and hope.

From their respective hiding places, Kendra, Nathan, and Beck kept a steady watch on the street.

"So far, so good," Kendra said.

"Copy that," replied Beck. He was scanning both ends of the street in five second intervals.

Look left, count to five.

Look right, count to five.

Repeat.

All he saw was a desolate street that was a mere shadow of its original self. Long gone were the days when industry ruled the town, jobs were in abundance, and there was real money to be made by those willing to work hard enough to create it.

Rachel reached the mouth of the alley and stopped, her heart pounding. She'd done it. She'd worked her plan to perfection, and not only had she successfully eluded Roman and his vile band of cutthroats, she was free from the wrath of their boss. Going forward, the unfettered feeling of freedom would be hers once again. During her brief stay in Canton, she'd made a vow not to waste it like she had before. First, she'd get settled. Then, she'd get busy. With hard work and careful planning she'd accumulate the resources she needed to craft an even more prestigious life.

Better cars.

Better clothes.

Palatial homes in pristine settings.

Maybe even some on foreign shores.

Her dream dissolved when she saw a human form emerge from the alley, seemingly drifting above the ground. As it drew closer she could make out the familiar details: the heavy cloak, as dark as the night, made from a course fabric that resembled the fur of a black wolf; the hood, loose-fitting and deep, pulled down to obscure the courier's face.

He stopped at the edge of the shadows where the darkness met the light. Without uttering a word, he raised his hand, palm up, and summoned the white envelope that she was clutching against her chest.

She stepped forward and gave it to him willingly, then closed her eyes and took a deep breath. In her mind she imagined that she was passing through a portal, into a world of peace and tranquility. Her agonizing trek, at long last, was finally over—a realization that was as startling as it was uplifting.

Her feeling of euphoria was shattered when someone grabbed her right arm, then her left, and wrenched them back behind her body. Her eyes blinked open and she saw the courier pull back his hood, revealing his face for all to see.

"Hello Ms. Denny," Roman said. "Or do you prefer Goudas? I can't tell you how pleased I am to see you. It's been a very, very long time."

"Let-me-go!" she shouted, struggling to break free.

306

Bolan increased his grip.

Cafferty and Rodano stepped out of the darkness from behind Roman and joined Bolan, the three men forming a makeshift triangle around Rachel.

Trapped, with no chance of escaping, she looked to the sky and screamed out in frustration—a painful wail that echoed up and down Jericho street. She caught her breath and eyed Roman with contempt. That's when she heard a sharp *CLICK!*

Everyone turned to look as Scottie Rios emerged from the alley, gun up and pointed at the back of Roman's head. "Let her go," he said. Before anyone had time to draw their weapons, he pressed the barrel of the gun against Roman's temple. "Guns on the ground or he's history."

From somewhere behind him came the sound of a bullet being racked into the chamber of a rifle. First, one. Then another. Shawn and Derrick Quinlan appeared, their oversized bodies emerging from the shadows like a pair of Macy's Thanksgiving Day Parade balloons. Shawn's nose was hastily covered by a strip of cotton gauze. "You heard the man!" he barked, pointing his Remington 700 rifle at Cafferty, "Guns on the ground!"

Derrick pointed his Winchester Model 70 rifle at Rodano. "NOW!"

As all three men complied, Rios jammed the barrel of his gun under Roman's chin, forcing it upward. "That means you too boss man."

Roman reached beneath his cloak and produced a 9mm pistol. Rios snatched it out of hand and shoved it in his waistband, then shoved Roman aside and went to Rachel. He pulled her away from her three captors, then motioned to them with his gun. "You three! Over there next to the wall. If your backsides are touching brick, I start shooting."

"Do as he says," Roman commanded.

Reluctantly, all three men walked over to the building and leaned back against the brick. At the same time, Derrick stepped forward, gathered their handguns, and handed them to Rios. He, in turn, passed them to Rachel. "Here, you're in charge of these."

As she deposited them in her backpack, he pulled Roman's gun from his waistband and handed it to her. "Now," he said, eyeing Roman, then Bolan and his crew. "Everyone stay where you are." He took Rachel by the arm and took a step back. "Anyone moves, Roman gets the first bullet. And we have plenty more for the rest of you."

The Quinlan brothers were standing slightly ahead of him like a protection detail: Shawn's rifle pointed at Bolan, Cafferty, and Rodano; Derrick's rifle aimed squarely at Roman. As they began a slow retreat, Roman raised his hand in the air as if hailing a taxi.

"Uh, Rios?" he called out. "Before you go, a question?"

Rios halted, as did the Quinlan brothers. "Yeah? What is it?" he asked. "And make it quick. We have someplace to be."

"Are you familiar with the Battle of Trenton?"

"The what?" Rios said, frowning. He turned to Rachel. "What's he talking about?"

"The Battle of Trenton?" Roman repeated. "1776?"

"Never heard of it."

"That's a pity," Roman said.

"Oh yeah?" Rios said, defiantly. He raised his gun. "How about

I—"

CRACK!

The pistol fell from his hand as he screamed out in pain and clutched his left knee.

"You got a big mouth, you know that?" Kendra asked, standing directly behind him. She cocked her bat back and swung again, this time smashing his right knee. He opened his mouth to scream but the pain was so excruciating that no words came out and he collapsed on the ground, writhing in agony.

Shawn Quinlan spun around, gun at the ready, but Beck already had the jump on him. He delivered a vicious elbow strike that connected with Shawn's forehead and knocked him out cold.

Derrick had also turned, but he never made it all the way around as Sisson took him down with a flying kick to the head.

In all the commotion, Rios lunged for his pistol that was lying on the ground three feet away. His fingers were closing in on it when Magnus appeared, seemingly out of nowhere, and kicked it away. "I thought I locked you in the trunk," he said.

Nathan, Gina, and Louise watched from across the street, peering over the front hood of the Mercedes. It was an impressive show as Rios and the Quinlan brothers were neutralized in a matter of seconds without a single shot being fired.

As they were being handcuffed by Bolan, Cafferty, and Rodano, Rachel stood frozen in place, stunned by the realization that the meeting with the courier had been nothing but a ruse, cleverly orchestrated by a 13-year-old girl.

Nathan saw her standing there, defeated, with her backpack dangling from her left hand. "The guns!" he said, jumping to his feet in a panic.

"What's wrong?" Gina asked.

As he took off running toward the alley, she climbed to her feet and went after him. "Nathan, wait!"

Rachel stood, frozen, as Nathan grabbed hold of her backpack and ripped it out of her hands, the disoriented look on her face betraying her feelings of anger and betrayal. When she saw Gina, her bewildered expression melted away and she slowly raised her right hand, which held Roman's 9mm pistol—the one gun she hadn't deposited in her backpack. "You," she hissed, pointing the gun at Gina. "You did this."

"NO!" Nathan shouted, stepping directly into the line of fire. "It was me. I did it."

Rachel blinked hard, trying to process the words he was saying.

He let the backpack fall to the ground as he stepped closer. "I didn't want to do it, really I didn't," he said, playing desperate. "You gotta believe me."

"You?" she said, her thoughts spinning. "But…why? Why would you do that?"

"I had no choice," he said. "They made me do it."

"Made you?" Rachel muttered, her confusion mounting.

"I'm not like that," he said. "Really I'm not. Ask anyone. Ask my mom. She'll tell you. I'm not a mean person."

She'd heard enough. Her anger surged and she raised the gun, bringing it inches from his forehead. "Nice try, kid. You almost had me. But now you're gonna pay."

She straightened her arm, taking aim, when he leaned to his left, grabbed the barrel, and twisted it back toward her. At the same time he slammed his other hand against her wrist with a powerful chop that bent it sideways, producing an audible *crack!*

Now *he* had the gun.

It felt oddly light in his hands, and using a firm two-handed grip he levelled it at her chest.

"Whoa, whoa, whoa," Beck said, rushing over to Nathan's side. "Let me have that before you shoot one of us by mistake." He eased the gun out of Nathan's hands as Bolan and Cafferty moved in and handcuffed Rachel.

Roman, still dressed in the cloak, eyed the day's catch, handcuffed and battered on the ground, then walked over to where Beck, Kendra, and Nathan were standing in a group, along with Louise and Gina. "You did it," he said to Gina, visibly impressed. "I had my doubts, but you pulled it off, just as Jameson said you would."

Gina shrugged, playing shy. *Eh…it was nothing.*

"What's he talking about?" Nathan asked Kendra.

"Shhh!" she said. "Listen."

Roman directed his next words at Beck, Kendra, and Nathan. "The three of you are free to go. All of the charges against you will be dropped. I'd say you redeemed yourselves, and then some," he added, looking over at Rios, who turned out to be a bonus acquisition.

"What charges? Nathan asked.

"See those guys, Bolan, Cafferty, and Rodano?" Kendra said, pointing at each of them. "They're federal agents."

"Wait-a-minute," Nathan said, realizing where he'd seen them before. "Those are the three guys from Smitty's."

"That's right. You helped us assault three federal agents. Put *that* in your diary!"

"F-federal agents? But...w-we didn't know..." he stammered.

"Serious assault with a deadly weapon on a federal agent is a Class C felony," Beck explained. "It's punishable by up to 20 years in prison."

"Deadly weapon my ass," Kendra snorted. "It was a baseball bat!"

"Twenty years in prison...*and*...fines up to $250,000," Roman noted.

The color went out of Nathan's face and his jaw fell open.

"The only reason the three of you aren't in jail right now is because of the deal I made with Jameson," Roman said.

"You made a deal? With *Jameson?*" Nathan said, shell shocked.

"When Bolan, Cafferty and Rodano were interrogated," Beck told him, "they identified themselves as federal agents. Jameson was notified and he immediately called their boss."

"Him," Kendra said, pointing at Roman.

"You... made a deal?" Nathan said, still struggling grasp the idea.

"That's right," Roman said. "The whole thing was Jameson's idea. After I explained the pending charges against you, and Harper Denny's criminal past, he suggested a plan that would suit both our interests. "

"Harper who?" Nathan asked.

"That's Rachel's real name," Gina said.

Nathan shook his head, dizzy, as the story took yet another confusing turn.

"In Jameson's proposal, the three of you wouldn't assault any more of my men. In turn, I wouldn't send any of them after you or Ms. Denny. Lastly, and this was the kicker, all charges against you would be dropped, but only if you delivered Harper Denny to me. It was payback, so to speak, for your physical assault on Bolan, Cafferty, and Rodano."

"I was wondering what happened to those three guys," Nathan said. He turned to Kendra, confused. "You told me they'd be turned over to the police!"

"They were," she said. "I mean, they *are* the police if you catch my drift."

"You're saying they got turned over to themselves? That makes no sense. And *you!*" he said, pointing a guilty finger at Gina. "There were federal charges pending against me and you said *nothing?*"

She looked at Kendra and Beck, beseeching them. *Uh…a little help?*

"For this to work, no one could know," Beck said. "Most of all, you."

"Ex-cuse me?"

"We couldn't tell you because we knew what would happen," Kendra said. "You'd pester Gina to no end and our window would close."

"What window?"

"The deal I made with Jameson was only good for one week," Roman said. "After that, if I didn't have Harper Denny, assault charges would be filed against you."

"I would *not* have pestered her," Nathan grumbled. He looked at Gina. "Tell them."

"What? You want me to lie?" she said, smirking.

"Nathan, one of these days you're going to figure it out," Kendra said. "Gina is one extremely smart cookie. She can do amazing things, when she's not being *BOTHERED!*" She accentuated the

313

last word with a hard stare.

"Yeah, well, someone should've told me," he muttered.

"I have to say, Jameson was very convincing," Roman said. "He assured me that Gina would pull it off. He also told me *you'd* be in the mix somehow—the one and only Nathan Cole."

"In the mix indeed," Nathan mumbled, shooting a nasty look at Gina.

"No thanks required," she said.

"Still, despite his belief in the two of you, and your now-famous detective abilities, I wasn't completely sold," Roman explained. "I know that sounds like a slight, but it's not. Trust me. It's just that, after chasing a fugitive like Harper Denny for as long as we have, only to have her slip through our fingers time and again, we couldn't afford to take any chances."

"That's why you had *him* tailing us," Beck said, pointing at Magnus.

"I needed to be sure that you were keeping up your end of the bargain."

"And that we hadn't made an alternate deal," said Beck.

"That's right. I had Magnus tailing Kendra because she was spending the most amount of time with Denny. I figured if Denny learned she was walking into a trap, she might attempt to harm the people who were involved, starting with Kendra—the first 'domino' as I was calling her."

"Harm *me?*" Kendra snickered. "*That* would've been comical."

Gina nudged Louise. *We need to go.*

"Yes, well, it's very late and I should get Gina home," Louise said. "Mr. Roman, if you need anything from either of us, please don't hesitate to call me."

"I'd certainly like to congratulate Gina's parents on her fine work," he said.

"NO!" Nathan and Gina blurted out, in unison.

"Uh…what they mean is, it would be best if you work with me directly," Louise said, politely. "Jameson can provide you with my contact information."

Walking quickly, nearly running, she and Gina made a beeline for the car.

Time was running out and they had to hurry.

If they weren't already too late.

20

The Shepherd of the Seven Hills

"Where to?" Louise asked, after she'd started the car.

"See that first mill building?" Gina said, pointing at the far end of the street. "Right next to it is an access road."

Louise chirped the tires on the pavement as they sped away from the curb, which drew the attention of Roman and his crew who turned to look as she raced down the street. When she reached the building in question, the one that occupied the front right corner of Mothram's sprawling eight-factory grid, she turned into the access road.

It was packed gravel that had been mostly ignored, and the car bounced and pitched as they rode over it. They passed Mothram Way, the narrow corridor paved with cobblestones that ran the full length of the complex, dividing the front four buildings from the back four. Seeing them up close, they looked like a miniature city.

"Okay, up ahead, after this next building, take a left," Gina said. "Actually, you have no choice."

Louise slowed as she approached the turn, then eased around the corner. On their left were the four brick buildings that comprised the back half of Mothram's eight-building grid. To their right, a wide strip of overgrown grass and tangled weeds that skirted a four foot chain-link fence. Just beyond the fence was a pair of train tracks.

There were no street lamps along the backside of the complex. As the headlights cut through the darkness, each of the buildings was slowly revealed, along with the cobblestone alleyways that separated them. The first two had been converted to office buildings while the last two had been gutted and were awaiting renovation. Louise drove past the third building when Gina said, "This is it."

"How do you know that?" Louise said, pulling the car over onto the grassy strip. It was a question she'd been meaning to ask Gina ever since she'd laid out the timing and location of the meet-up with Roman and his men.

"It was something Rachel told me," Gina explained. "She was describing how she met the courier seven years ago. Her memory was spotty, but she remembered being on a narrow road. She said the courier just appeared, that he stepped out of the darkness and into the moonlight. We were just on Jericho Street. Did any sections of it look dark to you?"

Louise shook her head in awe, once again amazed at how Gina could hold onto a single word or phrase that, at first, appeared to be completely random, but when put into context could provide a critical clue.

"Either I'm right or I'm completely delusional," Gina said, staring past Louise at the darkened alley.

"Let's go find out," Louise told her.

They got out of the car and made their way across the narrow access road, then stood side by side at the opening of the alley that separated the last two buildings in the row. The moon was perfectly positioned between them and was making the tops of the cobblestones shine like brushed steel. All around them the air was still, and there wasn't a sound to be heard.

They waited without speaking for a full minute. Then another. With no forewarning whatsoever, it happened. The courier drifted effortlessly out of the shadows just as Rachel had described, the moonlight revealing the tops of his shoulders and the hood of his cloak. For several seconds he just stood there, observing them. Then he spoke, in a deep, cavernous baritone that was eerily calm and reassuring.

"I remember you," he said to Louise.

She had never stood before the man and wasn't sure how to respond, or *if* she should respond. Were there rules here? Some protocol she was supposed to follow? If so, Helen had never shared that information with her.

"From long ago...when she started," the courier said, seeing her apprehension.

Helen had started her quest 12 years ago, and it dawned on Louise in that moment that she might have met this man, conversed with him on more than one occasion, or even dined with him, never once knowing the covert service he provided. It was a curious irony that she wouldn't soon forget.

"And you…" he said to Gina. "I know you."

She stared up at him, stunned. "Y-you do?" she said, summoning the breath to speak.

"You and your friend found the architect."

"That's right."

The discovery in question surrounded the baffling disappearance of Alastair Raven over 150 years earlier. It was a blockbuster news story that had swept the nation like wildfire, and despite the time that had passed since they'd solved the mystery, the media still refused to let it go.

"And now you've found *me*," the courier said, his tone implying that there must be a reason for her being there.

"I just wanted to tell you…" she began, the words almost too heart-wrenching to voice.

"That she's gone? Yes, I know."

A solemn pause followed—a reverent moment of silence for the woman who had served as a champion for the oppressed, unselfishly putting herself in harm's way time and again for the women whose lives she'd saved.

"There's something else," the courier said.

"Yes," Gina replied. "She was my grandmother… she…"

"Chose you, to continue her work," he said, helping her find the words.

"That's right," Gina said, astonished. It was like he was peering directly into her mind and reading the blueprint of her life.

"And in time you will," he said, kindly. "When you're ready."

"Hopefully, we can avoid incidents like tonight," Louise muttered to Gina.

319

"Yes. Tonight was...unusual," the courier said.

Gina and Louise shared a look of astonishment. *He was watching? He saw what happened?*

"That whole thing...it was...complicated," Gina said, feeling the need to explain it, hoping he wasn't offended that they'd impersonated his persona to trap a hunted fugitive.

"No matter," he said, without malice. "It's done."

"What now?" Gina asked.

"Should you need me, you know where to find me. And you know when."

With that, he gazed up at the night sky and slowly melted into the shadows, gliding as fluidly as if he were nothing more than a shadow himself.

21

Discovery

Wednesday, 8:00 a.m.

Gina stood just inside the garage door watching Nathan punish the heavy bag with a flurry of stinging left-right combinations. A full day had passed since the Jericho Street fireworks and since that time he'd said a total of four words to her. Six, if grunts could be classified as dialogue.

"So, this is the way it's going to be?" she asked.

He responded with another flurry. *Whap-whap...whap-whap... whap-whap.*

"Fine, have it your way," she said. "What are we looking at here? A few days? A week? A month?"

"Go ahead, make jokes," he said. *Whap-whap...whap-whap... whap-whap.*

Wow! Four words, she thought. It was start. "Call me crazy but I thought you'd be happy that the charges were dropped," she said.

The truth was: he was more than happy; he was ecstatic. But more than anything he was relieved, not that he was ready to admit it to *her*. "You should've told me," he mumbled.

Whap-whap.

"I could've helped you."

Whap-whap.

Whap-whap-whap.

She crossed the room and stood where he could see her. "You *did* help me," she said, her voice filled with a warmth that conveyed the honest appreciation she felt. "You provided a safe place to hide Rachel, and that allowed me to do what I had to do. Then you saved us from Rios and his two Neanderthals. You did more than help. Handing Rachel over to Roman never would've happened without you."

He stopped punching. "Really? You could've told me what you're doing. You could've let me help you find the guy in the cloak, whoever he is. And could've told me about *the federal charges!*" He paused for a beat and then said, "I thought we were friends."

"We *are* friends," she insisted. "*Best* friends."

"Oh yeah? Since when do best friends keep secrets from each other?"

He had a point.

Out in the street, a horn honked.

"Come on, we gotta go," she said. "She's here."

She left the garage first and waited outside the door. When he emerged moments later, they walked together down the driveway, not a word spoken between them. When they came to Louise's

Mercedes, parked at the curb, she slid in the front seat and he climbed in the back. Over the car's speakers, Schubert's *Symphony No. 9 in C Major* played softly.

"Good morning," Louise said, brightly.

"Isn't it, though?" Gina replied, unable to contain her joy. The drama surrounding Rachel Goudas, or Harper Denny as she was once again being called, was finally over. Her fate was now in the hands of the Massachusetts District Attorney. She was his problem now.

"Tell me again, what are we doing?" Nathan grumbled.

"Discovery," Louise said. She pulled away from the curb, the Mercedes cruising smoothly down the street as if riding on a cushion of air.

"What is that, exactly?" Nathan asked.

"Discovery is the imparting or exchange of previously undisclosed information."

"Great," he mumbled to himself as he stared out the window. "More things no one told me."

"I'm sorry, what was that?" Louise asked. She lowered the volume of the music.

"Nothing."

She looked over at Gina, who waved it off. *Pay no attention to him, he's grouchy.*

Louise nodded her head. *Got it.*

Twenty minutes later they walked into Louise's office in East Cambridge. Jameson and Kendra had arrived early and Louise's assistant, Gertie, had shown them into the palatial office. Jameson was standing at one of the large picture windows, taking in the panoramic view of the Charles River. Kendra had set up the coffee service she'd brought from her shop and the room was filled with the intoxicating aroma of freshly brewed Ethiopian Guji coffee. Two nearby tables, each one six feet long, held a diverse assortment of muffins, bagels, mini frittatas and egg tarts, croissant mini quiches, fruit, and juices.

Gina hadn't eaten breakfast and went straight to the food table to peruse the offerings while Nathan walked over to the window and stood beside Jameson. Beyond the river that sparkled in the early morning sunlight, the Boston skyline rose up like a row of jagged teeth.

"Quite a sight, wouldn't you agree?" Jameson asked.

"It's a river," Nathan said. *Big deal.*

"Did you know that two centuries ago, the Charles was a tidal river?"

"A what?"

"A tidal river," Jameson said. "It was surrounded by hundreds of acres of salt marshes and mudflats."

Nathan shrugged. *Yeah, whatever.*

Jameson noted the sullen look on Nathan's face. "You're angry," he said.

"That's an understatement," Nathan muttered.

"Let me guess. You're mad at Gina because she didn't tell you about the federal charges hanging over your head."

"Bingo," Nathan said, his eyes fixed on the skyline.

"I can understand why you might feel that way," Jameson said, "but I'm not sure you've thought it all the way through."

"What's to think about? She betrayed our friendship. She betrayed *me!*"

"Did she? You know, if not for her you'd be in a jail cell right now, awaiting the ruling of the Grand Jury. My guess is, since you're a first-time offender, the penalty would be reduced to court-mandated community service. Do you know what that is?"

"No."

"Well, first you and your parents would sign a contract agreeing to it. Then you'd have to complete an online evidence-based education course. After that, you'd be assigned a caseworker who would supervise you. A legal babysitter if you will. Of course, you could always refuse, at which point you'd be arraigned in Juvenile Court. I can assure you, that's not a place you ever want to be."

Nathan said nothing as Jameson's words of caution sank in.

"I'm just saying, you might want to go easy on Gina," Jameson told him. "What she was able to accomplish was nothing short of remarkable." He turned from the window and saw Beck walk into the room. Seconds later, when Phillip Roman and Magnus arrived, he and Louise walked over to greet them.

"Good morning," Roman said to each of them, shaking their hands.

Magnus offered a curt nod.

"Looks like the gang's all here," Roman said, scanning the room. "What about the parents?"

"At this point, there's no need to include them," Jameson said.

"Are you sure about that?"

"Positive," Jameson replied.

"It's better if we speak with them privately," Louise said. *Some of them anyway.*

"Okay, well, why don't we get started?" Roman said. He moved to the middle of the room and addressed the whole group. "Good morning folks. First off, Louise, I want to thank you for allowing us to meet here in your office. And to the rest of you, thank you for your assistance in bringing this very troubling case to a close. Your methods notwithstanding, it was an impressive trap you set: making Harper Denny believe you were all working together to help her escape; hiding her from Bolan, Cafferty, and Rodano; fooling her into thinking you'd removed them from the equation. Oh, that trick you pulled with her phone at Smitty's? I must say, that was very clever."

"She didn't want us to do it," Gina said, looking at Beck. "Remember last Sunday, when you were planning it at your house? She acted like she was worried about the three of you taking on Bolan, Cafferty, and Rodano because they were such savages…like you might not survive."

"I remember that," Kendra said. "She was trying to talk us out of doing it."

"That's right," Gina said. "The truth is, she didn't want you to go anywhere near them because she knew they'd identify themselves as federal agents. Once they did that, we'd have no choice but to hand her over to them."

"But didn't she assume the same thing after they were…you know…carted off?" Nathan asked. He didn't mention the Repository or the polite driver who picked up the three 'packages'.

"She did," Gina said, seeing through Rachel's odd behavior on the back porch. "That's why she fled."

"She fled?" Roman asked.

"Yes, and when she came back she was acting very strange. She wouldn't even step foot in my house. I think she wanted to confirm her suspicion that we knew the truth about her. For a moment I thought she was going to take off again."

"That was the most tenuous moment of this entire endeavor," Jameson said. "At that moment our deal was hanging by a thread. The whole thing could've blown up in our faces."

"Couldn't be helped," said Beck. "We took out Bolan, Cafferty, and Rodano before they could identify themselves as federal agents."

"Yeah, we didn't give them a lot of time to talk," Kendra said. "Come to think of it, we didn't give them any time to talk."

"But thankfully, Gina convinced her to stick around," Louise said.

"How did you do it?" Roman asked.

"I told her I'd found the transporter and that the meet-up was happening that night. Her troublesome journey was about to come to an end, which was a prospect that was too tempting to pass up."

"Well, I'm glad she bought it," Roman said. "I was under intense pressure to close the case, quietly, especially after what happened at Smitty's, which got the undivided attention of the local media. If they had uncovered the truth, that this woman had hoodwinked my agency for years, the fallout would've been, let's just say...severely damaging."

"Which reminds me," Kendra said. "You never told us which agency."

"That's right," Roman replied.

Jameson and Beck exchanged a knowing look.

"I have a question," Gina said. "Rachel...or Harper I guess I should call her now...said you guys were chasing her because she had something that belonged to your boss."

Before Roman could answer the question, the phone on Louise's desk buzzed. She went over to it and pressed the intercom button. "Yes?"

"He's here," Gertie said.

"Ah, just in time," Louise said. "Please show him in."

Seconds later the door opened and Gertie entered. Following behind her was a man in his mid 50s dressed in a formal business suit and tie. His height and military-style haircut made him a near match for Beck.

Almost.

Beck was a human fortress.

This guy was a water tower.

Gertie walked him as far as Louise, then nodded politely and excused herself.

"Good morning, I'm Louise Hayden," she said to him, extending her hand.

"William Tobin," he said, "but please call me Bill." They shook hands and then he turned to Roman. "This is all of them?" he asked.

"Yes," Roman said. He began the introductions with Jameson. "Bill, this is Jameson. He's the one who proposed the deal."

"Jameson, thank you," Tobin said, shaking his hand, "I've been overseeing the Harper Denny case for the past eight years. To say that I'm relieved to have it over with may be the understatement of the century."

"I just set things in motion," Jameson said, playing down his role in the whole affair. "It was these people you see here who actually pulled it off."

"Well, it was certainly an unorthodox plan but it worked and that's all I care about." He moved on to Beck. "You must be Beck."

"Yes sir," Beck said.

"We did some checking and your military record is very impressive. Is it true that you used an eight-sided club during the altercation at Smitty's?"

"Yes sir."

"It's part of the Taoist arts if I'm not mistaken."

"That's correct."

"I'd very much like to see it," Tobin said.

"No, actually you wouldn't," Kendra quipped. "Trust me."

Tobin looked at her, intrigued. "You must be…Kendra?" He said, making sure he had the name right.

She reached out and shook his hand, firmly. "You can call me bat girl."

"A very appropriate nickname," he said, nodding. "You play baseball, I take it."

"Softball."

"I'm guessing you bat somewhere around .350?"

"In your dreams, pal," she snorted. "Try .500!"

".500…wow," he said, eyes wide. "I'm impressed."

"Probably not the word Bolan and his boys used, am I right?"

"No, they used some very different words to describe you."

"No hard feelings?"

"Nope," Tobin said, without hesitation. "You acquitted yourself quite nicely." His eyes shifted to Nathan. "And you must be Nathan Cole, the boy I've heard so much about, which makes you," he said, pointing at Gina, "Gina McDermott."

They both nodded, uncomfortably.

"Luckily, the media didn't learn of their participation," Jameson said. "We'd prefer it stay that way."

"Their secret is safe with me," Tobin said. "What the general public doesn't know won't hurt them. That said, let me extend my heartfelt appreciation for what you both did to bring this case to a close. You know, in my line of work you hear things. Some of it you believe. Some of it you dismiss. And some of it…just some of it… takes your breath away. I have a sneaking suspicion that one or two of those breathtaking stories I heard have your fingerprints all over them."

Nathan looked down and kicked at the rug with his sneaker.

Gina gave her fingernails a close inspection.

Just as I thought, Tobin told himself.

"Bill?" Roman said. "Just before you arrived, Gina had a question. It was about you, actually, so perhaps you should answer it."

"I see," Tobin said. He looked at Gina. "What was your question?"

"When Harper showed up at my house last Saturday night, she claimed that bad men were chasing her. When I asked her why, she said they were sent to retrieve something of yours. Something you wanted back. She also implied that you were ruthless and you wouldn't hesitate to kill her to get it. When I asked her what it was, she flatly denied having anything and said that you were mistaking her for someone else."

"Ruthless?" Tobin said, grinning. "Yeah, I get that all the time. The truth is, she did have something I wanted. Would I kill to get it? No. That was a lie."

"One of many she told us," Louise noted.

"So…what was the thing?" Nathan asked.

"The name of her accomplice," Tobin said.

"Accomplice?"

"Scottie Rios."

"The guy in the Mustang," Kendra said.

"Before she went into hiding, Harper Denny and Scottie Rios were involved in a lucrative real estate money laundering scheme," Tobin said. "They specialized in high-price commercial properties. At the time, we knew Rios from another case, but we had no idea he was the one working with Denny.

"It was actually Jameson who suggested it," Roman said. "Truth be told, that's what sealed our deal."

"What's he talking about?" Nathan asked Beck.

"We knew that Rachel had been secretly texting someone, right?" he said.

"Yeah?"

"Roman's team knew it too. That's what allowed them to track her whereabouts. But what they didn't know was that she tried desperately to hide it, going as far as to lie about it, which suggested that her messages weren't to family or friends—she was protecting someone she didn't want anyone to know about."

"Like an accomplice," Nathan said.

"That's right."

"When Roman told me about Harper Denny's criminal past," Jameson said, "and that they wanted to not only get her but get her accomplice as well, I proposed that using Gina's trap could net them both."

"The thing you have to understand," Roman said, "is that Rios took extreme precautions to keep from being identified. For the longest time he existed as nothing more than a ghost. Then, two days ago, on Monday afternoon, when Magnus told me that he'd suddenly resurfaced and was pursuing Denny, Jameson's speculation was confirmed. I had Magnus track him down and he dispatched him that night as he was attempting to sneak onto the Canton property."

"Without the accomplice, this deal doesn't get done," Tobin said. "We would've just demanded that you turn Denny over to us."

"And face the pending charges," Jameson added.

"Correct."

"Wait a minute," Kendra said. "You say he was trying to sneak onto the property?" *Good luck with that.*

"Yes," Roman said. "His plan was to get inside and remove Ms. Denny, by force if necessary."

"Why?" Gina asked. "She believed her plan was working. She was almost home free."

"She had no idea he was coming for her. After Bolan, Cafferty, and Rodano disappeared, Rios sensed a trap. He was desperate to keep her from falling into federal custody for fear that she'd make a plea deal and trade information about him for a reduced sentence. Plus..." he said, looking at Gina, uneasily.

"What?"

"He had zero confidence that a 13-year-old girl could fool the feds and whisk Denny away before we caught up with her."

"Zero confidence? Hah!" Gina exclaimed. "How's his confidence now?"

"Hold on," Kendra said out of the side of her mouth as she chewed a mouthful of bagel. She held up her hand, gesturing for them to wait while she swallowed. "You said Magnus 'dispatched' him?" She pronounced the word like she wasn't sure what it meant.

"Yes."

"If he was 'dispatched', how did he end up in the alley? And who were those two cavemen he brought with him?"

"Cavemen?" Beck said, eyebrows raised.

"Excuse me. Cave *persons.*"

Roman looked at Magnus. *Go ahead, you tell them.*

"I waited in the woods and intercepted him as he was nearing the back fence of the property," Magnus explained. "His car was parked nearby and I stashed him in the trunk. Little did I know that the Quinlan brothers were waiting nearby. They discovered him and freed him."

"The Quinlan brothers?" Kendra muttered. "That sounds like a circus act."

"After freeing Rios," Magnus said, "they followed us to Worcester and hid in the maze of alleys."

"Which allowed them to sneak up on me without anyone seeing them," Roman added.

"By the way," Gina said. "That thing you asked Rios? It was brilliant."

"What are you talking about?" Nathan asked. "What thing?"

"The Battle of Trenton? You didn't get that?"

"Get what?"

She gave him a pitiful look. *When are you going to pay attention in school?*

"What?" he asked.

"In 1776, General George Washington led a surprise attack on a group of British-sponsored missionaries in Trenton, New Jersey. *Hello…ground control to Nathan.* "You don't remember studying it in class last year?"

"Last year?" he said. "No." *More like, never.*

"He snuck up on them, which is what Beck, Kendra, Magnus, and the other agent were doing."

"His name is Sisson," Magnus said.

"When I saw the four of them sneaking up on Rios and the Quinlan brothers," said Roman, "I tried to buy them some time by posing a historical parallel."

"Did anyone tell Rios that?" asked Beck.

"No, he's been a little distracted."

"I have a question," Louise said.

"Shoot."

"We all know that Rachel was in hiding for the past seven years. When did you actually find her?"

Tobin looked at Roman and nodded. *Go ahead.*

"As you know, we had access to her phone activity," Roman said, "which, in this case, was limited to an old work phone."

Louise assumed as much since Helen had confiscated Harper's personal phone—a safety precaution she followed with each of her "shadows" before they went into hiding. Still, she had to be sure.

334

"There had been no activity on the line for a number of years, but little over a week ago one of our electronics specialists got a hit."

"Did she say why she started using it again?" Beck asked, baffled why someone in hiding would do such a mindless thing.

"She was running out of money," Roman said. "The whole time she'd been hiding she'd been living off her savings. Living rather extravagantly, I might add. When her funds started to dwindle, she reached out to Rios, the one person she knew could help her pad her bank account."

Louise raised her hand to get Roman's attention. "You mentioned real estate money laundering?"

"Yes. Rios provided the money and Ms. Denny used it to purchase commercial properties. Because she was able to see the listings before anyone else was privy to them, she moved on them first, undervaluing the property before buying it, then overvaluing it when it sold. The process allowed them to clean large amounts of money and generate enormous profits. For her part, Denny was handsomely compensated."

"Wouldn't such repeated transactions raise a red flag somewhere?" Louise asked.

"Ordinarily, yes, but they used a 'cleanskin'."

"A what?" Gina asked.

"A third party who handles the money transfers. In this case, it was one of Denny's old college friends, Allison Reed, who created Reed & Croft Financial Services. Reed set up an off-shore account and handled the deposits and withdrawals. With no prior criminal record, she was virtually invisible."

"As you can see, this was a case with a number of layers," said Tobin. "Your combined efforts not only delivered Harper Denny, you also netted us the person she was working with, in one tidy little bundle I might add."

"When Rios intercepted us," Gina said, "she claimed she had no idea who he was."

"I don't doubt it," Tobin said. "For some time now, we've been tracking a very well established drug ring that operated up and down the East Coast. We knew they were cleaning vast amounts of money, we just didn't know how they were doing it."

"That's where Rios got the money," Beck said.

"Yes. *Lots* of money."

With no further questions, a casual air fell over the room and the generous spread of food and drink became the main focus. Tobin took that opportunity to direct Louise and Gina away from the others where he spoke to them privately.

"So, let me see if I have this right," he said to Gina. "Harper Denny, aka Rachel Goudas, sought you out based on something your grandmother did for her seven years ago?"

"Yes," Gina said. "My grandmother, Helen Bainbridge, secretly helped women who were being pursued by very bad people."

"Helen Bainbridge, the author?"

"That's right."

Tobin's face seemed to freeze, his look of astonishment set like a plastic mask.

"Are you familiar with the archetype of the Ferryman?" Louise asked.

"No, I can't say that I am."

"It's a timeless figure in storytelling. The Ferryman acts as a guide or aid to another character in a transformative journey through uncertain realms, helping them to reach a specific destination. According to Buddhist teachings, the Ferryman is a metaphor for a champion of compassion, which is what Helen was for each of the women she helped."

"And the help she provided these women…?"

"She made them disappear."

"Well, she was very good at what she did, I'll say that much," Tobin noted. "For years we couldn't find Harper Denny, not until she started using her old work phone. We located her in North Carolina, and from there we tracked her through Ohio, New York State, Vermont, and finally, Massachusetts. The question I have is why did your grandmother help her all those years ago? Harper Denny was a wanted criminal."

"Con man might be a more accurate description," Louise said. "Hers was a house of lies and deception. She lied to Helen, she lied to me, and she lied to Gina."

"She told me terrible men, *enforcers,* were chasing her," Gina said. "She claimed that if they caught her, she'd wind up dead."

"Her biggest lie of all," Louise said, disgusted.

"This imaginary hooded figure who could whisk her away to safety, that was ingenious," Tobin said. "How did you come up with *that?*"

Gina looked to Louise for guidance. *Can I tell him?*

Louise nodded. *Go ahead.*

"He's not imaginary," Gina said.

"You're saying he's *real?*"

Gina nodded.

"A hooded figure? Operating in the shadows? Helping innocent people escape forces of evil? That sounds like something straight out of a Marvel comic book."

Phillip Roman appeared at his side and they stepped away and spoke in hushed voices.

"Okay, give me a minute," Tobin told him. He walked back to Louise and Gina. "We have to go," he said, "but before we do, there's something I want to give you." He reached into his jacket pocket and took out a business card. It had his name and a private phone number. No title. No company or agency name. No street address. "I owe you one," he said, handing Gina the card. "If you ever need my help, call me. I mean it."

"One?" she said. "Uh, don't you mean three?"

"Three?"

She looked at him without speaking, suggesting he was smart enough to figure it out on his own.

"Well, let's see," he said, counting off on his fingers. "Harper Denny, that's one. Scottie Rios, that's two." He paused to think, then shrugged, unable to come up with the third.

"Allison Reed?" Gina said. "The cleanskin?"

"Oh, right," he said, with an embarrassed smile. "How about this? Call me anytime you want, day or night. Consider it an open invitation."

"It may be awhile," she said. "Are you sure you won't forget me?"

"Gina McDermott, I will never you forget you. On that you have my word."

"Okay, then," she said, slipping his card in her back pocket.

She reached out and shook his hand.

"Deal."

22 ~~Federico Garcia Lorca~~

A Short Essay

After Tobin left with Roman and Magnus, Jameson and Louise convened a meeting with Nathan and Gina at the dark walnut conference table next to the long row of windows. Given the nature of what they were going to discuss, Beck and Kendra were asked to join the meeting as well.

Once they were seated, Jameson said, "Again, I want to thank each of you for helping to resolve the Rachel Goudas matter. Needless to say, these last few days have been taxing on all of us."

You can say that again, Gina thought.

"Now that we're past it, there are things we need to discuss with both of you," he said, looking directly at Nathan and Gina. "Would you like to start?" he asked Louise.

"Actually, I believe Gina has something she'd like to say."

As all eyes turned to Gina.

"I just wanted to say thanks," she said. "You guys were amazing. The truth is, I couldn't have pulled off the trap without you and I am forever grateful for your assistance." She paused momentarily, then continued. "For some time now, I've been keeping certain information from you concerning my grandmother and the amazing quest she undertook, one that she kept concealed from her friends, her readers, and the rest of the world. I believed that if I shared it with you, your lives would be in jeopardy. But after speaking with Louise, we both agreed that you each deserve to know, especially given what we just went through. Will it put your lives in danger? Maybe yes, maybe no. That's for you to decide. But after seeing how this group pulled together, I think it's fair to say that danger has another thing coming."

"Damn right," Kendra said, pounding her fist on the table.

"What quest?" Nathan asked.

"The one I refused to tell you about six months ago," Gina said. "And for that, I'm sorry. You were right, this morning, when you told me that best friends don't keep secrets."

And then she told him about the six women.

All in danger.

All desperate to escape the sinister men who were pursuing them.

And how her grandmother, Helen Barnes, known the world over as Helen Bainbridge, provided each of them a swift and silent exodus from their predicament.

"That crusade has now been handed down to me," she said. "What that means going forward is uncertain. I'll just have to wait and see where the road takes me."

"If I didn't know better, I'd swear you were talking about my grandfather," Nathan said.

"And rightly so," Jameson noted. "It was your grandfather who helped Helen get her start."

"He also helped her set up her nationwide network of safehouses," Louise said.

"She called them safe havens," Gina told Nathan.

"Safe havens, indeed," said Louise. "For the women she helped, they were the first step into a life without fear. But that wasn't all. Henry Hammond helped her in other ways, guiding her as she began her 'quest' as Gina so rightly put it."

"The night she showed up, Rachel implied that she knew my grandfather," Nathan said.

"She met him," Louise explained. "It was seven years ago, when the arrangements were being made to hide her. Helen was still learning the ropes, so to speak, and he counseled them both on the level of secrecy that had to be maintained if any of it was going to work."

"I guess she missed the part about not using her cellphone," Nathan muttered.

"Hiding someone from the rest of the world is a very precarious proposition," Louise said. "There are pitfalls lurking around every corner. Fortunately, Henry Hammond and Helen Bainbridge perfected it to the degree that the people they helped were able to survive."

"Which brings us to the underlying purpose of this discussion," Jameson said. "You've both entered a world overrun with hidden secrets and potential danger. You've endured incredible challenges and have survived them with amazing guile and determination. You solved the mystery of Alastair Raven, found the killer of Charles

Warren. You took on the worldwide criminal Eduard Dampierre and his sister Ginette, ultimately exposing their vast criminal empire. You then identified their replacement, Asher Rickman. And in what was both tragic yet healing for the Hammond family, you brought closure to the unsolved deaths of both Sarah and her father Henry."

"Needless to say, you've been quite busy," Louise said. "We think it's time you both stop and take a breath."

"Indeed," said Jameson. "Live your lives. Be 13 years old. Embrace each day with excitement and hope. School starts in, what, another week? Let it be the respite you so desperately need and deserve."

"School? Exciting? Yeah, right," Nathan mumbled.

"I can't wait!" Gina said, flashing her eyebrows at him.

"That's because you're a geek."

"I prefer bluestocking if you don't mind," she said, raising her chin proudly in the air.

"Here we go," Kendra muttered.

"What, pray tell, is a bluestocking?" Nathan asked.

"Look it up," Gina told him. "In fact, you should write a short essay on the topic. Just think, your new teacher will be impressed and you'll earn extra credit, which, I might add, you're going to need… big time."

"Oh, I'm going to write a short essay all right, about being a geek!"

"You're going to write it about yourself?"

"No," he fired back. "You!"

"I think we're done here," said Beck.

343

"Yes. Quite," Jameson said. "But before you go, know this." He looked from Nathan to Gina as he spoke. "The waters that lie ahead for both of you are going to get wider and deeper. Much deeper. You can stay the course, or you can turn back now. That choice I leave up to you."

Nathan and Gina looked at each other and smirked.

Turn back?

Now?

I don't think so.

23

Treasured Time

It was nearly noontime when Louise dropped Gina off at home. With her stomach comfortably full from feasting on the exquisite offerings at the meeting, she went out to the back porch and stretched out on the wicker couch with her copy of *The Crown Killer.*

While the Rachel Goudas circus had left town for good, Louise spoke at length about it being a cautionary tale, one that Gina should consider a valuable learning moment. "Don't trust every person you meet," she said. "Yes, you'll encounter legitimately desperate people, those who are being unfairly persecuted by forces they can't repel. But be wary of those like Harper Denny, whose story was a cleverly woven blanket of deception."

As she recalled those words, she couldn't help but wonder where she'd be without Louise Hayden there to guide her. With a soft breeze wafting through the porch screens, carrying with it the enticing aroma of a nearby Jasmine bush, she abandoned any thoughts about the future, settled back into the couch cushions, and began to read. Unlike before, when she'd analyzed every sentence and every poetic stanza for a hidden clue, this would be reading for reading's sake, treasured time that had been sorely missing from her life during the previous week.

In no time at all she became immersed in the saga of Nikki Nolan and the decayed bodies that continued to be unearthed at the Grafton Reservoir.

Pages flew by.

Then chapters.

Noontime quickly became one o'clock.

Then two o'clock.

At 2:30 she paused long enough to get a glass of water from the kitchen, then it was back to the couch. At four o'clock she finished, leaving her another hour and a half before her parents got home from work. She considered her options momentarily, then tucked the book in her backpack and rode to the library.

As usual, Patty was working at the front desk. She was dressed in a pale yellow sundress with a repeating pattern of small black and white flowers. At first glance it looked like a tsunami of tiny panda bear heads. When she saw Gina enter the building, she set aside what she was doing, clasped her hands together, and held them to her chest. "So?" she said, grinning like Gina had juicy gossip to share. "What did you think?"

"It was very...arresting," Gina said, sliding the book across the counter.

"Yes! That's exactly what I thought," Patty said. She picked up the book and began turning pages, pausing briefly to read a sentence here, a sentence there. "Nikki Nolan is so amazing," she said. "The way she found the connection between the victim? That was genius. Me? I never would've thought to look in their cars. How about you?"

All right, you want to do this? Gina thought. *Let's do it.* "I was wondering why anyone would keep a receipt in their car in the first place," she said, "or a bookmark for that matter."

"Right?" Patty said. She leaned forward and spoke softly like she didn't want anyone else to hear. "Do you want to know what I think?"

I don't know…do I? Gina thought.

"I think each of the victims did that on purpose."

"Huh?"

"They didn't trust him," Patty said, matter-of-factly.

"Didn't trust who? Nigel Hewitt?"

"Yes. I mean, come on, the man was unbalanced. Every time one of the book club members challenged him about one of his…what did Roxy call them…?"

"Interpretations."

"Yes, his interpretations. Every time someone discounted one of them, he became a totally different person."

"True, but that's not what made Nikki think he might be the killer," Gina said. "The bookstore bags, receipts, and bookmarks they found in the victims' cars were circumstantial at best. It was the other part of his personality, the side she called 'the charmer', that nailed it for her. It was the whole reason she joined the book club. She wanted to watch him, study him…"

"I thought she was falling for him," Patty admitted.

"*Falling* for him?" Gina exclaimed. *Wow! My grandmother sure fooled you.*

"It was so sweet," Patty said. "The way she started arriving at the meetings before anyone else, sitting in the front row, never disagreeing with him. Then she began flirting with him, complimenting him on his clothes..." She paused and looked across the room, dreamy eyed, imagining for a moment that she was Nikki Nolan. "And then," she gushed, "he asked her out on a date." She pressed a hand to her chest. "So romantic."

"So, you think she transformed him," Gina said.

"Absolutely. He was a sinking ship, emotionally, and she swooped in and saved him—a classic love story."

"Uh-huh...but then..." Gina said, popping Patty's lovestruck fantasy bubble.

Patty shook her head begrudgingly. "Then his true nature emerged. I should've seen it coming."

"You mean, after she started challenging him?"

"Yes. I couldn't understand why she was acting that way, purposefully trying to provoke him."

"She was setting him up," Gina said. "She knew he would never admit to killing the people who had angered him. She believed that, in an uncontrollable rage, he'd snap and say something to incriminate himself. And what do you know? It worked."

"Yes, but she nearly paid for it with her life!" Patty said, relieved that her favorite Helen Bainbridge character had survived to see another day.

"That she did," Gina replied.

"I really thought she was done for," Patty said, sadly. "When he pinned her on the ground and tried to crush her windpipe with the crown of the book…"

"You thought she was *done for?*" Gina said. "I was *waiting* for that to happen. I figured she had O'Brien and a handful of other officers hiding nearby, ready to jump in if Hewitt attacked her."

"Well, it's a good thing she did," Patty said, setting the book aside. "Now, I won't ask if you're going to read the next book because, well, you're a Helen Bainbridge fan. Of course you're going to read the next book. All I *will* say is this…"

A devious grin crossed her face.

"Just wait. You're not going to *believe* what happens next."

Explications

BANANA CONSOLE DESK, described in this story, is based on an actual model made by ErgonomicHome.com, based in Houston, TX. It was first introduced in 1995 for computer-intensive environments where ergonomics and productivity are important. The front and back surfaces are curved to embrace the human form and respond to the dynamic movements of the computer user. Eight electric motors allow the front and back tops to adjust vertically and independently of one another. The design helps to reduce stress and strain on the computer user's wrists, forearms, neck, shoulders, back & lumbar region. It reduces eye fatigue by having a minimum viewing distance from the computer user's eyes to the monitors of 24".

DUMBELLS can be traced back to ancient civilizations in Greece, Egypt, and India. In Greece, a similar device called a "haltere," was U-shaped and made from stone or metal. In Egypt, they were crafted from stone or sand-filled bags and used for strength training. In ancient India, wrestlers and warriors increased their strength and stamina by using a large stone with a hole in the middle (for grip), called a "Nal."

THE SEVEN HILLS of Worcester, MA, include: Hancock Hill, Green Hill, Chandler Hill, Bancroft Hill, Mt. St. James or College (Pakachoag) Hill, Newton Hill, and Union (Sagatabscot) Hill.

12-6 ELBOW STRIKE, also referred to as a "twelve to six elbow" and "downward elbow strike," is a strike used in the combat sport of mixed martial arts (MMA). The name is based on the concept of a clock and refers to bringing the elbow from straight up (12 o'clock) to straight down (6 o'clock). This type of strike is illegal under the Unified Rules of Mixed Martial Arts.

"GET OUT OF DODGE," is an idiom meaning to leave a difficult or dangerous environment with all possible haste. It references Dodge City, KS, and was popularized by the TV show "Gunsmoke" that aired from 1955-1975.

KOSCIUSZKO CIRCLE was named after Tadeusz Kosciuszko, a Polish military leader who fought on behalf of the Colonials during the American Revolution. It was designed by Frederick Law Olmstead and Arthur Shurcliff and built in 1927. It is part of the Old Harbor Reservation Parkway and in 2008 was added to the National Registry of Historic Places.

FORAGE CAPS were small cloth caps worn by British cavalrymen in the 18th century when undertaking work duties such as foraging for good for their horses. The term was later applied to all "undress" caps worn by men of all branches and regiments as a substitute for the full-dress headdress.

BIRD'S NEST FERNS *(Asplenium nidus)* belong to the Aspleniaceae family and originate from the rainforests of East Africa, Asia and Australia. True to its name, its funnel-shaped leaves form a kind of nest. In its natural environment it's an epiphyte, a non-parasitic plant with no attachment to the ground that grows on another plant for physical support (ex. in the canopy of trees), providing shelter for certain amphibians.

LOW EARTH ORBIT, (LEO), according to NASA, is an Earth-centered orbit with an altitude of 1,200 miles or less. Such an orbit is near enough to Earth for convenient transportation, communication, observation and resupply. It is also the area where the International Space Station currently orbits and where many proposed future platforms will be located.

LEOPARD CRAWL is a military-specific crawl where an arm is advanced with the diagonal knee, allowing the smallest silhouette with most limbs touching the ground.

"YOU PAYS YOUR MONEY AND YOU TAKES YOUR CHOICE," is an informal saying inferring that one is responsible for their own decisions and can't blame anyone else if they aren't successful. Its origin is believed to be British and was first seen in print in an 1846 issue of *Punch*, the weekly British magazine of humor and satire, in a cartoon entitled "The Ministerial Crisis." Mark Twain used the saying in 1884, in his novel *Adventures of Huckleberry Finn*.

THE CATACOMBS OF ST. CALLIXTUS were the official cemetery of the Church of Rome in the 3rd century AD. Approximately half a million Christians were buried here, among them many martyrs and 16 popes. The catacombs are named after the deacon St. Callixtus who, at the beginning of the 3rd century AD, was assigned to the administration of the cemetery by Pope Zephyrinus.

IMEI (International Mobile Equipment Identity) numbers are a unique 15-digit serial number used by carriers to identify a device on a mobile network. Every mobile phone in the world is equipped with one. Mobile network operators and law enforcement agencies can use the IMEI number to track devices on their network and aid in locating stolen phones.

BUBBLE BATHS date back to ancient Rome. The first commercial bubble bath solution in the United States emerged in the 1940s and was introduced by a Chicago-based company, Chemtoy. In the 1960s, Harold Schafer and the Gold Seal Company developed Mr. Bubble, which quickly became a household name.

EULA MAE PITMAN is a fictional character.

CINNAMON has been proven to repel snakes without harming them. Cinnamon oil, in particular, is much stronger than the powder alternative and can be beneficial to gardens due to its antibacterial and antifungal properties.

WAX LIPS are a candy made of colored and flavored wax that resemble large teeth and lips. They were first introduced in 1924, by confectioner John W. Glenn, who came to the United States from England in 1888 and grew up in his father's wholesale candy business.

"DOLLARS TO DONUTS" is an American idiom that originated in the mid 1800s and reached its peak in 1915. The phrase expresses the sentiment that the speaker is so confident that he or she is right about something and will put forth dollars to the listener's doughnuts in a wager where the dollars have a much higher value than the doughnuts.

ASA MOTHRAM, THE MOTHRAM BLOCK, MOTHRAM MAZE, JERICHO and BEECHAM STREETS in Worcester, MA, are fictitious creations by the author.

PARLOUR PALMS (*Chamaedorea elegans)* come from the rainforests of Mexico and Guatemala. They have been popular houseplants since the 1800s. The name is derived from their common placement in Victorian households, notably, in the parlor room.

MONEY LAUNDERING in the general sense is the process of disguising financial assets. It involves transforming monetary proceeds derived from criminal activity into funds with an apparent legal source.

THE DAILY DOUBLE is a betting system in horse racing and dog racing where the bettor makes one bet on the winners of two races. It was first introduced in 1931 at Connaught Park Racetrack near Ottawa on the third and fifth races, with a winning $2 wager paying $47.95. In time, racetracks began offering the wager for the first two races of each day's program as an enticement for spectators to arrive early.

PEQUITSIDE FARM in Canton, MA, is a 33-acre parcel of land that was originally part of the Ponkapoag Indian Reservation. It was named Pequitside in 1885 when the land was purchased by mill owner Charles N. Draper. In 1971 it was sold to the Town of Canton which uses it as a conservation/recreation facility for community organizations and events. It features a picnic and passive recreation area, protected wetland area, playground, walking trail, community garden, and areas for youth soccer and lacrosse.

"HOPE FOR THE BEST, BUT PREPARE FOR THE WORST," originated in the 18th century and has no literary attribution. The phrase first appeared in print in the 1833 book *The Wondrous Tales of Alroy,* by British novelist, essayist, and twice Prime Minister of the UK, Benjamin Disraeli.

SNOWFLAKE RIMS are a cast-aluminum wheel option introduced in 1977 by the Pontiac Motor Division of General Motors. The design featured a single casting, cross-fin pattern which resembled a snowflake. They were most popular on the Firebird and Trans Am, but could also be ordered for the Grand Prix and Sunbird.

THE CLAWFOOT BATHTUB, so named for the ball and claw design, was developed in Holland and was inspired by the Chinese motif of a dragon clutching a pearl. The design emerged in the mid 1800s with two designs: a lion's paw clutching a ball, and an eagle's claw clutching a ball. The lion style was popular in England while the eagle claw was popular in the United States.

18 US. CODE 111 states that it is a federal crime to "commit an assault, resist, or impede certain officers or employees, and covers simple assault, aggravated assault, and serious assault with a deadly weapon."

DRACAENA is a genus of approximately 120 species of trees and succulent shrubs and a member of the family Asparagaceae. The name is derived from the Ancient Greece *drakaina,* meaning "female dragon." They are a rugged and carefree houseplant with elongated, variegated leaves, giving them a robust and tropical appearance. They can tolerate low light conditions and are widely used at home and in an office setting.

EIGHT-SIDED CLUBS, true to their name, have eight sides running the length of the weapon. The style is traditional in Taoist arts with the eight sides representing the eight Trigrams (symbols of the cycle of yin and yang energy present in all things) and the Pa Kua (Bagua), one of the three main Chinese martial arts of the Wudang School founded in the early Yuan dynasty.

CAVALRY SCOUTS were established shortly after the creation of the U.S. Army in 1775. Prior to Army soldiers getting involved in a situation, Cavalry Scouts are sent ahead to survey areas where the enemy may be situated, providing important information such as the number and position of enemy troops, notable environmental features, and navigational information.

SMITTY'S BACKYARD BARBEQUE is a fictional restaurant.

Chapter Page Illustrations

With the underlying theme of poetry in the story, the chapter page illustrations are the signatures of famous poets. True to the person to whom it belongs, each signature is as unique as it is artistic.

Chapter 1   Geoffrey Chaucer (1343-1400)

Chapter 2   Sir Walter Raleigh (1552-1618)

Chapter 3   Edmund Spenser (1552-1599)

Chapter 4   Sir Philip Sidney (1554-1586)

Chapter 5   Christopher Marlowe (1564-1593)

Chapter 6   William Shakespeare (1564-1616)

Chapter 7   John Donne (1572-1631)

Chapter 8   W.B. Yeats (1665-1939)

Chapter 9   Jonathan Swift (1667-1745)

Chapter 10   Oliver Goldsmith (1730-1774)

Chapter 11   Johann Wolfgang von Goethe (1749-1832)

Chapter 12   William Wordsworth (1770-1850)

Chapter 13   Sir Walter Scott (1771-1832)

Chapter 14   Lord Byron (1788-1624)

Chapter 15   John Keats (1795-1821)

Chapter 16   Ralph Waldo Emerson (1803-1882)

Chapter 17   Elizabeth Barrett-Browning (1806-1861)

Chapter 18   Henry Wadsworth Longfellow (1807-1882)

Chapter 19   Thomas Hardy (1840-1928)

About the Author

Alfred M. Struthers lives in Peterborough, New Hampshire. In addition to crafting books that inspire, teach, entertain and make a difference in the lives of readers both young and old, he is a singer/songwriter, woodworker, photographer, and avid collector of Vermont river rocks, beach pebbles on the NH coast, and fossils that line the streambeds in and around Cooperstown, New York.

To find out what he's been up to lately, visit:
thirdfloorbooksllc.com.

Coming Soon!
Book 10 in the Third Floor Mystery Series

The Parcener's Tale

Nathan was approaching the garage door when he saw it. The way it was hastily wedged into the crack between the door and the frame suggested that the person who left it there had been in a hurry. Otherwise, they would've simply knocked on the front door or called ahead. The size and shape were unique, and the moment he saw it he knew it was a calling card, or a visiting card, a holdover from 18th century France. And that told him who had put it there—the man he'd met in the W. Heffron Antiquarian Bookstore in Boston, a friend of his grandfather who had introduced himself as "the keeper of things that must not be found."

He opened the garage door and let the card drop into his open hand. The front he'd seen before, the name all too familiar to him.

It was the handwritten message on the back that gave him pause.

The Ophidian vault has been compromised
Take all necessary precautions
He's coming for you next